"Trade?" repeated Ryszard. "What do you trade for?"

Walker needed to convince Ryszard that he and Hairy had something of value. Or at least keep Ryszard confused long enough for Hairy and Walker to escape. Especially if he and Hairy were destined for the dinner menu.

"That spear for instance," remarked Walker. "I made it," replied Walker.

"You mean to say you made this?" asked Ryszard, who couldn't help but sound impressed, yet also dubious.

Ryszard shook his head in wonder.

"You should keep it then," suggested Walker, he assumed he wasn't going to get it back anyway. "A gift to you, for saving us from those two brutes."

"No, no, you are too kind," replied Ryszard.

"Please, I insist."

"The knife in your belt," continued Ryszard. "Another example of your craft?"

"Yes," agreed Walker, casually handing it over before Ryszard could take it.

"An amazing weapon," said Ryszard unable to hide his admiration. "Beautiful."

By **Peter Alan Thelin**

Hairy and Walker, In the Valley of the Auroch

The Laughing Demons, a Hairy Walker and Aygul Story

Hairy and Walker

In the Valley of the Auroch

The characters and events in this book are fictitious.
Any similarity to real persons, living or dead, is purely
coincidental and not intended by the author.

ASIN: B07WG3Y83B

Publication date: August 15, 2019

Language: English

Publisher: Amazon.com/Kindle

Printed: Amazon.com

Independently published (August 15, 2019)

Print length: 282 pages

ISBN: 9781686816949

Hairy and Walker

In the Valley of the Auroch

A Hairy and Walker Story

Written and illustrated by

Peter Alan Thelin

Hairy and Walker

In the Valley of the Auroch

ISBN: 9781686816949

DEDICATION

To my wife Sue, for putting up with me.

And thanks to my friend Lisa Brill and my wife Sue Rosenof for help editing my lousy grammar.

CONTENTS

Peter Alan Thelin

AURIGNAC —HURRIANS

(HOMO SAPIENS)

LITTLE HAWK
HAIRY
FATHER
MOTHER
STRIDER
WALKER/LITTLE FOX

WALKER'S BROTHER
(HOMOHABILIS)

WALKER'S UNCLE

*

VADI KABILE (VALLEY TRIBE)—HURRIANS

(HOMO SAPIENS)

AYGUL	MOON ROSE (FEMALE)
BAGHADUR	WARRIOR
BAHADIR	ONE WHO IS BRAVE AND VALIANT
CENGIZ	STRONG
HOSMUNT	CLEVER PERSON
OSMAN	CRANE-LIKE GAME BIRD
OSMANEK	CHIEF
TABIB	PHYSICIAN
TAICHI	LARGE ONE
TAMRAZ	LARGE ONE
TARKAN	HE WHO IS BOLD AND STRONG
VOLKAN	VOLCANO

*

ELVES

(HOMO-ERECTUS)

THE ELEVES HAVE NO NAMES

1

*

TROLDFOLK— (VALLEY TRIBE)—TAL STAMM

(NEANDERTHALS)

ARICK	NOBLE LEADER
BABAK	SMALL FATHER
BERNT	AS STRONG AS A BEAR
CADMAEL	WAR CHIEF
CAEL	SLIM
DOLPHUS	NOBLE WOLF
EVELINA	LONGED FOR
GINO	WELL KNOWN FIGHTER
HAGAN	FIRE
HORST	MAN OF THE FOREST
HUBERTA	WOMAN WITH CLEVER MIND
NEFIN	NEPHEW
ROLF	WOLF COUNSEL
RYSZARD	HUNTER—POWERFUL RULER

PROLOGUE

It was spring, and the days were growing longer, even now, when it was early evening, and the sun was still above the rim of the valley.

But here, tall white cliffs of fractured limestone loomed overhead and cast deep shadows.

Along the base of the cliff, the trail undercut the mountain. Trees grew thick surrounded by dark green vegetation. It was a sub-tropical jungle and pleasantly warm. The atmosphere here was a tangible thing. It was alive with movement and shafts of sunlight angling through the trees illuminated clouds of midges and pollen and reflected off fleeting birds. The air was full of the sweet-sharp fragrance of pine needles, fennel and juniper bushes and the lively sounds of birds, frogs and cicadas looking for mates.

The forest floor was carpeted in dark green moss. It flowed over fallen trees and stumps like water. There were weathered rocks—themselves home to blue, green, red and yellow lichens. Clusters of mushrooms and fungi in all the colors of the rainbow punctuated the shadows. A woodpecker announced its presence with its rat-a-tat-tatting, and a fox—oblivious to that noise, slunk between the trees, stalking an equally oblivious vole.

In contrast to this symphony of nature, a very alien sort of creature passed by.

A human.

A girl.

Slim, with chestnut-colored, shoulder-length hair.

In contrast to the furred, feathered or scaled creatures of the forest, the girl was covered in dead skins.

She wore a loose tunic, soft-leather sandals and carried a short spear for protection.

Stopping before a gnarled old oak, she looked about expectantly.

All about her, the forest moved like the parts of a dream.

Water in the stream, leaves on the trees, clouds of midges, tapping woodpeckers, hunting foxes and furtive voles. These all followed patterns repeated endlessly, outside of time.

The girl was different. She was focused, with purpose distinct from merely existence.

The girl was aware of her surroundings in a philosophical fashion different from the mere survival of the forest denizens.

Looking through the lush green canopy, patches of blue were visible. Down on the ground, the dark shadows covered mosses, ferns and detritus.

The girl was beginning to grow anxious. Hearing the snap of a twig, she turned in time to spot another alien picking his way along the forest trail.

Sighing with relief, the girl recognized her new friend, the mysterious young man. The tree was their planned rendezvous, and he was late. The girl rushed to his side, took his hand and relaxed, now that she was in his company.

The young man reached inside his cloak and withdrew a beaded necklace. Bits of bone, carved into the faces of animals and threaded onto a leather cord, he presented it to the girl. She clapped her hands together in delight.

The girl's smile was dazzling as she beamed with pride—no one had ever given her such a gift—she felt a warm glow grow within her chest. Everything about her new friend was special and she hugged the necklace to her, and though she lacked the words, she tried to thank him, and now wished she had thought of bringing a gift for him too. But the act of giving appeared to make him happy enough.

In the Valley of the Auroch

As delighted as all this was, the girl was still practical enough to feel wary. She may not be a part of the forest, but she knew that the night belonged to predators.

That, and that neither of their families—their tribes—would be happy if they knew they were sneaking off like this, meeting a stranger.

It had been an entire moon since the girl had first met the boy. So long, and yet so short.

She had been on her way to the river, to wash and collect water. The young man had just appeared—stepping out of the forest.

At first, she was frightened. She'd never even seen a stranger before. But then he'd smiled—the biggest, brightest smile she had ever seen—and her fear evaporated, transformed into something else.

Initially it was just curiosity. He had just stood there, looking at her from a safe enough distance and made no move in her direction.

He was just a boy.

The girl knew all the boys of her tribe, had known them all her life, (and was even related to most of them).

But this boy was unfamiliar. He was someone new and, in a slightly scary way, exciting. His skin was shockingly pale. His hair was the color of dried grass and lighter than that of the boys of her tribe. It hung down over his face, partially covering his brown eyes shaded by heavy brows. He was also heavier than the boys of her tribe. There was an unfamiliar quality about him, which she found alluring.

Working up her courage, they approached each other. Unlike the people of her tribe, he was barefoot. He dressed in animal furs, not skins. The boy appeared shy but was trying hard to hide his anxiety. When he smiled, the white of his teeth split his face from ear to ear. His attempt to be friendly seemed earnest and very endearing.

Their first meeting was short—if she didn't return soon, her family would come looking for her and they may not understand.

They couldn't speak each other's language, but the boy made hand signs and indicated that he would return the next day. She nodded and tried to indicate she understood. They started their own private ritual—to meet, again and again. Always by the river—always in secret, and always exciting.

The differences in their languages were a challenge at first, but they were young and quickly figured their way around that. She pointed to herself, the moon and a red flower to show that her name was Aygul and that it meant Moon Rose.

In a more complicated procedure, and by miming himself only larger, the boy explained that his name—Nefin—meant son or nephew.

By fits and starts—they picked up a little of each other's languages and began to get to know each other. But the day Aygul suggested Nefin follow her home to meet her parents the boy became nervous.

She had to admit, her tribe was suspicious of strangers, and Nefin probably had a point. But then Nefin asked Aygul to accompany him to his home instead—to come to his village and meet his family.

Aygul found that she had the same reservations; in their worlds, visitors were rare, scary and even dangerous.

They decided to keep meeting together, away from adults, and in secret. And so now here they were, alone, together.

The young couple walked through the forest, Nefin taking her hand while they played a game of pointing at objects for the other to name.

As the sun was getting low Aygul placed a hand on Nefin's arm, and signaled it was time to leave.

But Nefin appeared nervous, something was in the air and his anxiety was starting to rub off on Aygul. Was it her imagination or had the forest grown quieter? Aygul thought she knew all its sounds by heart. Maybe it was just nerves—the shadows were playing with her mind.

Nefin glanced around in a curious fashion and Aygul tried to ask what was wrong. But her voice seemed too loud. Maybe one of them had been followed. Aygul was certain no one had followed her.

Taking Nefin's hand, Aygul led him back the way they had come, while anxiously peering through the trees.

They were almost back to the ancient sycamore when a shadow separated itself from the darkness and the forest itself crashed down on them

CHAPTER ONE

It was noon as the two men crested the rim of the valley and stopped to behold a truly breathtaking sight. An immense emerald-green canyon snaked into the distance. The gorge looked to be days long and was bisected by a ribbon of blue and white—a sparkling river. It provided a vivid contrast to the forest's greens and white limestone cliffs. There were sheer precipices, broken crags and defiles of shattered stone, and all under a blue sky the color of a robin's egg. It had an ancient look—and it was—older than time as measured by man. Older than the two travelers could comprehend, though they had a sense of it. The broken weathered rock spoke of countless generations of animals marching back and forth across space and time. It was an old, old land, and yet at the same time ageless. Broken only by the seasons—it would be unchanged long after everyone alive was gone.

The valley stretched out of sight—to disappear around the crumbling peaks and cliffs. It was the wilds of nature.

Far down on the valley floor, from the travelers' vantage point, the trees looked like nothing more than moss. The fuzzy green forest twisted back and forth as it followed the river. The canyon cut like a knife through the earth, revealing layers of white, brown and black and long stains in the limestone from countless rains. From this height the river looked peaceful—lazy—even serene—but the travelers knew better. On closer inspection it would be alive, home to fish and beaver and otter.

The river could crash over rocks and falls to quench the thirst of the untamed landscape. Spent, it would slow as it reached the dry scrub land and open fields.

Here on the heights the air was clear and crisp. A breeze rustled the trees—and was accompanied by the lonely cries of great hawks as they keened to each other and soared between the hidden eyries. The travelers were in the hawks' domain—this province high above the valley floor. While the sun blazed down to warm them, the wind chilled their skin. It was enough motivation to encourage the two to begin their descent.

In the Valley of the Auroch

Hours later, the travelers reached the valley floor and looked for a spot to relax. It had been an arduous hike down from the rim. But it was a whole different world here at the base of the cliff and a good place for a bivouac.

A light breeze ruffled the leaves in the trees; it carried the fragrance of pine and cedar while the ground seemed to emanate an earthy musk. It was the aroma of leaves that had fallen, and green ferns with long leaves dotted with spores. Everywhere thick, olive-colored moss blanketed the forest floor and enveloped tree-roots, stumps, fallen trees and branches in a soft and moist carpet. Even the rocks couldn't escape nature's palette as they were encrusted in red, yellow and blue-gray lichen.

Still young, the day had grown pleasingly warm, and shafts of bright yellow sunlight pierced down through the trees to illuminate an immense fog of swirling midges and other tiny insects. Birds sang to each other while squirrels chittered noisily at the travelers' passing.

The two travelers made an unlikely pair. The taller was an angular young man with dark wavy hair and a neat beard. He was dressed in a trim, tanned, deer-skin jacket with matching fringed leggings and a deer-skin cap, and was sitting on a flat knee-high rock. He was chewing on a licorice root—as was often his habit—and when he smiled—which was often—he had a brilliant smile. This dapper young man called himself Walker because—no surprise—it so happened that he walked a lot.

Walker was busy rummaging around in his pack and then—his face lighting up with that smile—found what he was looking for—the last of his stash—a carefully leaf-wrapped bundle—which he opened to reveal several exquisitely smoked trout fillets.

"Hairy," whispered Walker.

Walker was trying to get the attention of his small companion, the second traveler, who was sitting on a nearby log, busily inspecting and coiling a length of braided rope.

This fellow was quite a stark contrast to Walker. While he too was dressed in dapper deerskins, he was much smaller in stature and while his features were dark too, he was decidedly furry—hence his name. Hairy also had prominent brows, a flat nose, sharp teeth and almost no chin.

The two had been hiking the trail hard for days and although they had been carefully rationing their food, they were beginning to run low on supplies. Walker knew it meant they would have to devote some time in the near future to reprovisioning, but he hoped this valley—at the moment full of mystery and adventure—would be a bounty of lazy wild game as well as who-knows-what other opportunities.

In the meantime, it looked like they had at least one decent meal left. Now that he'd gotten Hairy's attention, Walker waved one of the smoked fishes and tossed it over. Hairy—quick-as-a-blink—snatched it out of the air. Hairy sniffed the treat and closed his eyes, smiling with pleasure. Opening his eyes, Hairy dipped into his own rucksack and tossed a small leather pouch to his companion.

Walker—hoping for berries or nuts— took a deep breath and opened this bag with some trepidation. In deference to Hairy's feelings, Walker maintained his smile and suppressed a sigh of disappointment. The pouch was full of brown, striped, squirming grubs—each the size of Walker's thumb. Still, he wasn't surprised. Grubs were easily Hairy's favorite food on the trail. And they were easy to catch—you could find them under any old log or in a rotten stump. Walker had to admit, grubs were nutritious and kept well—staying alive and squirming for days. And his furry little friend really seemed to enjoy popping the nutty, buttery bugs between his big teeth—grinning with pleasure with every swallow.

Suppressing a grimace, Walker tossed a fat grub into his mouth. To stop its wriggling, he bit down quickly, doing his best to ignore the bug-guts now sticking to his teeth.

Popping his licorice stick back into his mouth to kill the taste, Walker gathered up some bum-fodder and stood up to embark on a trip to the latrine. He looked about the clearing and nodded to his little friend.

In the Valley of the Auroch

"Any trouble I should know about?" asked Walker.

Even a trip to relieve yourself demanded that a person remained vigilant. This valley was truly terra incognito—and it was important to stay alert, and Walker didn't know what manner of creatures stalked this particular forest. One of the advantages of traveling in pairs was that it usually dissuaded all but the fiercest predators. Stepping behind a tree for privacy meant taking a risk, but Hairy was Walker's early warning system.

In response, Hairy stopped nibbling his fish and looked up, beetling his brows in concentration. Hairy—a man of very few if any words—waved casually in the direction that the sun would set into—west—and waggled a hand, a mime of a swimming fish, across his chest and then outward—Hairy-speak for—"That direction".

"What in that direction?" asked Walker as he himself strained to see into the undergrowth between the trees.

Hairy bared his front teeth and now mimed stroking a pointy beard—which he didn't have—several times, then held both palms up as if comparing the weight of two objects—again, Hairy-speak for—leopard—maybe".

Walker had spotted leopard and wolf tracks earlier on their hike. Under the circumstances, leopards didn't worry him. This forest was lush and there would certainly be plenty of game for the noisy predators.

On returning from his ablutions, Walker considered their situation.

"I might as well refill our canteens and make tea," said Walker, and pointing off towards the river, "You got any particular insights in that direction?"

Instead of directly answering, Hairy paused to take another nibble of trout. As he chewed, he appeared to grow thoughtful while his big ears twitched—Walker's hearing was fine, but for his part, he couldn't hear anything but the sounds of birds, frogs and bugs.

Walker couldn't tell if Hairy was just enjoying the fish and choosing to ignore the question—an annoying habit of his—or really concentrating. But finally, Hairy shrugged— "No."

"You want to make camp by the river?" asked Walker. "Maybe we can catch something along the way to go with the tea."

Hairy nodded and stood to collect his things.

Walker shouldered his spear and began to gather up his tools and equipment too. He also absentmindedly began to whistle.

Hairy looked at his taller friend and shook his head. He had issues with Walker's whistling, especially when they were in unfamiliar territory. Shrugging, Hairy finished rolling his things into a bundle and then hefted it over his shoulders. Finally, he picked up his rabbit-stick—basically a small spear—along with his carefully coiled rope and nodded to Walker that he was ready.

Walker wrapped his tooth-cleaning sticks up into a leather parcel and stored them deep in his pack for safe keeping, then repacked the remaining food and slid his arms through the straps on his bag before straightening and signaling he was ready too.

Hairy turned to leave but abruptly froze—a peculiar sight that caught Walker's attention. Hairy raised a fist.

Walker stopped whistling.

Walker dropped his voice to a whisper and asked, "What?" But Hairy was ignoring him—having gone all quiet and intense.

"What?" repeated Walker.

Hairy turned slowly, scanning the trees. Then, as if noticing Walker for the first time, he barred his teeth and slowly raked an open hand over his head.

"Lynx?" whispered Walker and tightening his grip on his spear.

Hairy shook his head violently—creeping backwards a step—and raked his open hand over his head again. "Lion," sighed Walker feeling his heart drop and taking an involuntarily step back himself. "How close?"

But instead of a verbal response, Hairy began shuffling—very fast—in his quietest mincing way—across the clearing. Walker quickly fell into line, all the while looking over his shoulder. He didn't see anything yet, but by the time you actually saw a lion, it was too late.

On reaching the trees, they both broke into a casual, shambling trot—carefully avoiding anything like the panicked run which would provoke a lion's attack response. But as Hairy and Walker emerged from the forest they were brought to a stop by a wide, loud, fast-moving stream. The dense ground cover and steep riverbank blocked them from heading up or down river on land. Walker jabbed Hairy on the shoulder and pointed to the river, but it was much too wide to jump, and Hairy—who was terrified of water—shook his head violently.

In the Valley of the Auroch

Walker knew they had no choice and pulled the rope from Hairy's pack. He knotted the bitter end around his spear. Holding a few coils loosely in his left hand, Walker flung the spear toward the far side of the river. It sailed across but came up short and Walker retrieved it, pulling hand over hand, as quickly as possible. Hairy—looking back the way they'd come—was crouched, rabbit-stick at the ready—though little good it would do against a lion. Walker flung the spear once more and this time it reached the far side but slid free of the brush. Walker retrieved the spear again and—near panic—threw for all he was worth—so hard he almost fell into the river himself. He was rewarded to see the spear tangle in the crotch of a tree on the other side. Walker tugged hard and the rope held fast. Quickly wrapping the line around his arm, Walker grabbed his companion and flung him over his shoulder. Hairy—horrified—twisted his arms though the straps of Walker's pack and dug his fingers into Walker's jacket. Walker dove headfirst into the raging water. They were still in the air as the monster cat—all claws and teeth—leapt out of the trees, and just missed them as the pair splashed into the cold river.

The fast-moving water carried Hairy and Walker downstream and to the end of the rope, coming up with a hard jerk—the force practically yanking Walker's arm from his shoulder. The fast-moving current swung them clear across to slam into the opposite bank. Somehow Hairy managed to hold on, as Walker dragged them both—gasping for air—arm-over-arm—up and onto the sandy bank. Standing, Walker looked back across the river to see a gigantic and very angry cat—striped shaggy gray fur and enormous jaws full of long white teeth. The lion paced back and forth, roaring at them in frustration and flicking water from its paws—the spray sparkling in the sunlight.

The river was much too fast and wide for the lion to cross, but Walker and Hairy still couldn't take their eyes off it as they backed up slowly into the woods.

They were soaked and shivering from the cold water, and the garments were filled with river sand. They felt weighed down by their soggy things but it was warm, so they were unlikely to catch a chill. Still, the water had soaked their packs and would ruin their provisions. Hairy and Walker knew that instead of traipsing around in their wet clothes, they should take everything off to dry. After they'd hiked what seemed like a safe enough distance from the river, they settled on a small clearing under the warming sun.

Recovering from the immediate shock of the situation, Hairy automatically turned to gather kindling as Walker shrugged off his pack and bent to try to start a fire. They were both grateful it hadn't rained recently, and everything was dry.

"Well, that was more excitement than I needed before lunch," remarked Walker and finding himself smiling at finding themselves both still alive, "Good ears Hairy, you saved our skins today—again."

Hairy acknowledged the compliment with a weak smile—he was still a bit shaken after the impromptu dunking.

"Not that you didn't need a bath anyway," added Walker, struggling to remove his cloying garments, "But we should get out of these wet things before they shrink on us. Then we should go through our packs."

Hairy dropped an armload of twigs and leaves and promptly began peeling off his wet clothing.

Walker—naked as the day he was born—crouched and began to twirl a stick into a dry chunk of willow bark. This fire-starting technique could take a while, so Hairy helped by blowing on the tinder. Soon enough, they had a little smoke and Hairy added sprigs of dry moss until they saw a lick of fire. Walker added a few leaves and encircled the blaze with stones, adding more kindling as necessary.

Fire started, Hairy and Walker began rubbing themselves with leaves to dry. Next, they assembled a rack a short distance from the fire to dry their stuff on. Walker carefully arranged his deerskin leather shoes (with bear hide soles), fringed deerskin jacket, matching leggings and linen tunic on the rack to dry. Finally, he turned his attention to the contents of his wet pack. Walker removed the leather bundle and carefully unrolled it. Inside were half a dozen gleaming shards of obsidian in a variety of hues. Satisfied that none of his precious cargo was broken, Walker laid the bundle out to dry. Next, he fished out a collapsible leather teapot and his precious licorice sticks. Finally, and without much hope, he removed several leaf-wrapped acorn bread cakes. These were to have been the last of their old provisions for the next few days. But now they were ruined, disintegrated from the dunking. And on top of all that, Walker had accidentally dropped the smoked trout back at the previous clearing.

"Consarn it! So much for our provisions," remarked Walker, letting a few wet crumbs dribble through his fingers. "Damned mumblecrusted lion."

At the mention of the cat, Hairy turned to nervously eye the forest in the direction of the river.

In the Valley of the Auroch

"I don't think you need to worry about the kitty, Hairy," said Walker to soothe his companion's nerves. "That lion's going to have to travel some distance to find a shallow spot in the river if it really wants to cross. Hopefully it'll just forget about us long before then. Come to think of it, the lion was probably tracking something else when it chanced on our trail. I mean if it was stalking us, even you probably wouldn't have heard it in time. But you know, aside from the lion, this valley seems pretty quiet. Anything else around?"

Hairy got to his feet—standing full upright he was almost to Walker's shoulder. Hairy's wide nostrils flared as he sampled the air. Then, pointing off opposite the river, Hairy made hand signals, holding his hand in front of his face, a thumb on his nose and little finger in the air. He then raised his hand a few times while snorting—Hairy speak for unicorn—the big, bald forest rhinoceros.

"Figures it would be a unicorn, if it has a calf that might explain a few things—nothing big cats like more." Walker contemplated the sheer cliff behind them. "So, we're maybe between a lion and its dinner. Uncomfortable. And, now I'm all turned around. We need to get the lay of the land."

Quick-as-a-blink, Hairy began climbing a nearby, very tall sycamore, high enough to see over the tops of the surrounding forest. When Hairy was in position, he snapped off a twig and threw it down to Walker to get his attention. Walker shrugged.

"What?" he called.

In response, Hairy just pointed off into the distance.

Walker sighed and began climbing, though a bit slower and more laboriously than his hirsute little friend. Naked, he climbed until he'd accumulated a respectable number of scratches and the available handholds had grown uncomfortably thin. And as if that wasn't enough, a flock of crows turned up to caw derisively from the nearby branches, heckling the awkward intruder.

Looking down to the forest floor and then back up to Hairy, Walker said, "You know, it's times like this I'd appreciate it if you could find your voice." Of course, he didn't expect a response and proceeded to push aside the leaves to get a better view of their surroundings. "Okay, what did you make me climb all the way up here to see?"

Hairy ignored the sarcasm and pointed off down the length of the valley. Walker had to wriggle up a few more precarious arm-lengths, but there—off in the distance—he spied tendrils of smoke. And from the looks of things, it was a settlement.

"Damn, Hairy, it looks like this valley is already occupied," said Walker. "That's too much smoke for primitives. Just our luck we stumble across the perfect wilderness spot, and it's already got a settlement. And you know, it was probably the smell from their damned fires that the lion was following." He shook his head in frustration.

Walker was disappointed. This was supposed to be their quest for adventure. He and Hairy were on the trail of new and undiscovered lands. They were out there, living rough in nature's wilderness and declaring their freedom and independence. This was to be a physical pursuit of otherworldly encounters. But instead, this valley had already been discovered by someone else.

This was what Walker was running from. It seemed that the world was filling up with people. The Hurrian race was expanding, and it was spoiling the nature's wilderness in the process. Pretty soon there would be nothing left for adventurers like Hairy and him to discover. Dispirited, they both began climbing back down to evaluate their situation.

As he went, Walker thought to himself. Maybe there was a bright side here. Perhaps there were interesting new people who they might be able to trade with and maybe get something to eat.

Walker found that it was better to be positive and make the best of every situation.

On reaching the forest floor they discovered that their clothing and stuff were still wet, and it wouldn't do to meet the new neighbors naked. To kill time while waiting, Walker fetched their water bags and grabbed his spear.

"Hairy, I'm going back to the river for water," said Walker. "You climb back up and keep an eye on everything just in case."

As he retraced his steps to the river, Walker kept a wary eye out—he didn't want to run naked into a wolf if he could help it. The river was clear—no sign of the big cat—the rapids too much to bother with. And like he'd told Hairy, by now the lion had probably forgotten all about them and moved on. Nevertheless, it would still be prudent to remain vigilant, under the circumstances, only an idiot would completely drop his guard. Best to always play it safe.

Locating a clear eddy where he could see the bottom, Walker knelt, held his hair back and he drank his fill. Then he set about topping up the water

In the Valley of the Auroch

bags.

Finished, and picking his way back to camp, Walker kept on the lookout for fresh animal tracks. But aside from the wolf tracks, he wasn't seeing much of anything.

At least until Walker spotted a promising print in a patch of loamy soil. It was the big, flat impression left by a rhino. And it was heading away from the river. Walker felt better. The valley was beginning to seem weird—they hadn't seen any sign of game since they climbed down from the plateau. But Hairy was right, this was the track of a rhinoceros. Evidently, the beast had quenched its thirst at the same clear eddy and was moving deeper into the forest.

Aside from the one loamy patch, the ground was rocky and difficult for tracking game. Walker headed in the direction indicated by the rhino print. Coming around a thick stand of trees he came face to face with its owner.

"Nice monster," said Walker in his most soothing voice.

Only a few armlengths' away stood the wooly rhinoceros.

*

Little Fox peered over the edge of the stone he was clinging to and gasped—immediately losing his grip.

The big man on the boulder next to Little Fox caught him by the collar before he slipped too far and hauled him back up.

"Whoa, there Little Fox," he whispered. Little Fox was Walker's childhood name. "Your mother would never forgive me if I brought you home worse for wear."

The big man turned and looked at the smaller, feral looking child to his right. "And you, little Hairy, are you okay?"

Little Hairy beamed up at his stepfather and gave an okay sign. Little Hairy could climb like a spider.

The three were clinging to the side of an enormous boulder on the outskirts of an alpine field. It was mid-morning, the sky was blue, the sun was shining, the grass was green, the field full of flowers and the air crisp. Walker—Little Fox—gulped, then cautiously raised his head to look back over the edge of the rock. The image was hard for him to comprehend— there appeared to be fur-covered boulders moving slowly about the grassy field, each supported by what looked like stout tree stumps. And from each furry boulder's nose—Little Fox could only assume it was a nose—grew a giant horn. And there were a lot of these boulder things.

"Behold, the wooly rhinoceros," stated the big man. "One of the most dangerous animals in the world."

"Are we safe here uncle?" asked Little Fox. The big man was his uncle Strider, and Little Fox was feeling this excursion of theirs was more precarious than he was led to believe, that he hadn't been given enough information and so he was now looking around for quick escape routes.

"We're safe from the rhinoceros," chuckled Strider. "As long as we stay off the ground, cause these big rhinos can't climb."

Little Fox didn't think that any of the rhinos would have any trouble just reaching up and poking them with those long horns, right here on the side of the boulder if they became so inclined.

"You know, if your parents were here," explained Strider, "they'd be giving thanks to the ancestors and the forest spirits for providing us with such bountiful gifts as these great animals."

But Little Fox wasn't really listening to his uncle.

"Do you hunt rhinoceros uncle?" asked Little Fox. "They look too big."

"I have," replied Strider. "But they are very dangerous animals, and it is no small task."

Just then Little Fox spotted something even more diverting emerging from the trees—mammoths. There were several of the giants on the far edge of the clearing, noisily tearing branches off of the trees, stripping off the green leaves and shoving the greenery into their mouths. Little Fox was too young to be a hunter, but he still knew what a mammoth was. Were they in danger from getting poked by the big horns?

"Won't the rhinoceros poke the mammoths? Why don't they run away?" Little Fox asked, momentarily forgetting his own nervousness.

"Even though rhinoceros are quick to anger, mammoths and rhinos are friends," explained Strider. "Mammoths mostly eat leaves too high up in the trees for rhinoceroses. And rhinos mostly eat grass low down on the ground. Rhinos don't see very well, while mammoths see everything. The mammoths will roar if they see danger, like a pack of lions or wolves. And hearing the mammoths' warning, the rhinoceros will charge and drive off danger with its horns."

Little Fox turned his attention back to the rhinoceros. They were a contradiction to him. Huge, terrifying beasts, grazing peacefully in a field of flowers.

"Why do you even hunt rhinoceros, Uncle?" asked Little Fox, incredulous at the very idea.

"I have hunted rhinos before, but only in time of great need, Little Fox," explained Strider. "And even one rhinoceros is too much for a lone hunter. The horned beast can be quite fearsome. It takes many men to kill one, though it's true that they are very good eating."

Hairy pointed at the mammoth and mimed poking a spear, using the signs Little Fox's uncle had taught him.

"Yes Hairy," replied Strider. "I've hunted mammoths too. And it takes many brave men to hunt them as well. And lots of people to butcher and carry the meat back to the village. It takes even more to keep watch for wolves and jackals who would try to steal our kill."

"I would need a very long spear," added Little Fox.

"Or a very tall cliff," laughed Strider, "Sometimes the best techniques are not the most obvious, boy."

*

"Nice little beastie," said Walker to the hair-covered hill standing before him.

The rhinoceros appeared to be taking Walker's measure. It was more than half again taller than Walker at the shoulder, and certainly had nothing to fear from him, but the rhino didn't know that. It stood perfectly still, save a single twitch of an ear.

Walker spread his arms wide, palms up, hoping to appear non-threatening, and began to reverse course, very, very slowly.

"Don't bother your big, beautiful head about me," continued Walker in a friendly tone. "Just a buck-naked man on a stroll through the woods."

In response, the rhino's ears began moving and the beast let out its breath, blowing leaves off the path. Then, the moment passed, the rhino raised its big head and turned, ambling off into the forest.

Walker collapsed to his hands and knees in relief.

Opening his eyes Walker spotted another track in the sand between the pieces of gravel—human.

Alarmed, Walker jumped to his feet and picked up the pace. Returning to the impromptu camp, he was relieved to find Hairy lounging high off the ground in the bough of the sycamore. Maybe the humans were tracking the rhino and if so, it helpfully led them away from their camp.

Walker checked the drying rack and satisfied with the results, slipped into his deerskin leggings, tunic and jacket. He completed his outfit with a wide belt, from which dangled a row of leather strips, some knotted. Walker began repacking his kit before remembering the lost provisions. Hairy had descended from his perch and was repacking as well. All at once Hairy stopped and looked around frantically, keening softly under his breath. Evidently, in their haste to avoid the lion, he'd lost his pouch of grubs.

"Sorry Hairy," sighed Walker. "I'm out of corn cakes and dried fish too. It looks like we'll need to restock. It's weird, I haven't seen a track for a deer, antelope or boar. In fact, there's not so much as a rabbit. If it weren't for the squirrels, I'd think this place was dead. The only tracks I did find were from that rhino you sniffed out and I'd rather not run into that walking mountain again."

Walker looked off in the direction they had seen the smoke. "Maybe the natives are friendly, and we can beg a meal."

CHAPTER TWO

Visitors weren't always welcomed in frontier settlements as folks tended to be suspicious of strangers.

As such, Hairy and Walker approached the settlement from downwind and kept to the densest undergrowth for as long as possible.

There was also the problem that you never knew what kind of people you were going to find. If you were lucky, they might be folks setting up a trading post. But they could just as easily be savage inbred cannibals, religious nuts or end-of-the-world survivalist weirdos. Regardless, travelers like Hairy and Walker were well advised to proceed with the utmost caution whenever making introductions.

They ensconced themselves inside a thick stand of bushes. It would serve as an effective blind from which to observe the village. Their arrival displaced a collection of small birds, who quickly relocated nearby and chittered angrily at them for invading their territory. Hairy and Walker settled down to stake out the settlement and pass the time.

It had certainly been a disappointing few days. Every trail invariably led

In the Valley of the Auroch

to nothing. The valley was beautiful, even awe-inspiring, but also virtually lifeless—aside from birds, mice, squirrels and the rhino. But Hairy and Walker weren't going to replenish their provisions on mice and tiny birds. And the two of them weren't about to tackle a rhino. Walker was normally a pretty lucky angler, but he couldn't even pull a fish from this river. It looked like this valley was hunted out.

But there were people. Walker wondered what they managed to live on.

"This is all fine for you," Walker said. Hairy enjoyed grubs and caterpillars, of which there were plenty. "But I can't live on bugs alone and I'm not constitutionally suited to become a vegetarian."

It came down to two choices. Leave the valley and go looking for more fertile hunting grounds or see what the villagers had to offer. And Walker wasn't too optimistic about the latter. If there were already too many mouths to feed already, he and Hairy wouldn't be receiving a very warm welcome. The most likely scenario was that they would be chased off as trespassers by the apprehensive country folk. Still, it was worth the effort. If it didn't work out, they could still always just leave the valley hungry.

Now, on closer inspection, Walker was surprised at the size of the settlement. It was big enough to be called an actual village and looked fairly organized. There was a couple dozen clay and straw-daubed, grass-thatch roofed huts. He noted water troughs and storage bins. There were grinding stones for making flour and lots of stone-ringed fire pits. Walker guessed there could be well more than a hundred souls in the village.

And in the center of everything was a large hut—a longhouse; it was a tall and wide structure covered with a heavy thatched roof. Smoke from inside curled up from a pair of openings in the roof.

Walker noted a number of drying racks between the huts, some with hides and others with fish and even meat. Meat! There were skinned rabbits and hare hanging from the rack.

Walker didn't have Hairy's nose, but even to him the village reeked— like a lot of unwashed people living in close proximity to each other.

"That lion we bumped into could have been following the smell from this place," whispered Walker to Hairy's nodding agreement. "And it looks like these people might be Hurrians." So far, most of the people Walker and Hairy had run into since setting out on their travels were Hurrians. Walker was one himself, at least his people called themselves Hurrians, which is why he knew the name. "But that doesn't mean they're friendly."

It might have seemed to be a peaceful settlement, but Walker spotted what looked like sentries at all four corners of the village.

"Suspicious folk," said Walker, pointing them out to Hairy. "Typical, but I wonder what they have to be suspicious about?"

The dwellings were all clustered along a quiet brook—a tributary off from the main river. The stream provided easy access to water for the community. Men and women dressed in mismatched animal skin and/or straw-mat wraps went about their daily business. Babies played in the dirt, and toddlers toddled. Hairy nudged Walker and pointed—a tall, coarse-looking fellow with a thin face was hitching up his leggings as he emerged from a tall conical tent.

"Well, they got themselves an outhouse," observed Walker and, wrinkling his nose, pointed at another example farther off. "I guess these are cultured folk."

Hairy raised his big eyebrows questioningly.

"You know, for dropping a shite away from prying eyes," explained Walker.

Walker's attention was suddenly diverted by a remarkable sight; a boy ambled into view with a little animal on a rope—it was a baby auroch! The diminutive forest beast even had ridiculously little horns—just bumps protruding from its head. The creature was thickset with the beginnings of a hump on its back and covered in short gray hair. The child was a little taller than the auroch. But the little calf would eventually grow into a monster. It was astonishing to see it on the end a measly little length of twine—and led around by a little kid, no less! Walker was utterly flabbergasted; the creature looked completely docile. The idea that a brute of the forest would just allow itself to be led around by a boy—a boy its mother could crush without a second thought—was beyond belief. Yet, the kid appeared totally indifferent to any danger as he led the little auroch up to a roughhewn water trough and just stood there, shooing away flies while the wild little beastie drank.

Hairy seemed to be equally flabbergasted—his mouth hanging open in dumbfounded bewilderment. Hairy elbowed Walker in the ribs and pointed at the pint-sized beast.

"I know, I know," agreed Walker, "I wouldn't have believed it myself. What I don't get is, with animals so scarce around here, why haven't they eaten it yet? You think it's on tonight's menu?"

In the Valley of the Auroch

The baby auroch must have been thirsty because it drained half the trough. Satiated, the beast looked up and the kid took that as a signal and turned to lead the beast away.

Hairy nudged Walker again and pointed to the shaggy little monster. He raised his thick brows questioningly.

"I know, I know it's tempting," agreed Walker. "But the locals might object if we invited their pet to be our dinner."

Hairy shook his head in confusion.

"Just because they haven't eaten it yet doesn't mean they're not planning to later," added Walker.

Hairy and Walker settled back to see what else they could learn. Walker pricked up his ears as a fellow emerged from the longhouse and walked, relatively close by, in the direction of the outhouse. This gave Walker the opportunity to get a good look at one of these people. The man looked the part, he was Hurrian for sure. Walker's disposition soured somewhat.

"It looks like I have some country kin here," observed Walker. "They're Hurrians, Hairy, and aside from having a baby bull, I guess they're normal." But Walker was also disappointed.

He and Hairy were on an exploration. This was supposed to be the wild frontier. But it seemed that wherever they went, they just found more people. The world they were exploring was filling up and soon there wouldn't be any wild places left.

Like it or not, these folks were already here, and Walker figured they might as well make the best of it.

Still, trading relations or not, normal looking or not, Walker wasn't taking any chances, even normal looking people could surprise you.

Just as Walker had this thought, he noticed a tall thin woman exiting the longhouse. She walked to a rack of drying meat and filled up a shallow wicker basket before returning inside. Walker's stomach growled as he watched this feast disappear from sight. He and Hairy had only had a few nibbles since they started out and the day was wearing on. Maybe there was something they could do about that. Hitching up his gumption, Walker turned to his little traveling companion.

"Okay, it's time to see how friendly these valley people are, but stick close to me in case there's any trouble."

They backtracked out of their blind and hiked around until they reached what looked to be a well-used path leading back toward the village.

Since it's never a good idea to show up anywhere empty-handed, Walker knelt and searched through his pack. He produced a carved wooden charm—a standing bear with its paws folded over its chest. It had been given to him as a child—whittled by one of his dad's friends. He'd brought it along for just such an occasion. It would make a nice gift and would pay double, as Walker had never liked the guy who carved it.

Walker removed his spear's obsidian tip and leather handgrip, while Hairy tossed his rabbit-stick into the bushes. Hitching up their pants, they headed to the settlement, using their spears like walking sticks and with their free hand open, loose at their side. Making no further attempts to conceal themselves, they stopped at the edge of the village. A group of villagers hurried over at the sight of the newcomers.

Walker raised his free hand and smiled a broad greeting. Growing up, his parents had taught him a few of the different Hurrian languages and Walker was hoping these folks spoke one of them.

"Hello, and good spirits be with you," Walker began with what was a pretty safe greeting. "We're travelers from a far-off land visiting your beautiful valley."

Of the group of men and women who had gathered, five individuals— all dressed in what looked like worn deerskin and fur—stepped forward to get a better look at them.

The villagers nodded to Walker—a guarded greeting—but narrowed their eyes at the sight of Hairy.

Walker had been taught that it was simple courtesy to provide a warm welcome to visitors. Tradition held that you should assume all guests are tired, hungry and thirsty. It was these 'good manners,' that governed civilized culture and Walker hoped these folks followed the same rules.

The tallest of the group took a step forward. He was a gray haired, big nosed, broad-shouldered fellow, dressed in what looked like a deerskin with a bear fur cloak and heavy sandals. Walker noticed he moved with a limp. Gray Hair raised his hands but remained silent. Walker hoped he knew their language, or this could take forever. With a sign for Hairy to stay put, Walker took a step forward as casually as possible. Gray Hair raised a hand to stop him and leaned forward.

"Why do you travel with an ape?" asked Gray Hair. He spoke in one of the older dialects and with a peculiar accent.

So that's the way it was going to be.

"He's not an ape," Walker replied. He used as friendly an inflection as he could manage. "His kin are prairie folk, he's just small."

Hairy, for his part, didn't appear to take offense.

Gray Hair stared at Walker for a moment, then turned an unfriendly gaze back on Hairy.

"He has got an ape's face. His kind used to live all over this valley."

"Really?" replied Walker, ears pricking up, "Where did they go?"

"They're gone," was Gray Hair's curt reply. "A long time ago."

Disappointed, Walker shrugged and decided it was best to ignore Gray Hair's rudeness for the time being. His mom had taught him to be tolerant when dealing with strangers. "Well, like I said, Hairy's people were prairie folk. I've known him since we were kids."

Gray Hair humphed and limped back to his group. Walker waved a friendly greeting to the crowd. No one waved back. Walker nodded encouragement to Hairy, acting more confident than he felt. Gray Hair turned back to his visitors taking a few steps in their direction, apparently having reached a decision.

"Well, I suppose you must be hungry after your travels," said Gray Hair. He sounded annoyed at this imposition. "You might as well come inside for a spell."

Relieved that courtesy finally trumped racism and bad manners, Walker nodded to Hairy and followed their hosts into the longhouse.

The big hut was dim; the light from a fire and smoldering torches chased the shadows around. The ventilation was poor, and the place stank from the smoke, rancid grease, cold ash, mildewed lumber and unwashed people. But it was warm, and the aroma of braised meat, hot fatty stew, and baked bread was enough that Walker almost swooned. Gray Hair waved them towards a circle of old logs arranged around the blackened fire-pit stones. There was a lanky woman in a dirty tunic standing by a patchwork curtain dividing the house. Gray Hair pointed at her, and she vanished behind the curtain.

Walker and Hairy settled themselves uncomfortably on a smooth thick log. Sitting in a corner, an unkempt gent in a scruffy fur vest was blowing tunelessly on a gnarled flute. He was off any key and the noises he produced assailed Walker's senses like the buzzing of cicadas. Gray Hair joined them opposite the smoky fire, still eyeing Hairy inhospitably.

"Welcome to our village; good spirits be with you." said Gray Hair in a strained display of diplomacy. With a hand to his chest, "I am Osmanek. We are the Vadi Kabile."

"Good spirits be with you as well," answered Walker.

Walker, drawing on his understanding of the dialect guessed Vadi Kabile meant; valley tribe—not the most original name for a village, but maybe that was on par with folks in the wilderness.

"I am headman of the village," added Osmanek. Which, Walker translated as; chief.

"And I am Tabib," said another, older, tattooed fellow in a feathered cloak. "I am the medicine man of our tribe." Walker knew Tabib translated as; medicine man. No imagination at all. Evidently Hairy and Walker had stumbled onto the village of the literal. Was that a trait of fundamentalism?

"Tell me, is it common to travel with apes where you're from?" This from a smaller, beardless gent garbed in a brown bearskin. Apparently, this guy's prejudices overcame any manners he'd ever been taught.

Repeated insults. To Walker, these back-country yokels were proving to be short on civility. He was above that sort of behavior. As rude as his hosts were being, it would be even ruder for a guest to point out his host's shortcomings. Though Walker had to admit, there were plenty of folks' back home who looked down their noses at Hairy; maybe he shouldn't be so quick to judgement.

"I can't answer for everyone," replied Walker, "but I enjoy traveling with Hairy. We've been through a few scrapes together and he's the best tracker I've ever met. I'm glad to have him along."

But from the sour look on his face, chief Osmanek was apparently little interested in being polite company.

A brown-haired, brown-eyed woman of indeterminate age, wearing a patched rabbit-skin garment and sporting a pretty bead and coral necklace emerged from behind the curtain bearing a wide basket filled with acorn cakes, dried fish, smoked rabbit and slices of fried puffball. The lanky woman Walker saw earlier reappeared with several bowls of gray liquid that smelled like fermented sorghum. One bowl was presented to Walker, the second to Osmanek. The drink was milky and had a sweet-sour odor. Walker screwed up his courage and sampled the earthy, slimy beverage.

In the Valley of the Auroch

Disgusting.

Walker smiled as politely as possible—as he'd been taught—and bowed his head in appreciation for the drink.

"Yum," he said, "and thank you for your hospitality." Walker continued, trying to suppress his natural tendency toward sarcasm. He passed the bowl to Hairy, "And for this great feast."

Osmanek nodded in return and took a sip from his own bowl. Walker could tell the grayed haired gent tried to suppress any reaction, but a twitch escaped his control. The chief didn't think much of the drink either. When his turn came, the little beardless guy winced, unable to stifle his reaction— was this some kind of test or an example of bad country cuisine?

"I am Walker." he said, bowing his head, "And my companion is called Hairy."

Hairy looked up, more or less expressionless unless you knew what to look for.

"My name is Taichi," replied the little beardless gent. Walker knew that the name literally meant; large one, evidently Taichi's parents had been wishful thinkers. "Good spirits be with you."

A muscular chap with a hollow face and a wolf-skin vest said, "I am called Tarkan," which meant He who is bold and strong.

"And I am Volkan." said a tall man with very long braided hair. His name meant volcano.

"And I am Osman." added a powerful looking, big-nosed man with a pointy little beard. He was wearing a heavy bearskin cloak held together with wooden toggles.

Walker raised an eyebrow, "What does Osman mean if you don't mind my asking?"

"Bird with a large beak." replied Osman. "Good spirits be with you," he added as an afterthought.

"Yes, and you too, thanks." said Walker.

The brown haired, brown eyed woman of indeterminate age returned to hand Walker a small basket of dried fish and another of fried puff balls. Walker sniffed a piece of the fish and concluded its best days were long past. He selected a slice of puffball instead but took a bite as small as he considered would appear polite. It was a wise choice; the mushroom was slimy and bitter. To forestall any involuntary wince, he busied himself digging the carved bear totem from his jacket.

"A small token of our appreciation for your hospitality," coughed Walker, making a great show of offering forth the charm.

"Yes, well, it is seldom we have visitors," replied Osmanek. Walker wasn't surprised considering the quality of the food. Osmanek nodded his thanks for the gift. "Especially as talented as the carver of this piece."

"Thank you for your kind words," replied Walker, and quickly passed the basket to Hairy, "and for this generous banquet," he added diplomatically.

"Not at all," replied Osmanek, who, stone-faced, bravely took a small bite of fish. He was less successful at squelching a grimace. "It is our honor to be able to offer you something of our bounty. These are hard times. What brings you to our valley?"

Walker took a nibble of acorn cake. It was jarringly bitter and the grit crunching between his teeth brought him up sharply. Hiding a reaction, Walker smiled and continued.

"Hairy and I are explorers, on a quest to see new worlds. We chanced upon your valley. It was the smoke from your village that drew us here."

Pointing and smiling to admire the hanging torch over his head, Walker dropped the corn cake behind the log. "We were hoping maybe to trade for food and water."

"I'm afraid we don't have much to trade," replied Osmanek. "As I said, these are hard times. The spirits of the forest have been testing us."

"Does your…Hairy speak?" asked Tabib.

"Hairy's a man of few words," replied Walker. He turned to accept a new basket—with increasingly diminished expectations. The basket contained small pieces of dried something. Hare? Rabbit? Rat? Wasn't sure.

"You said quest?" repeated Osmanek, and eyeing his own corn cake suspiciously, "and new worlds? Where are you from then? What is your clan?"

"The Aurignac," answered Walker proudly. But the name elicited no reaction. Strange. Surely everyone had heard of Aurignac.

"Arg-nak?" said Volkan.

"Arrow-nak?" tried Tabib.

"What is this Ar-ge-nak?" asked Tarkan. "Is that your village? Where is it from here?"

"Aurignac," replied Walker, speaking the name slowly and distinctly, as if just repeating the name should explain everything. "On the coast, by the sea. You haven't heard of it?"

"No," answered Osmanek.

"By what see?" asked Taichi.

"THE sea," Walker explained. But this explanation was only met with empty stares. He added, "The big body of water stretching on to the horizon?"

"A lake?" asked Taichi.

"Sure, I guess," agreed Walker. He decided to give up and move on. "Anyway, it's a long way from here."

"How long?" asked Osmanek, "How many days travel?"

"More like a fortnight," replied Walker. "More than a fortnight's hike from your land."

"A fortnight?" Osman repeated the word in disbelief.

"You must be protected by demons to venture so far by yourselves," said Taichi.

"No." said Walker, "we're just good hikers. But we also stopped a lot. You know, sightseeing."

"Perhaps it was because you swallowed a wandering forest demon," said Tarkan, his eyes growing wide, "and it is that restless spirit that makes you roam."

"No, I've been running away from home since I was a kid," explained Walker, hoping to avoid being ritually exorcised. "Hairy and I are explorers, adventurers. Just a couple of guys out in looking for new places."

"It sounds like a restless spirit compels you," added Taichi.

"Maybe. Look—isn't that how you folks got here?" replied Walker. "Didn't one of your relatives go off looking for the great unknown? And that person discovered this valley in the process."

"So, you're scouts?" asked Osmanek, leaping to another conclusion.

"Not professionally," answered Walker, and looking to Hairy for help.

31

"We're explorers, adventurers, it's sort of the latest thing."

"A young man's rite of passage?" asked Osmanek, ignoring Walker's reply.

"No, just the two of us out on a long hike," Walker said in an effort to make things simple.

"So, what is it you're looking for again?" Osman asked.

"The last of the wild frontier. Before it's all gone."

"Gone where?" asked Taichi. "Where is it going?"

"That's just a figure of speech, it's not actually going anywhere," explained Walker. "I mean before the whole world is settled and filled with people. Before there's a village around every corner."

"Did your village shaman send you on this quest?" asked Tarkan.

"No." answered Walker.

"Ah! I know." said Osmanek, snapping his fingers, "You're a young man. Is this a bachelor's quest, to find a wife?"

"No, I'm not on a bachelor quest either," replied Walker. "Though I'm sure my parents would probably be happy if I did bring home a girl."

"So, you just abandoned your people to do this exploring. For no reason?" asked Taichi, "Don't you have any responsibilities back in your village?"

Walker thought Taichi sounded too much like his dad.

"I think they'll do just fine without me," replied Walker.

"So, tell us then," said Tarkan. He waved off Osman, who was trying to pass him a basket of gamey dried rabbit. "What new places you have found on this quest?"

"Well, I thought this place was new," answered Walker, trying to ignore Hairy's attempt to pass him the bowl of goop. "Until we saw that you folks were already here."

"You thought this valley was new?" asked Taichi. "That you had discovered it?"

"It was new to us," replied Walker. He was encouraged by the change in the direction of the conversation. "And it seemed like a really great find until we crossed paths with a lion not far from here."

In the Valley of the Auroch

"A lion?" repeated Osmanek snapping to attention, "Where?"

"Yeah, farther up the gorge, just the other side of the river," answered Walker. "It was probably drawn to the smoke from your cooking fires."

"More likely it was following you two," snapped Osmanek. "And now you've probably led it here, endangering everyone."

The villager men exchanged anxious looks, and at a nod from Osmanek, Osman and Tarkan exited the longhouse.

"Hey, the lion didn't follow us across the river," said Walker. "Anyway, that was a day ago. By now it's probably moved on looking for other game."

"Maybe you didn't see the lion follow you across the river," said Osmanek. "But there are shallows on the river. So now, thanks to you, we have a lion in the valley."

"It was just one lion," added Walker. "A valley this big, there must be more lions up in these hills."

"No," replied Osmanek, "there aren't. We've seen to that. But now, thanks to you, that has changed."

For a few moments everyone sat in an uncomfortable, embarrassed silence. It was finally broken by the sound of Hairy, gulping down a mouthful of fish.

"Get out," said Osmanek, rising to his feet.

A finger of time later, Hairy and Walker found themselves back outside. Once again, they were facing an unfriendly crowd. Muscular, hollow-faced Tarkan, garbed in his wolf skin vest shoved a sack into Walker hands.

Suppressing an urge to look inside—which would be rude—Walker nodded thanks.

Osmanek, believing Walker and Hairy had endangered the village, stood at the edge of the encampment, making no attempt to hide his irritation.

"Well, thank you for your hospitality," said Walker. He even bowed. Then, hoisting the bag, added, "and thank you for your generosity."

Osmanek leveled a stern gaze at the interlopers and shook his head.

"May the spirits keep you safe on your travels and for your... quest or whatever. I hope you find whatever it is you're looking for."

"Yes, well, good spirits be with you too."

But Osmanek didn't hear him. He had already turned on his heels and limped off.

Tarkan, Volkan and Osman on the other hand, remained, arms crossed, to make sure the travelers got the message.

Walker managed to maintain his smile. He wasn't going to let these yokels' lack of manners drag him down to their level. He nodded to Tarkan for the bag of vittles, waved to the crowd, and then turned and followed Hairy off down the trail. When they were comfortably out of sight of the settlement, Walker opened the sack and took a whiff.

The tang of the rancid contents jerked him upright and he passed the bag to Hairy.

"Well, that was a waste of time. All because we got chased by a lion?" Walker said, shaking his head. "Well, sorry Hairy. At least we've got plenty of water, and maybe we'll get lucky and bag a rabbit or squirrel before dark."

Hairy made a wiggling motion with a finger and pointed to a fallen tree.

"Yeah, we can look for some grubs, too," said Walker. "But let's wait till we're farther from the village. They'll be happier when they think we're out of their valley and honestly, the feelings are very mutual. Still, I'd sure like to know where they found that little auroch."

It was nearly afternoon, so they picked up the pace—it got dark early down in the valley. Still, they weren't about to abandon the river until they'd replenished their supplies. They left the trail and doubled back in the opposite direction—careful to give the village a wide berth—and headed towards the part of the river farther from the settlement, where they were more likely to find fish or game.

Presently Hairy tugged on Walker's sleeve and pointed to some freshly churned-up soil on the trail. Stooping for a better look, Walker recognized the tracks—auroch. The tracks looked pretty fresh and were from more than one animal.

"Well, now we're talking. An old auroch might just be doable. Right, Hairy?"

If they managed to stumble across an auroch they'd be set for a fortnight. To properly butcher such a big animal and preserve all the meat would mean making camp for a few days. But Walker figured they could find a spot far enough from the village to avoid conflict. Hairy set off tracking the beast, Walker on his tail, so to speak.

As the afternoon wore on, the tracks led Hairy and Walker back in the direction of the river. From all the turned-up soil it indicated that this was the aurochs' private watering hole. But it seemed that the aurochs had turned back into the forest.

It was odd that the aurochs were so close to the village. Big animals tended to avoid people. All this raised Walker's curiosity. But there was no mistake, the tracks led back in the direction of the settlement.

Then Walker remembered that kid with that auroch on a rope. Was that a coincidence? Could these folks have caught and tamed themselves some forest animals? Maybe that was why Osmanek was so anxious about the lion. And it might explain what the lion was doing in the valley; it wasn't tracking Walker and Hairy at all. The lion was tracking the auroch calf—a lion delicacy.

"Okay Hairy, maybe we'd better keep an eye open for that lion after all."

But from Hairy's posture, Walker could tell he had already reached the same conclusion.

By afternoon, they had picked up more tracks. This trail did indeed lead them to the aurochs.

And then they saw them. There was a couple dozen of the monsters—young and old, and they were all grazing together in a single open field along the cliff face. The field was between the cliff and a long rock defile. It was like a natural pen with the cliff on one side and the boulders on the other. The rocks were too big for clumsy critters like aurochs to climb over. They were big heavy brutes and couldn't manage such terrain. This was certainly odd.

Walker had seen herds of animals before. Elk, bison, even mammoths, but auroch were normally solitary animals.

But then Walker saw the log. It had been set between the forested cliff face and the rocky defile and was blocking the narrow entrance into the field. These animals weren't here on their own accord, they had been confined.

The heavy log was set waist-high and formed an effective barrier since aurochs can't jump—at all. They were trapped on what was essentially a big ledge overlooking the raging river.

Walker started to move forward to get a better look, but Hairy grabbed his arm and pointed to a leaf covered lean-to on a ledge above. There was a pair of leather-shod feet protruding from the crude shelter. Reexamining the gully with fresh eyes, Walker saw Osman, propped up with his back against a tree, looking mostly asleep himself. Farther off, Walker spotted a kid—the one from the village. He was slouched against a rock, quite asleep. Were these fopdoodles supposed to be watching this herd?

Well, well, thought Walker, this certainly explained a lot. Including where that auroch calf in the village had come from.

"What's the deal with these people and aurochs?" asked Walker.

It was pretty obvious that the scobberlotchers hadn't noticed Hairy and Walker. But just to be safe, they settled into the brush to wait.

After a while, they were satisfied that the idiot guards really were asleep on the job and wouldn't notice them.

Walker turned his attention back to the animals. Was there something special about these particular creatures that he was missing?

The aurochs looked normal enough—essentially giant antelope. Tall, hump-backed, clumsy looking, very heavy-set antelope. But with ridiculously large horns on their heads. Ridiculous, and not to be trifled with. Each horn was longer than Walker's arm. An auroch could skewer a leopard with those things. A big bull could even give a lion a bad day.

Yet the villagers had somehow tricked these critters into this trap and managed to barricade the entrance before the beasts got back out.

CHAPTER THREE

"So, the Vadi Kabile folks have got themselves some aurochs," whispered Walker. "But what are they doing with them? What is so special about these animals?"

Walker already knew the answer. Besides the one rhino he'd encountered, he hadn't seen much sign of any other game in the gorge. Could the people of the village have killed off or driven all the big animals away? Maybe there were just too many mouths to feed for even a big valley like this.

Folks living off the land had to keep moving around, following the herds from summer to winter feeding grounds. Walker's own people pulled fish from the sea, a seemingly inexhaustible bounty. But by settling in this land, the Vadi Kabile had probably killed and eaten most of the big game. So, were these auroch the only animals left? It made sense. A rhinoceros was probably too much for the Vadi Kabile to handle, but they'd managed to trap aurochs and were now keeping them for food.

But the desperate villagers were afraid of losing these animals too. No wonder they had been short-tempered. They had trapped these aurochs here to keep them handy but that also made them easy for a predator to find.

Hairy and Walker

In the Valley of the Auroch

Walker had to give the Vadi Kabile credit; it was an innovative solution to the predicament they'd gotten themselves into. And somehow the villagers figured out that aurochs would tolerate each other in their makeshift prison. Still, Walker thought, with all those deadly horns in one place, this was one dangerous venture.

This whole affair bothered Walker on a gut level. The auroch belonged in the forest. It was natural for people to hunt them, but to Walker, it was like the Vadi Kabile were somehow "stealing" the animals from everyone else.

Maybe it was Walker's attitude that didn't make sense. After all, these people had settled into the valley, but did that mean that all the game in the valley belonged to them? Where did their territory end? Did any animal that wandered into the gorge belong to the Vadi Kabile?

Maybe Walker was just being slow to accept a new idea. If this was the Vadi Kabile's answer to feeding their village, who was he to question it? But to Walker it felt wrong, like they were trapping a cloud or caging a lake.

The problem, as Walker saw it, was that the village was just too big, there were too many people for this valley to support. The Vadi Kabile should have moved on to healthier hunting grounds.

So why did the Vadi Kabile feel the need to set guards for the herd? The animals sure didn't look like they were trying to escape. Were the villagers afraid the lion would try to take an animal? It would have to be a pretty stupid lion to jump into the middle of a bunch of aurochs. No, the guards were in more danger from the lion than any of the aurochs were.

Walker noticed that Hairy was wringing his rabbit-stick in frustration. He was probably beside himself, at the sight of so much prime game in a single confined space—it was almost more than he could handle. Walker placed a sympathetic hand on his companion's shoulder.

"I know how you feel," said Walker, "but the Vadi Kabile's are already suspicious of us. If they catch us trying to make off with one of their precious aurochs, we'd be asking for more trouble than it's worth. Better we just head back to the river and hope for a squirrel or something." Then to appease his friend, "And maybe some grubs too."

Hairy lowered his stick and shook his head in disappointment.

They picked their way back to the clearing where they'd dried their clothes earlier. It looked like as good a place as any to camp for the night. After carefully hanging their gear high enough up in the sycamore tree to protect it from scavengers, they set off hunting—and gathering. Hairy got lucky, succeeding in surprising a distracted squirrel, beaning it with his rabbit-stick. Walker—true to his word—found Hairy some nice fat grubs under an old log. This, combined with some edible moss and some pine tea provided a passable evening meal. As the sun sank below the hills and the moon took its place, Hairy and Walker grabbed their bedrolls, gathered some leaves for extra bedding, climbed the sycamore once more to find a couple of secure spots, and turned in for the night.

In the Valley of the Auroch

Back in the Vadi Kabile longhouse, Osmanek sat on a log by the fire, rubbing his leg. It was cramping up on him after the day's exertions. In younger days, he'd run down deer and bison, and then carried the day's kill on his back while climbing the gorge. Now, even though he'd seen twice as many seasons as his aides, it embarrassed him that he felt he no longer carried his weight. These days Osmanek's contributions were intellectual rather than physical. He led his tribe through experience, and today was just such an occasion. He signaled Tarken, Volkan, Osman and Tabib to join him.

"So, what did you think of our visitors?" he asked Tarken while throwing another log on the fire.

"I noticed you didn't tell them about the aurochs when they mentioned the lion," replied Tarken. "What did you think of them?"

"I think the one calling himself Walker is an idiot," said Osmanek. "But they're both probably harmless enough. And the aurochs are none of their business."

"Well, if there's a lion around, that would explain a few things," said Osman. "Like the missing animals.'

"Indeed," replied Osmanek. "But a lion can't have carried away an auroch. It would've just eaten its fill and left the rest where it lay. And there would've been signs of a struggle, blood everywhere. But there was nothing, and no drag-marks. Anyway, would even a starving lion jump into the middle of an auroch herd?"

"No, it wouldn't," agreed Volkan. "Under normal circumstances. There are too many aurochs, too close together for even for a lion to tackle. No cat would be that reckless. But these aren't normal circumstances, are they?"

"I think if there's a lion in the valley, those two idiots are in more danger than our animals," offered Tabib.

"Agreed," replied Osmanek. "But now that we know for sure, it would be best to keep the women and children inside the village. And post a couple more sentries. No one goes out alone anymore."

"My daughter has been spending much of her time in the forest by the river," said Taichi. "She likes to do her sewing by the water. Is she in danger?"

"I would advise you to keep her in the settlement until we know more," replied Osmanek.

"So, then what happened to the missing aurochs?" asked Osman. "Did they get out on their own? We watch them all the time."

"It only takes a moment," said Tabib. "Your people must have fallen asleep."

"Maybe the strangers took them," replied Osman. "Maybe they've been in the valley longer than they let on."

"I said we needed more men," added Volkan. "It's too much to expect us to watch the animal's day and night."

"I doubt those the strangers took the aurochs," said Osmanek "They would have hardly turned up here if they had. I doubt there's a lion about. There isn't enough game left in the valley to tempt one. But if there was one, I guess sooner or later it would come after our herd. And then the men will need to watch out for themselves, or they will end up as dinner."

"I think if a lion wants an auroch it's best not to argue with it," said Tabib.

"If there's a lion, we will deal with it if it comes to that," stated Volkan.

"You could kill a lion?" asked Osmanek.

"Lions may be spirit animals," replied Volkan. "But a few men with spears should be enough to chase one off."

"We should send scouts up the river," said Osman, "in case the lion crossed down river. We could spot the tracks and know which direction it would be heading."

In the Valley of the Auroch

"Just as long as you go no farther than the great arch," warned Tabib, returning to what was for him, a sensitive subject.

"That arch is just a pile of rocks," said Osman. "It's time we explored the rest of the valley."

"No! The arch is a warning from the forest spirits," said Tabib shaking his fists. "It is their gate, and it separates our world from theirs. This part of the valley and its bounty is ours, but the rest of the valley belongs to the spirits."

"Well, all of the bounty is gone from our end," declared Tarken, "Except for our aurochs. I think its time we explored the rest. We are sure to find more game upriver."

"No. We are being punished for our gluttony," said Tabib. "We must learn to live within our means. This end of the valley is ours, but the great arch represents the gateway to the domain of the spirits. As before, they will punish anyone who intrudes into their sacred hunting grounds."

"Aren't you going to say anything about this?" said Volkan, looking at Osmanek.

"Yes," said Baghadur. "It's time we went upriver."

"For now, the aurochs are sustaining us," replied Osmanek. "Tabib is right, we must learn to live within our means. We don't even have to hunt anymore. As long as we don't kill all the aurochs at once, everyone will have enough to eat. I say, we wait and see."

"All the more reason to take care of what we have then," added Volkan. "More eyes on the herd and spears for the lion."

"Maybe the lion was sent as a punishment as well," remarked Tabib.

Walker stretched and yawned, which in turn woke Hairy. Shafts of morning sunlight illuminated their nests high up in the tree long before it reached the ground. In no hurry to start their day, Hairy and Walker lounged back, and, entertained by the twittering early birds, watched as a troop of wolves nosed around last night's campfire. Walker chewed his licorice stick and absentmindedly tied another knot on his belt.

Eventually, the wolf pack wandered off and Hairy and Walker climbed down to the forest floor. After a trip to the river to complete their morning rituals, Hairy returned to start a campfire and Walker hung a pot for pine-needle tea. Gathering up their tools, they both set off scavenging for breakfast. Walker collected young cattails and fiddleheads from the river—they could be peeled and the hearts eaten raw—and a handful of blue sloe berries—ripened early in unseasonably warm weather. Hairy surprised Walker with a handful of grouse eggs.

They took their time over breakfast while planning their next move, both agreeing it was time to leave the valley for whatever lay over the hill.

And after burying the remains of their campfire they broke camp and headed off for the opposite side of the valley, hoping to be on the summit by early afternoon. Ruminating on their recent experience, Walker articulated his feelings concerning the Vadi Kabile's' folly.

"This is what happens when people settle into a new area," remarked Walker. "They kill or chase away all the big game. People just weren't meant to live so close to each other."

Hairy signed in response— "What about our family back home?"

In the Valley of the Auroch

"That's different," explained Walker. "Our people fish. The sea is endless and inexhaustible. And our hunters—like Stride—follow the seasons and the game. Keep everything in balance."

Hairy and Walker enjoyed a pleasant hike and chanced across a line of carpenter ants crossing their path—each carrying a tiny piece of leaf or flower like a colorful little parasol—on their way back to their nest. The travelers crouched down to watch the industrious procession; the ants' single-mindedness made them oblivious to observation.

Continuing on, Hairy spotted a walking-stick bug as long as his arm. And Walker couldn't resist trying to bean an angry red squirrel with Hairy's rabbit-stick, but only succeeded in chasing it off.

But as they pushed their way through the brush near the far slope, Hairy put a hand to Walker's chest and dropped to a crouch. Walker knelt to follow Hairy's gaze. Ahead through the heavy undergrowth was a medium sized auroch on the end of a rope, being led through the forest by a trio of elves.

"Elves!" whispered Walker, "and an auroch. What is it with the aurochs in this valley? They must be really good eating, because everybody seems to have them."

Hairy held his hand up, motioning and with his index finger— "What do you want to do?"

Walker shrugged, "follow them?"

Hairy saluted and thumbed his chin— "Why not?"

Hairy and Walker waited till the elves were out of sight, and then proceeded to follow in their tracks—it wasn't difficult. While elves hardly left any trace of their passing, even a small auroch made quite an impression.

"Elves," whispered Walker. "Apparently this valley is quite the crossroads."

Walker had caught glimpses of elves before. They were nomadic people, primitive and skittish around strangers. Years ago, Walker had been on a hunt with Strider when they'd spotted an elven hunting party in a clearing.

Elves were generally a little taller and leaner than the average Hurrian. Always naked, they were covered head to toe in body fur. Elves had prominent brows, low foreheads, broad faces, wide noses, sharp teeth and next-to-no chins.

Frankly, Walker had to admit, they looked like taller versions of Hairy.

This discovery consumed Walker with curiosity.

First, he and Hairy find the Vadi Kabile hidden auroch herd. And now

In the Valley of the Auroch

they stumble across this group of elves with an auroch of their own—it had to be one of the Vadi Kabile' aurochs, right? Had the elves somehow managed to liberate it from under the villagers' noses?

But where were they taking the beastie? If they were just planning to chop the auroch up, they were far enough already. But they must have something else in mind.

And once again Walker was astonished to find that an auroch—albeit a smallish one—was just allowing itself to be led along, and this time by a trio of elves. Apparently, all you needed to capture an auroch was a rope and the proper demeaner. Maybe Strider had been wasting his time throwing spears.

As if following the elves through the forest wasn't strange enough, it took an even more unexpected turn; the elves appeared to be heading up the trail for the tree line.

Hairy and Walker continued to follow the group, but as the elves reached the limestone cliffs, the trail altered to snake along the edge of the dense forest. Walker and Hairy found themselves in danger of being exposed or rounding a corner and running directly into the elves. At some point the trail would reach the plateau.

Perhaps the elves were heading to their camp.

By noon Hairy and Walker were looking back down into the valley. Walker paused to admire the long blue river twisting off around the bend and disappearing into the forest. The trail they followed continued through scrub and brush to the very top of the gorge. Could the elves be leaving the valley altogether? Were they taking their prize and going home?

As they emerged from the last of the forest, they were treated to a cloudless sky as blue as a robin's egg. Breathing deeply, Walker felt the clean and refreshing air in his lungs and on his face. They followed a trail carpeted with small blue flowers providing an intoxicating lavender bouquet to the hike.

It was an interesting change from the musty banks of the river bottom. Here they were far above the pine and cedar scent of the forest. There was a slight chill in the air, but the hike kept them warm. Shortly, Hairy and Walker found themselves on a ridge looking down to the river below. The trail led to an open stony saddle between the hills, and a stand of small scrub. From the path's well-travelled look, it was in regular use.

Hairy prodded Walker and pointed up to an enormous hawk— a raptor big enough to take down a deer. The great bird soared between the peaks not far above their position. It was mostly white with dark spots and stripes, its wings blackish towards the tips with an unusually long tail. The hawk banked, tilted its head and focused a yellow eye on them.

"Stick close, Hairy. I think we're safe as long as we stay low."

Walker spoke in a voice he hoped was more reassuring than he felt. He tightened his grip on his spear.

As they crossed back into the trees, the trail spanned a patch of loamy gravel and Hairy dropped to examine the trail more closely. It hadn't rained in some time and the tracks were stark in the loose earth.

The path continued on between tall broken rock towers. The towers formed a natural gateway between the hills and spikey cacti. Walker figured that there could be caves in the nearby cliff faces. Those would make handy elf lodgings. They continued along the trail and passed between the towers and through a boulder-filled notch to emerge into the sun—surrounded by hairy elves with pointy spears.

In the Valley of the Auroch

Recovering quickly, Walker flashed his best smile and raised a hand.

"Hello, good spirits be with you." Walker's mother had taught him the common elf language, he hoped that these elves spoke it. "We just travelers, here to see beautiful valley."

The elves—glaring at Hairy and Walker suspiciously—didn't answer, but they didn't kill them. Walker took that to be a positive sign.

But the elves hadn't lowered their spears or altered their grim, toothy expressions.

On close inspection, Walker saw that this was probably a family, five elf men and six elf women carrying a bunch of elven babies with a few toddlers scampering about.

The elves' spears—which Walker was being given an excellent opportunity to examine—were crude rough-hewn devices, little more than heavy sticks with pointy ends.

Not at all like the caliber of Walker's weapon—an arrow-straight yew, tall as a man, stained with a combination of beetle juice and pine tar and rubbed to a high sheen.

His spear sported a razor-sharp obsidian tip and a tooled grip halfway along its balanced shaft. On the walking end, there was a tough hide button to protect the wood.

But while the elves' spears might be unsophisticated, Walker had no doubt that—at this range—they could be lethally effective.

And Walker's mother had always said, be polite and you'll find that most

Peter Alan Thelin

people will respond in kind. Thinking fast, Walker spotted a child peeking out from behind a mother's legs. He waved the kid a friendly greeting.

But instead of the gesture breaking the ice, it triggered the elves to advance, menacingly.

Uh-oh.

"Nice kid," said Walker.

This innocent remark prompted an unexpected response. All the elves exchanged angry looks and glanced back and forth from Walker to the child.

"Why you follow us?" demanded the lead big angry elf, speaking in the simple elven language, "What want with children?"

The heavily armed elves took a menacing step closer—spears shaking angrily, or nervously—either condition problematic.

Walker had only made reference to the child in an attempt to seem friendly. But it looked like he'd hit a nerve.

Walker quickly reconsidered his strategy. He had to say something to quell any homicidal intentions, and quickly, before he and Hairy ended up skewered on the elves' spears.

"We not follow you," Walker replied in Elf, "And We not want anything of your children—I being polite. You know, little talk?"

The expressions on the Elves' faces didn't change.

"Like say; nice family you have. And happy meet you, if you not point spears face."

Again, nothing.

"I Walker, my friend Hairy?"

Perhaps Hairy's feral appearance was adding to the Elves' confusion?

"We travel from faraway land," Walker continued and waved in the general direction of everything outside the valley. "We only passing through."

But it was obvious from the looks on their furry faces, that the Elves were very reluctant to engage Walker in conversation. Especially as it was interfering with their original plan to stick him with spears and be done with it. At least now Walker suspected that they were struggling with that last part.

But then, as if compelled by some primal force, the universal sense of courtesy Walker's mom told him about started to kick in. The Elves began to respond—almost it seemed—against their will.

"Walker?" replied the biggest guy reluctantly. "Hairy?"

"Yes," said Walker. "You name?"

"What name?" asked the elf, shaking his head. "We no name."

Interesting, thought Walker. He'd never heard anyone mention an Elf by name. Could it be that Elves didn't use names? Walker wondered what life would be like without one.

"Name tribe?" asked Walker.

"No name, family."

Amazing. Walker wondered if the lack of names was specific to this family or all Elves were like this. But while talking to the Elves seemed to be alleviating tension to some degree, Walker noted that they still hadn't lowered their spears. Once again, he flashed his smile. This time he put a hand to his chest and bowed, "Greetings family."

"We ask—why you follow us?" demanded another, taller Elf.

"Not follow you," lied Walker again. "We travelers. We climb hill to see land below."

"Why follow us," repeated the big Elf. "You hunt us?"

"Hunt you? No, no. Why we hunt you?" asked Walker. "We follow animal track up hill. We hope kill animal for meal. We hungry."

"Animal? What animal?" asked the taller Elf.

"Hairy spot deer track," lied Walker thumbing back the way they'd come. "Hairy great tracker, Very great tracker."

The Elves exchanged curious looks.

In fact, it looked like Walker had said something funny and the Elves were sharing a private joke. As if to say; this Hairy of yours mistook auroch tracks for deer? And this Kobold is supposed to be a great tracker?

Kobold?

Walker hadn't expected the Elves to call Hairy a Kobold—basically a little Elf. Well, no accounting for manners.

Walker was also pleasantly surprised to find he could almost read the

Elves' thoughts on their furry faces. Maybe it was their similarity to Hairy. Anyway, it was making this part of his job a little easier.

"Yes, we very hungry. Not much animal in valley. We follow deer track. But now, so hungry, we eat squirrel."

Walker figured if it would preserve their lives, he was happy to play the fool.

And just like that, the Elves were laughing. The big Elf even elbowed the taller one. Walker gratefully noted that the Elves had even lowered their weapons. Whew.

"You lucky find squirrel in valley," remarked the tall Elf, "No animal here. People in village hunt all long ago."

"Oh?" replied Walker. All the hunters Walker grew up with loved to give their advice about hunting. Maybe the same was true for Elves.

He made a pouty face and said, "That sad. You not know where we look then?"

And sure enough, the Elves were just like all the other hunters Walker knew. It appeared that hunting was the Elves' favorite pastime. And they all had opinions on the subject. They put their heads together and some serious Elf hunting-talk ensued; fingers were pointing in different directions while their spears were all but forgotten. Walker made a mental note that if he ever again found himself in a similar predicament, he should probably lead with this tactic.

The big Elf stepped forward.

"No animals above trees, you waste time look," the big Elf explained. "But little animals down in valley, upriver."

Walker knew that the Elves could just be sending them off on a wild auroch chase, but that was better than the alternative.

"Maybe you find squirrel there."

"Upriver?" responded Walker. He was trying hard to look earnest, "You say, people of village? They friendly?"

"Yes," said the tall Elf.

But the big Elf—perhaps having a moment of conscience —qualified the statement; "but there very bad people in valley. Not go past great bridge."

In the Valley of the Auroch

"Upriver," echoed another, reinforcing the big Elf's advice and pointing down into the valley. "Not go past great bridge."

"Great bridge, huh?" Walker wondered what they were talking about. "Yes."

Hairy elbowed Walker and pointed to the sun, which was now getting low on the horizon.

"Oh, day grow long," said Walker nodding to Hairy. "We go now make river before night."

"Back way you come," said the taller Elf, pointing behind Walker. "First trees, go left. Downhill to river. Not miss it."

"Good," agreed Walker. "Thank you for help. Sad about no deer."

"Here!" One of the elf women stepped forward and handed Walker a small leather bundle. "For trail."

"Oh! Thank you," replied Walker, genuinely touched. "Safe travels you."

With that, he smiled once more to the Elf kid and turned to walk—as nonchalantly as possible—back the way they had come. They were halfway across the sandy saddle before either chanced a look behind. When he was sure they were in the clear, Walker gently punched Hairy on the arm and let out a sigh of relief. Remembering the leather bundle, Walker undid the wrapping to discover two impeccably cured slices of auroch jerky.

As they walked and chewed, Walker considered their situation. A magnificent valley, but with practically no big game. The village full of annoying people calling themselves the Vadi Kabile and their herd of wild aurochs. And now the Elves.

It was certainly an unusual situation. And ordinarily he and Hairy would spend weeks exploring a place like this. But not only wasn't there anything to eat, they didn't feel welcome.

And as beautiful as it was—and this valley was truly spectacular—it was just turning out to be a waste of their time.

"Well, Hairy, I say we leave all these folks and their aurochs and see what's over the next horizon."

Hairy nodded— "Agreed".

By the time they reached the valley floor, it was almost dark, and they decided to just have a quick dinner and look for a safe place to sleep. After all, there could still be that lion or the usual wolves and leopards about.

Tomorrow would be another day and they were anxious to put this valley behind them.

Hairy pointed to a stand of tall saplings that would provide good shelter. There was a resinous scent of pine in the air—an aroma that always made Walker smile.

Hairy nodded and crouched to start a fire. Walker erected a cooking crane out of stout sticks, from which he hung their collapsible leather cooking pot, filled it with water from the river and a handful of crushed young pine-needles. Being that it would be their last night in the valley, he splurged, adding a sprig of mint from his bag. Tea on, Walker turned his attention to flipping stones in search of some nice grubs for Hairy. And just to top off their day of frustration, it began to rain.

Hairy and Walker

In the Valley of the Auroch

Walker pointed to a gnarled old oak, big enough for the two of them. Hairy grabbed his gear and followed Walker up the tree. Somewhere out in the forest, a jackal began to laugh.

CHAPTER FOUR

They woke with the sun, high above the forest floor, the warming rays burning off the water from last night's rain.

Walker chewed on his licorice stick as he watched the morning dew turn to steam.

Fully awake, he tied a new knot in the fringe on his belt. Then he and Hairy gathered their things, climbed to the ground and retired to the river for their morning ablutions.

Returning to the campsite afterwards, Hairy busied himself rolling up their sleeping rugs while Walker worked to restart the fire—a more difficult chore after the evening rain. When the fire was finally up and going, Walker erected a cooking crane and hung the collapsible leather tea-pot which he filled with the remaining water.

Finished with breakfast, they decided to try a little last moment provisioning independent of each other. Hairy grabbed his rabbit stick and tiptoed off into the bush while Walker picked up his spear and headed back to the river.

By early afternoon they were both back at camp, Hairy, a rabbit in one hand—the last in the valley? —and a fresh bag of grubs. Walker held up a respectable sized fish and a branch full of sloe berries.

They set about preparing their dinner and were both so busily involved with their culinary responsibilities that neither noticed the arrival of the villagers until it was too late.

Walker looked up to see Osmanek lead a large group of armed men out of the brush to surround the makeshift camp. Hairy stumbled forward, prodded by Volkan, holding a spear.

Now what was all this about?

"Don't move," admonished Osmanek. Walker shrugged. His own spear was too far out of reach to be worth making the effort anyway.

Leaning back against a stump, and clasping his fingers behind his head, Walker slowly shook his head and let out a sigh.

"I'm afraid I've only just put the tea on," he explained. "And I'm afraid we don't have enough for everyone."

Taichi stepped forward and angrily kicked over Walker's pack. Walker saw that a few of the other men from the village were beating the bushes surrounding the campsite. While outwardly appearing relaxed, Walker was tensed, ready for action.

"Where is she?" growled Osmanek.

It was a question that caused Walker some confusion for several reasons.

First, who was the "she" Osmanek was referring to? The auroch the elves had taken? And did the Vadi Kabile use personal pronouns when talking about their aurochs? Did they give the animals names, too?

And secondly, did Osmanek honestly think that Walker and Hairy would be stupid enough to steal one of their aurochs and just hang around waiting to be caught? That was just insulting.

"Who is this 'she' you're you're referring to again?"

"Don't try my patience," warned Osmanek.

"I told you strangers were dangerous," added Taichi, shaking with rage. "They've probably killed her by now.'"

"Whoa, just a moment," sputtered Walker. "We didn't kill anybody—anything." Walker turned an eye on Taichi. "And if we had, do you think we'd be sitting here eating bugs?" he gestured to Hairy's handful of squirming grubs.

"Cannibals!" exclaimed Taichi jumping forward with his spear. "Kill the strangers!"

"Wait, what?" asked Walker, himself jumping to his feet and raising his hands to calm everyone down. Cannibals? Just what do these country yokels do with their aurochs anyway? "Who said anything about cannibals? All we've eaten so far is berries and bugs."

"Liar!" screamed Taichi.

"Where is she?" demanded Osmanek, himself shaking in anger.

"Who? What? Look, there's nothing else here," answered Walker and waving to invite everyone to look, "See for yourself, where could we hide a whole auroch?"

"Who said anything about an auroch?" yelled Osmanek, "Where is the girl?"

"What girl?" asked Walker, now completely confused. "Who said anything about a girl?"

"Aygul!" answered Taichi, who was now being restrained by Tamraz, Tarkan and Volkan. "What have you done with my Aygul?"

"Wait, who?" Walker stammered, "You're not here asking about an auroch?"

"What auroch?" asked Osmanek lowering his voice and narrowing his eyes, "Why do you keep asking about an auroch?"

It occurred to Walker that everyone here—himself included—seemed to be talking at cross currents. He thought they were here about the Elves' auroch, while the Vadi Kabile were obviously here about some girl. Walker decided this would be a good time to just shut up and let these idiots talk.

"Nothing," said Walker shaking his head. Hairy was shaking his head too.

"You said, auroch," said Osmanek, backtracking, "Why did you say auroch?"

"Well," drawled Walker, still trying to work out what was going on. "It's just that since we arrived in your lovely little valley, we've seen a lot of auroch tracks, that's all. They're all over the place. So, I just assumed you were here about aurochs. What's all this about a girl?" And turning to Taichi, "Who by the way, we would never have eaten. I mean, do we look like cannibals to you?"

"She's, my daughter!" exclaimed Taichi, now wringing his hands on his spear. "My daughter. She's gone!"

"Well, I'm sorry to hear that," replied Walker. "And hey, I understand how it looks; Hairy and I are strangers," nodding to Hairy, "Out here on the frontier it's only natural for you to suspect us."

"A reasonable assumption for us to make under the circumstances," agreed Osmanek. "Wouldn't you say?"

But while it was true, that it might be a reasonable assumption, thought Walker, it was obviously the incorrect one. For the simple reason that he and Hairy really had nothing to do with the disappearance of this Aygul girl. But simply being innocent probably wasn't going to be good enough for these people. Walker knew that he had to convince his already biased interrogators that they were barking up the wrong tree.

"Yes," replied Walker. "But it really is just a coincidence."

"Then, where is she?" asked Tamraz.

"Well, I don't know," replied Walker. "But there are plenty of other possibilities as to why your girl is missing."

"I say we start making them tell us what they've done with Aygul," replied Tamraz.

Osmanek, shaking his head added, "You see, stranger, we don't believe in coincidences."

And frankly, Walker usually didn't either, nevertheless, in this case it was true.

"We're wasting time talking to these two—get rid of them," said Taichi.

"No, it would be a mistake killing Hairy and me," replied Walker, now carefully standing up and speaking in a clear, measured voice. "Think about it. If we had anything to do with your daughter's disappearance, well, then you've already got us. But if she's lost or hurt somewhere, then yes—you're wasting valuable time."

"Or maybe she's been taken by the lion that you led into our valley," growled Volkan. "In which case we should kill you for that."

"Lion?" said Walker seeing where this was headed. "I told you that I didn't think the lion crossed the river."

But the assembled villagers didn't appear to agree with Walker's assessment. At least no one was poking him just yet.

"Maybe your little Aygul's just lost, wandering around out there somewhere."

"Aygul knows the forest like the palm of her hand," answered Taichi. "She wouldn't get lost."

"Okay," agreed Walker. "Then maybe she's hurt, injured. Kids get themselves into all kinds of trouble. Right? It doesn't have to be lions."

"It would still be a mighty big coincidence," said Osmanek in a low voice, "Aygul getting lost just when you two show up with a story about a lion."

"I'm sure there are lots of other things that happen at the same time," replied Walker, thinking furiously. "But that doesn't mean the lion is responsible. We've been tracking game for several days and haven't seen any lion tracks, have you?"

"No. There are no lion tracks anywhere around our village," admitted Osmanek. "Now that you mention it, we only have your word that there was a lion at all."

"Well, there you go," said Walker, trying to suppress a self-satisfied look from taking over his face. But then he had a thought regarding what might have really happened to the girl.

"What?" asked Osmanek. "I saw something change in your expression. What do you know?"

Walker cursed himself.

"Just that there are other odd things that Hairy, and I have observed since arriving in your valley," replied Walker. "And maybe one of those has something to do with what happened to the girl."

Hairy's big eyebrows rose a notch at this revelation as well.

"Just what does that mean?" said Volkan, shaking his spear and baring his teeth. "Explain."

Walker nodded to Hairy to reassure him, took a deep breath and set about trying to convince these guys of their innocence; it would be a hard sell.

"Listen. This may or may not have anything to do with your missing girl. But yesterday Hairy and I came across the tracks of an auroch not far from your camp."

"Again, with the aurochs?" asked Osmanek. Alright, what about auroch tracks?"

Walker decided the best course of action would be to stick closely to the facts. "This wasn't just any auroch, it was an auroch on a rope, being led by a party of Elves."

Hairy chimed in with fingers like horns on the side of his head and then fingers wriggling like legs—auroch—while miming being pulled by a rope—a rather confusing set of signs.

Osmanek watched Hairy for a moment and then shook his head dismissively. By the looks he exchanged with the others, this information wasn't coming as a complete surprise.

"So, you've seen these Elves," said Osmanek. "With an auroch?" He looked deep in thought. Then, "Still, even if that was so, what would that have to do with Aygul?"

Judging from Osmanek's reaction, Walker guessed he was at least on the right track.

"Bear with me a moment," replied Walker. "Hairy and I followed these Elves out of the valley. We tracked them all the way to the hills." He pointed toward the cliffs far overhead. "Unfortunately, they ambushed us before we actually found their camp, but we managed to escape."

"What does any of that have to do with Aygul?" cried Taichi, a confused look on his face.

But Walker could see that Osmanek was getting the idea.

"Elves," muttered Osmanek, glancing at Osman.

"So, you already know about the Elves then?" asked Walker, not really surprised.

"We're aware of them, yes," agreed Osmanek. "But what do these elves have to do with Aygul? Elves generally avoid other people altogether."

"Well, if Hairy and I encountered the elves, maybe Aygul did too," explained Walker. "And maybe the elves grabbed her to keep her from talking."

"And you know where the elves are?" asked Taichi. "You can lead us to them?"

"Sure," agreed Walker. But as he said that it occurred to him that if this was what had really happened, it was unlikely that the elves would have bothered dragging the girl all the way back to their camp. After all, Walker hadn't seen the girl with them. Maybe they killed Aygul and stashed her body somewhere in the forest. And it was still conceivable that she really was just lost or had gotten herself hurt, and this really was all just a big coincidence.

But if either of those scenarios were the case—and Walker considered them just as likely—then they wouldn't find Aygul in the elves' camp. In that case the Vadi Kabile would probably forget about the elves and shift the blame back to Hairy and Walker somehow. Still…

"Yes, I can tell you where their camp is," Walker said. Considering how quickly these guys were to anger, it was best for him just to let them focus on one thing at a time.

"No," declared Osmanek. "You will show us where their camp is. You'll lead the men there."

Walker's idea had been to send the villagers off looking for the elves, while he and Hairy made their escape in the opposite direction. Walker didn't want to be anywhere around if these guys got to the elves' camp and didn't find the girl.

"We have only your word for any of this," said Osmanek, "So, it will be you accompanying the men."

This wasn't working out the way Walker had planned. And Osmanek had a good point, apparently, he wasn't a complete idiot. In response, Walker quickly improvised a modification to Osmanek's plan.

"Sure, we'd be happy to lead you folks to the camp. But this is too many men," explained Walker, waving to include the large group. "A group this size, traipsing up and over the gorge would raise a cloud of dust visible across the valley. The elves would see us long before we saw them. If we go with you, it should be just a small party."

Walker liked this new argument because it had the advantage of actually being true.

"Oh? Then how many would you suggest?" asked Osmanek.

This was encouraging progress, thought Walker. It was better to go along with Osmanek and then suggest modifications, than to simply reject everything he suggested.

"Hairy and I could handle this on our own," explained Walker, trying to look and sound concerned. He didn't have much hope Osmanek would accept this suggestion, but it was at least worth trying. "And the sooner we go the better. The girl may not have much time."

"Why would we trust you?" asked Taichi. "My daughter means nothing to you. And the elves ambushed you once already, what's to stop them from doing it again?"

Walker ignored the first half of Taichi's objection and concentrated on the second.

"The elves had the element of surprise before," he argued. "But they don't anymore; we know where they are now. And they won't be expecting us back."

There were nods and murmurings of reluctant agreement among the villagers at Walker's assessment.

"But, there's just two of you," explained Osman staring pointedly at the diminutive Hairy. "What could you do?"

"This time we'll have the element of surprise," replied Walker. "Hairy and I could sneak up on them. We'd just creep into their camp, and remember, they're a small group, too. We'd be in and out before they knew we were even there."

Osmanek stroked his gray beard thoughtfully, while studying Walker with an appraising eye. His scrutiny made Walker uncomfortable, but he made every effort to present a relaxed and confident appearance.

"Taichi is right, why would we trust you to rescue the girl?" asked Osmanek. "She doesn't mean anything to you. What's to stop you from running off the moment you're out of our sight? We have only your word for any of this."

Indeed—Osmanek wasn't a complete idiot.

"Okay," replied Walker, figuring this was the best he could have hoped for. "Then send a couple of men with us."

Osmanek grunted, and turned to Tamraz, Osman and Taichi for a huddled talk. After a few heated words, he turned back to address Walker.

"They don't trust you either," explained Osmanek.

"Look, you can see for yourself that the girl's not here," said Walker, waving around their camp. "And you admitted you already knew there were elves around. And I know there's something funny going on with the aurochs, so you probably know I'm telling the truth about that. I think at this point you can trust me that this is the best idea for finding the girl."

Walker's argument must have scored points because the villagers were exchanging confused looks, spears all akimbo.

Osmanek furrowed his forehead, big bushy eyebrows bunching like hairy gray caterpillars. Reaching a decision, he lowered his voice. "Alright, you'll lead Osman and Tarmaz to the elf camp, and your ape-man will remain with us as hostage until you return."

Walker's eyelids narrowed in a manner that would have caused anyone who knew him better great alarm. His breath slowed and his muscles tensed like knotted rope under his tunic.

"I don't think that's a very good idea," he said.

"I think it would provide you with the proper incentive to see this through," explained Osmanek.

"But we need Hairy," explained Walker, and looking to his friend, "He's the best tracker I know, and the elves are light on their feet."

"But you said you already know where they are," Osman pointed out annoyingly.

"I know about where they were," explained Walker, "And I said we didn't actually reach the elves' camp. They ambushed us before we got there. So, I need Hairy to find their camp and avoid any elves' lookouts."

In the Valley of the Auroch

"I'm a tracker," said Osman. "We don't need your ape."

"And I'm a tracker too," added Tamraz.

"And I don't mean to insult you two," replied Walker lying through his teeth and imagining the many fun ways he'd like to murder Osman, "but Hairy's the best tracker I've ever met and this is too important for the local talent."

Osmanek put out a hand to restrain Osman and the three of them huddled up once more. There were angry voices expressing strong opinions, and suspicious glances were cast in Walker's direction. In the meantime, the rest of the group resumed pointing their spears at Hairy and Walker.

"Alright, the four of you will go," explained Osmanek, turning back to address Walker.

"Three would be safer," argued Walker, without much hope. "It'll be difficult enough trying to sneak up on the elves."

"There are two of you," explained Osmanek, "And there will be two of us."

"Fine. We're strangers and you don't trust us. I get it," agreed Walker.

"You'll do it our way," said Osmanek, "and your little friend can demonstrate these superior skills of his."

"We'll start at dawn," declared Tamraz.

Walker knew this was likely the best outcome he could've hoped for. He'd managed to get Osmanek to make a lot of concessions and Walker and Hairy would have a better chance with only two others than the dozen that presently surrounded them.

Hairy prodded Walker and motioned towards the hill, stirred a brown finger around his palm then spread his hands. In response, Walker shook his head and used two fingers to point from his eyes to the forest. Hairy waved his hand in front of his face and pointed at the ground by their feet.

"What's going on?" asked Osmanek.

"Hairy thinks we should go now," Walker explained. Hairy provided them with a significant strategic advantage. "It could rain tonight and wash away any trail."

"Now?" repeated Tamraz incredulously, "It'll be dark before we reach the ridge. You can't follow tracks at night."

"Hairy can," explained Walker. "I told you he's the best tracker I've ever met. Hairy's eyes are better than ours in the dark. And Hairy thinks we'd have a better chance of sneaking up on them at night."

"And you really believe he can do this?" asked Osmanek.

"Hairy says he can," replied Walker. "Hairy doesn't lie. He wouldn't say so if it weren't true."

From the looks on the villagers' faces it was obvious they all had their doubts.

"Well, I couldn't follow a trail in the dark," argued Osman.

"But the moon will be brighter on the ridge," said Osmanek, stroking his beard.

"I guess we would have a better chance of catching the elves by surprise," agreed Tamraz.

"Are you seriously going to trust this mute ape?" asked Osman, "And this smooth talker?"

"What choice do we have?" asked Taichi; "I'll go, she's, my daughter."

"No Taichi, I will go," said Tamraz with a hand on the smaller man's shoulder. "You should go back to the village in case Aygul returns on her own."

"It's for the best," agreed Osmanek.

"All right," said Taichi.

"Fine," said Osman, not trying to hide his own suspicions. "Let's see this magical tracker in action."

"Then it's settled," pronounced Osmanek. "I suppose we'll have to trust you. You and the ape will guide Osman and Tamraz to the elves' camp and retrieve the girl. But be warned, if you run, we'll find you." Osmanek nodded to a man standing to the side. The villager bent down, retrieved Walker's spear and passed it to him.

Walker nodded to Hairy who turned to lead the group off, through the forest, in the direction of the ridge. Flanked by the two big villagers,

In the Valley of the Auroch

Walker swore to himself that once this business was over, Hairy and he would never set foot in this bescumbered valley again.

Walker, Tamraz and Osman followed Hairy through the growing shadows as the sun settled behind the hill. An earthy scent of musk, green plants and mildewed pine needles filled the air. It was largely thanks to Hairy's keen senses that they were able to follow the trail at all through the darkening forest. But Walker was a more than passingly good tracker himself—thanks to Strider's tutelage—and he too possessed surprisingly good night vision, though he wasn't about to let Tarmaz and Osman know that. Best to let the yokels continue to think they were dependent on Hairy.

Poor Hairy, thought Walker, this wasn't any of his fault. He was always going along with Walker's crazy schemes, like leaving the safety of their home to explore the wild world. Hairy had given up mom's home-cooked meals and hunting trips with Strider. Not for the first time in the last few days, Walker felt the familiar pangs of a nagging guilt.

CHAPTER FIVE

Hairy had been following Walker around since they were kids, almost from the time Strider had first brought him home. Walker remembered when he first saw his cousin. Strider had been on a hunt and came across the remains of a camp, and from the look of things, it had been a party of Kolbolds—an ape-man clan—but it looked like the camp had been attacked and the Kobolds were gone. Then Strider heard a sound, a whimper coming from a tree. Hidden among the leaves and clinging to a branch, Strider had spotted a furry little baby. Someone had placed the child there, probably in an effort to hide him.

From the baby's bedraggled appearance, it looked like the poor thing had been there for a while. Strider couldn't just leave him—what if the parents never came back?

And so, Strider had brought the furry little thing home.

Walker's aunt and uncle never had kids. Even though the baby was clearly not Hurrian, they were happy to raise the furry little guy as their own.

They named him "Hairy".

At first, young Walker—who had always adored his adventurous uncle Strider—had been annoyed by what he saw as the intruder. Hairy was now the center of his uncle's attention and Walker was jealous. Hairy grew fast. He got to go hunting with Strider and learn how to track animals and flint-knap rocks and all the other things Walker wanted to do.

Walker's parents insisted that he study to be a healer like his father. That meant he had to learn all about medicinal plants and herbs that grow freely in the wild. But when Walker caught Hairy eavesdropping on his lessons, it was the last straw and he got angry—wasn't it bad enough Hairy hogged all the time with Strider; did he want to be a healer, too?

"Little Fox, your cousin doesn't care about the lessons," Little Fox's mother had explained. "He's only interested in them because of you."

"What? Why?" asked Little Fox.

"Because he looks up to you!" she said.

That had left Little Fox gob smacked. The runt looked up to him. Little Fox was just a little kid too; no one looked up to him. Hairy was weird.

"Why would he do that?" asked Little Fox.

"Well, you're his big cousin," answered his mother. "He doesn't have a big brother to look up to, so he looks up to you instead."

"Huh?" For a kid, this was a lot to process. Little Fox actually did have a brother, but he was just a baby and did little baby things like cry and poop. Little Fox felt like an only child and had been on his own for as long as he could remember.

"But" he started.

"No buts," admonished Little Fox's mother. "Try being nice to Hairy for a change. It wouldn't kill you."

"But he doesn't even talk!" said Little Fox. "How am I supposed to be nice to him?"

"Maybe you should learn to sign," suggested Little Fox's mother. "You'll probably love that. It will be like the two of you your own secret language."

That was a thought.

"Okay, so how am I going to learn to sign?" asked Little Fox.

"Ask your uncle Strider," answered Little Fox's mother, "But, I'm sure Hairy would be happy to help you."

Despite his misgivings, Little Fox learned to sign quickly, especially since Hairy seemed to have a lot to say.

Hairy and Walker

In the Valley of the Auroch

Hairy wanted to show Little Fox everything—how to follow and identify animal tracks—how to throw a stick—how to stalk a mouse—how to knap stones into tools— how to climb trees—how to start a fire—how to find grubs—how to carve—how to find water—how to set a trap.

And Hairy wanted to learn from Little Fox, too, which made young Little Fox a little happier—knowing things that Hairy didn't.

And Little Fox's mother had been right, learning to sign was fun—he and Hairy could carry on conversations with no one being the wiser. They could sign to each other from across the whole village without anyone else knowing what they were saying. Little Fox's mother was constantly after the boys to stop signing during meals and such, but that just made it more fun. Before he knew it, Little Fox was spending nearly all his free time with Hairy.

Then there was the day Hairy jumped into the river.

They were playing on a tree overhanging the water when Little Fox slipped and fell in. He didn't think anything of it—living by the sea, Little Fox could swim like a fish—but when Hairy jumped into the water after him he didn't come up.

Little Fox thought Hairy was just playing and he paddled to shore, but then realized Hairy was still missing and started to scream for help. A couple of the older boys dove in and dragged Hairy out of the river—retching and gagging.

"What's wrong with you two?" yelled Little Elk, the oldest and angriest, "Elves can't swim!"

Little Fox socked him in the stomach.

"Hairy's not an elf!" he shouted before he was flung back into the river.

"He's more like an elf than one of us!" shouted the angry adolescent turning away. "And if you want to keep him alive you better keep him away from the river!"

Obstinate to the end, Little Fox tried in vain to teach Hairy how to swim—but Hairy just sputtered; he didn't seem to be able to move his arms the right way.

"Why can't you learn this?" Little Fox growled in frustration.

"Because his arms don't work like yours," explained Strider, walking over to comfort his boy. "He'll never be able to swim like you, Little Fox. Just like he'll never be able to throw like you either."

Little Fox had been noticing that. Hairy could only throw a rabbit stick underhand—like a girl. He did so with weirdly unerring accuracy, but Little Fox could throw the stick much farther, because he could throw it overhand.

"Why not?" asked Little Fox.

"Because Hairy's people are different than us," answered Strider, as if that should explain everything.

"But why?" Little Fox pleaded. He knew Hairy was different, but…

"They're just a different kind of people," explained Strider.

"Little Elk called Hairy an elf," tattled Little Fox, hoping for a better explanation.

Strider shook his head and patted Hairy's.

"No, Hairy isn't an elf," his uncle agreed, *"But, he isn't Hurrian either. Most folks call them kobolds, but I don't really know what Hairy's people called themselves. There aren't any of them around to ask."*

"Where are they?" asked Little Fox, consumed by this new mystery. Hairy was equally transfixed by this information.

"Gone," said Strider. *"There used to be a tribe living in the forest off toward the sunrise, but that was long ago. I really don't know what happened to Hairy's people. They just vanished over time."*

"So, why did Little Elk call Hairy an elf then?"

Strider shrugged and appeared to be very uncomfortable.

"Well, I guess Hairy sort of looks a little like a very small elf.

"But Hairy's just a little kid," argued Little Fox. *"That's why he's small."*

"Well, he's small for a young elf too."

Little Fox digested this information as they all walked home. How could Hairy's people be gone? Where could they go? Little Fox pictured them fading away, like fog in the morning sun. Was Hairy going to disappear too? This bothered Little Fox to such a degree that for days he didn't let Hairy out of his sight. But, then being a boy, his worry faded, and he mostly forgot about it.

Until the day Leaning Deer knocked Hairy down.

It was after the evening meal and all the kids were running around outside playing kickball. Hairy had the ball when Leaning Deer knocked him to the ground, grabbed the ball and ran off laughing, *"Stupid elf!"*

Little Fox beaned Leaning Deer with a rabbit-stick.

"You could've killed him!" his mother screamed at Little Fox as his father dressed Leaning Deer's head.

"I was aiming for his legs!" explained Little Fox.

In the Valley of the Auroch

"Well, you missed!" yelled his mother in reply and shook the bloody bandage in Little Fox's face. *"And this could've been much worse."*

Leaning Deer glowered at Little Fox from behind Little Fox's dad's back.

"He hit Hairy," explained Little Fox.

"Hairy can fight his own battles," responded Little Fox's mother, only slightly mollified. *"He doesn't need you hitting people with sticks for him."*

"But Hairy's too little to fight back," argued Little Fox.

"Well then, he'll just have to learn to deal with that," replied his mother.

"And he called Hairy an elf," protested Little Fox.

Little Fox's parents exchanged pained glances and his dad led Leaning Deer outside.

"Well then," replied his mother, *"Hairy's going to have to learn to deal with that, too."*

*

And now here they were again, Walker getting himself into trouble and dragging poor Hairy in with him.

They stopped at the edge of a moonlit clearing for the two villagers to confer. Hairy took the opportunity to signal privately to Walker; What was their plan?

That was a good question. If Walker had a plan, it was still a work in progress.

On the one hand, Walker wouldn't mind just pushing Osman off the mountain and washing his hands of the whole affair. After all, he and Hairy didn't have anything to do with the missing girl. They could just abandon the villagers here in the forest, far from the village, and make their escape. But Tarmaz had been pretty decent so far; he probably deserved better. And in the back of his mind, Walker wondered if maybe the lion had found its way across the river.

To be honest, Walker found himself growing increasingly curious about the missing girl. Of course, the Vadi Kabile were understandably worried about the kid, too, but could she really be connected with the elves and their auroch? Elves were usually pretty peaceful and had even let him and Hairy go. They were more likely to abandon the stolen auroch and run than they were to kill an innocent child.

Walker had managed to sell the villagers his theory about elves and aurochs, but Walker didn't really believe it himself. Still, he and Hairy had seen the elves stealing an auroch for themselves. And there was a missing girl. Was it all just a coincidence? If not, how did it all fit together? Walker agreed with Osmanek, he didn't believe in coincidences either.

So, although Walker and Hairy should have been looking for their opportunity to run for the hills—and certainly Hairy must have been thinking that—Walker's curiosity was getting the better of him.

He thought more about it. The elves had seemed angry, overly anxious, which was understandable; they'd just liberated one of the villager's aurochs.

And they thought—correctly as it turned out—that Walker and Hairy had been tracking them. But Walker hadn't seen any evidence that the elves had a Hurrian girl prisoner. And if the elves had taken (or killed) the girl they would hardly have been so nice to let he and Hairy go free.

So, was the girl dead, somewhere back down in the valley? Kids got themselves into trouble all the time; it didn't have to be elves or a lion. Heck, probably a few toothsome beasts—like tigers and wolves—were out looking for a meal with their regular game being so scarce.

In the Valley of the Auroch

And there was the little issue of what they were going to do if they found the elves and they didn't have the girl. Should he and Hairy just abandon the Vadi Kabile to fight it out with the elves? Or should they just push Tarmaz and Osman off the mountain if they got the opportunity?

What else could he and Hairy to do? Even pushing the villagers off the mountain might be easier said than done. If they waited until they reached the elf camp and came up empty handed, these two were going to be ready for a double-cross.

Hairy stopped and got everyone's attention with a raised hand. He then dropped to a crouch to examine the trail. He motioned for Walker to take a closer look.

Tarmaz followed, curious to see this great tracker in action.

"What is it? You find something?"

What Hairy found was a big, deep footprint.

"Just how big were these elves?" asked Tarmaz.

Even in the dark, Walker could see the track Hairy pointed out. There, in a damp patch of moldering leaves there was a very large footprint. Osman sighed—even he was impressed.

"That's too big to be an elf," remarked Osman. "It looks like an ogre track to me."

"I always hated that name," exclaimed an unseen speaker in a high-pitched voice. And then Osman fell to the ground from a knock to the head.

CHAPTER SIX

Osman and Tarmaz were both down and out.

Walker and Hairy jumped in response but were immediately seized by brutally strong hands. Trolls were materializing out of the surrounding forest; a number of big, hairy, heavy creatures, carrying long war-clubs.

Walker muttered to himself under his breath—this made three times he'd been caught unawares—idiot!

He swore that if he survived this, there wouldn't be a fourth.

With a mighty jerk, the biggest troll Walker had ever seen picked him up and left his feet dangling.

"Hmm, this one I do not know," mused the creature in a surprisingly child-like voice. It contrasted sharply with the owner's fearsome countenance. "Or that little one," the creature added, looking down at Hairy, in the grip of another, smaller normal-sized troll. "He looks like an elf child."

"No, I don't believe we've been properly introduced," Walker agreed. Don't panic, remain calm, that's what Walker's uncle used to tell him. Walker was seeing an opportunity and was going to make the best of it.

In the Valley of the Auroch

"My name is Walker by the way, and that's Hairy."

The huge pale face was covered in light-colored fur. Yet it was still ruggedly handsome; outlined in the moonlight. Deep-set eyes were shadowed by protruding brows, now furrowed in concentration. There was an intelligent look in the eyes, but also a ferociousness contrasting with the owner's eloquent voice.

"As I said, I am familiar with most of the villagers," explained the giant troll. "Including those two. But I do not know you."

"That's because we're new to your valley," explained Walker, in a sudden fit of inspiration. Evidently, the big troll had a problem with the Vadi Kabile, enough to knock them in the head. Whatever the reason, Walker needed to put some distance between him and the villagers, who this giant seemed to have had a problem with.

"New?"

"We're tourists!"

"But what are you doing out here in the forest, at night, with those two?" asked the troll.

"We were just trying to make the mountain-top before it got too dark," explained Walker. He motioned awkwardly towards the ridgeline as best he could with his hands pinned to his side.

For whatever reason, the trolls hadn't yet killed him and Hairy. For that, Walker was grateful. But he wondered why they were spared? Whatever the reason, he hoped the trolls would buy this innocent act long enough for him to come up with an explanation to get them both out of trouble.

"How did you come to be with these villagers?" asked their interrogator.

"Those two?" Walker asked and nodding towards the motionless bodies. "Oh, no-no, we weren't with them!"

Out of the corner of his eye, Walker saw Hairy nodding at Tarmaz's spear, adding some subtle hand movements.

"They ambushed us," Walker exclaimed, as Hairy's inspiration hit.

This was a chance to put even more distance between he and Hairy and the two villagers.

"Hairy and I were minding our own business, just walking along this trail, when that big brute with a spear jumped out from behind a tree and demanded to know what we were doing out here."

"They ambushed you," repeated the giant slowly. "Both of you?"

"Yes, well, to be honest, I'm not much good with a spear," replied Walker. He managed to give a weak shrug. "And as for little Hairy, well…"

Hairy managed to make himself appear even smaller in his troll's grasp and shrugged/nodded in agreement.

"So then, the villagers were waiting behind a tree just to ambush unsuspecting strangers who might be wandering by?" asked the big troll, "out here at night?"

"I wouldn't know why they were hiding behind the tree," replied Walker innocently. Suddenly, he had an idea; "But, now that you mention it, they did question us about aurochs, even accusing us of stealing one if you can believe that. I mean an auroch! How can somebody steal a wild animal? Have you ever heard anything so ridiculous? They might as well have accused us of stealing their trees. The big one was just pointing to some tracks when you arrived."

"I heard that one mention something about elves," said the big troll. "What was that about?"

"I don't know," answered Walker, "Maybe you can ask him when he wakes up?"

One of the other trolls rolled Tarmaz over. Even in the dark, it was obvious he wouldn't be waking up ever again.

"Oh dear," murmured Walker. He feigned a swoon for added measure. "Well, I suppose it was nobody's fault. After all, accidents happen."

"He was not a friend of yours then?" asked the smooth-talking giant.

"No, no-no."

"And you are not upset that he is dead then?"

"Oh no, no. Frankly, you've done us a favor," replied Walker. There was more truth to that than he cared to admit. "Actually, I would enjoy the chance to push him off a cliff myself if you hadn't come along. Not that I could, what with the two of them waving those big spears around and all."

The troll seemed to ruminate on this information. After a few moments, he carefully lowered Walker to the ground.

Next, the troll made a great show of smoothing Walker's rumpled jacket.

In the Valley of the Auroch

Walker rubbed his bruised arms to get the blood flowing again and took the opportunity to examine his interrogator.

Trolls as a race tended to be shorter and stockier than the average Hurrian—but this guy was big, bigger than any troll Walker had ever seen. Strider had told Walker trolls were about as strong as apes—which meant this guy must be the strongest of the bunch.

"Well then," said the big troll, in a voice dripping with concern, "How rude of me. You must be terribly frightened by all this." he added, waving about.

"Oh, no, no," replied Walker, pleased with the troll's change in attitude but guessing that this guy was nobody's fool either. "I understand how these things can happen. There is nobody to blame, really. Like I said, accidents happen."

"But I have failed to introduce myself," exclaimed the eloquent giant. "I am called Ryszard the Powerful. And this is my brother Rolf." Ryszard motioned to indicate a rather unfriendly looking shorter troll. Rolf had a large, bulbous nose and even heavier brows. "And these are my associates, Cael and Dolphus."

"Charmed I'm sure," replied Walker. He was wary of Ryszard's sudden change in attitude. All at once, this troll was being a gentleman? It was obvious Ryszard was trying to manipulate Walker, but why did he bother? He and Hairy were already at his mercy. What Ryszard hoping to gain by this? If this was supposed to be subterfuge, it was pathetic. Walker was sure Ryszard wasn't seriously buying Walker's innocent act either, but this performance was mildly insulting.

Walker also wondered if he might have just stumbled onto the answer of the missing girl.

Yay for him.

"We are the Tal Stamm," said Ryszard, completing the introductions. Walker knew enough troll to guess Tal Stamm meant valley family. It seemed the trolls weren't any better at the name game than the Vadi Kabile or the elves.

So, if this was turning into a strategy game, it was Walker's turn to make the next move.

"Pleased to make everyone's acquaintance," replied Walker, endeavoring to maintain his innocent demeaner. "What a lucky break it is for us we ran into you."

"Yes indeed," agreed Ryszard. "You two, all alone out here in this dark, dangerous forest. You could get lost or hurt if you were not careful. I insist you return with us to our camp. You can continue your journey in the morning, in the safety of daylight."

"Oh, that's so very nice of you. You're really too kind," replied Walker. What did this Ryszard guy want? How could Walker talk their way out of this predicament? "But you've been so helpful already, we wouldn't want to inconvenience you further."

Hairy nodded vigorously in agreement.

"With these ruffians taken care of," he continued, "Hairy and I should be fine from here on. We'll just be on our way."

"Oh, but I insist," said Ryszard, grabbing up Walker's spear and pointing off into the forest, "After you."

Shite.

In the Valley of the Auroch

So, thought Walker, it must have been these guys the elves had tried to warn him and Hairy about. Great. Why didn't they just tell him to look out for trolls?

Encouraged along by some less-than-gentle spear-jabbing from Rolf, Hairy and Walker were ushered through the dark forest.

The path was invisible to Walker; it seemed to parallel the river as it wound through the valley. The trolls were either very familiar with this route, or they could see in the dark like Hairy could. Walker guessed probably both.

Their path followed the river; it appeared they were avoiding the sandy banks and staying just inside the forest. It was the right technique if you were trying to avoid leaving tracks. The pine-needle strewn forest floor hid most of the evidence of their passage.

The moon was fully up now and now its light filtered through the trees, providing enough illumination to allow Walker safe footing. Looking up, he could see the white limestone cliffs through the forest canopy; the mountains looming over their midnight stroll.

Walker noticed Hairy surreptitiously placing his thumb against his forehead—hand open, then cupping one hand atop the other and splaying his fingers out. Walker got the message.

"No, I don't think this is the kind of trouble dad warned me about," Walker whispered back. But he had to admit that it probably was.

Hairy repeated the gesture but thumbing his chin this time.

"Don't go bringing mom into this either," replied Walker feeling exasperated. "If it was up to her, we'd spend the whole summer picking medicinal flowers."

"What are you two talking about?" asked Rolf in his singsong, yet oddly menacing voice.

"Nothing in particular," replied Walker, "Hairy just talks too much,"

"Something you would like to share?" asked Ryszard.

"No," sighed Walker, looking down at his friend and reminding himself every word mattered here. "Just idle chit-chat."

"Good," replied Ryszard. "I would not like to see the evening disturbed by acrimony between friends."

Walker thought it wouldn't be prudent to suggest killing the two Vadi Kabile guys had already disturbed the evening to a dramatic degree.

"Is your camp much farther?" he asked while trying to sound nonchalant.

"Not far," replied Ryszard. "So, Walker, what brings you to our valley?"

Walker was wondering when Ryszard was going to ask him that. He had been trying to come up with a reasonable answer. Osmanek hadn't been satisfied with Walker's explanation. Apparently not everyone understood his quest for adventure. But, considering the casual way Ryszard and friends had ambushed Osman and Tarmaz before dragging the bodies into the bushes, Walker worried that if Ryszard had the same suspicious reaction, it could prove fatal. Walker had another idea.

"Trade," he replied.

"Trade?" repeated Ryszard. "What do you trade for?"

Walker assumed that the only reason he and Hairy were still alive is because Ryszard was curious and didn't see them as a threat. That, or he was saving them for dinner. Some people believed that trolls were cannibals.

Walker needed to convince Ryszard that he and Hairy had something of value. Or at least keep Ryszard confused long enough for Hairy and Walker to escape. Especially if he and Hairy were destined for the dinner menu.

"That spear for instance," remarked Walker.

The big guy had been quietly inspecting Walker's weapon.

"Yes, it is truly remarkable. Such beautiful workmanship. Where did you get it?" asked Ryszard with undisguised admiration.

"I made it," replied Walker.

"You made this?"

"Mother insisted I learn a trade."

Walker wasn't bending the truth too far there.

"I wasn't much good at hunting, so I tried knapping and woodwork."

"You mean to say you made this?" asked Ryszard, who couldn't help but sound impressed, yet also dubious. "And you are proficient with it then?"

"Oh no," lied Walker. "I couldn't hit the broadside of a mammoth. I'm just a traveling tradesman. That's a sample of my merchandise."

Ryszard shook his head in wonder.

"You trade? You travel and trade spears like these?" the big man shook his head in wonder. "It is so beautiful."

"You should keep it then," suggested Walker, he assumed he wasn't going to get it back anyway. "A gift to you, for saving us from those two brutes."

"No, no, you are too kind," replied Ryszard.

It seemed Ryszard was also good at this game, and he seemed to be enjoying toying with Walker.

"Please, I insist."

"The knife in your belt," continued Ryszard. "Another example of your craft?"

"Yes," agreed Walker, casually handing it over before Ryszard could take it.

The knife was impractically long. It too was obsidian, which was terribly fragile to be practical for such a long weapon. But the knife of black glass blade glistened like flowing water in the moonlight. It was really just a toy; Walker was proud of the work he'd put into it and liked the look of it.

"An amazing weapon," said Ryszard unable to hide his admiration. "Beautiful."

Obsidian had the sharpest edge of any material, and the knife was deadly sharp. But it would be uselessly brittle in a fight against these trolls. Better it was in Ryszard's hands if it came to that.

"Obsidian does make for a pretty weapon," agreed Walker. He wondered how he could make use of this development. And then he had an inspiration. "You can keep that one too, if you like. I can always make more."

Ryszard stopped in his tracks. The sounds of the night birds, frogs and crickets filling the void.

"How?" replied Ryszard, immediately attentive, eyes growing large.

"I've got my flint-knapping tools with me. And flints shouldn't be hard to find around these parts."

Ryszard narrowed his eyes suspiciously, turning the knife to reflect the moonlight. "My people make hand axes from stone, but this is made of something else."

"Yes, it's obsidian—stones found around volcanos. It's more brittle than the average stone but produces the absolute sharpest edges. I have some raw pieces in my pack."

The troll carrying Walker's pack stopped walking and his compatriots turned to regard his burden with awe.

"Perhaps you could give us a demonstration of your craft. It is not often we find ourselves with such talented visitors."

Sure, thought Walker, not if you brain them all first. But this was an encouraging development. The conversation had changed, and Walker felt that the advantage had now shifted to him. He'd better be careful not to squander this opportunity.

"Oh, you'd all be bored."

"No, no we would not," responded Ryszard. There was a new, insistent quality to his voice. He looked to his associates who were all nodding in eager agreement as well.

Walker was keenly aware that to frontier people, entertainment—in any form—was almost as valuable as food. Could he navigate a way out of their predicament though a simple display of knapping? Maybe it could save the two of them when brute force could not.

"Well, if you insist." He might as well see how far this would get him. "But I'll need a few things. I can't work in the dark and it's getting late; I'll need more light."

"Of course, of course! Whatever you need. You must be tired and hungry. Tomorrow will be fine. At our camp."

"It's the least I can do to repay your hospitality, "said Walker. Now he was feeling a little better about their situation. And he silently thanked Strider for all those flint-knapping lessons. But what, he wondered, should his next move be in this dangerous game?

Troll brother Rolf grunted to get the group's attention and they resumed walking along their invisible trail. The circle of trolls tightened possessively around their illustrious guests and Ryszard seemed distracted admiring his new toys. As the eclectic band crossed a moonlit clearing Walker noticed the ground covered in straggling vines adorned with pretty pink and white flowers. It made him think of his mother.

*

"Here you are little Fox, why aren't you ready?" asked Walker's mother. "We're about to start."

Young Walker was rooting around his mother's workshop, looking for his knife. He was sure she'd hidden it again.

"I don't want to pick flowers," he sulked; "it's girl's work."

Walker's mother sighed and shook her head in resignation. How many times had she and her boy played this game?

"This is important, Little Fox. Medicinal herbs are the basis for Shamanism."

"But I don't want to be a Shaman," argued Walker for the umpteenth time. "I want to be a hunter like Strider."

"I know you admire your uncle Strider," responded his mother gently. "But a hunter's life is very difficult—it's a young man's profession. A person can be a healer long after a hunter retires."

"I'm not going to retire, I'm still a young man," snapped Walker. "And Uncle Strider says I have great potential."

"He says that because he's your uncle and he loves you," replied his mother. "And anyway, you're too young to go hunting."

"But that's why I have to train now!" said Walker, feeling he scored a point there.

"No, that's why you need to do the lessons I give you," argued his mother. "Your father was younger than you are when he started his training."

"So, because father's a Shaman I have to be a Shaman?" asked Walker, angrily repeating that complaint, but already knowing what his mother's reply would be.

"You are his son, his apprentice," replied his mother. "A father passes his knowledge down to his son, so he can carry on his work. It's tradition, and a good livelihood. Your father being a Shaman has put bread on the table and a roof over your head."

"Maybe I don't want a roof over my head," said Walker.

"What would you do, Little Fox," began his mother, "sleep outside like an animal?"

"Little Hawk is his son too," replied Walker switching strategies. "Maybe he can be the Shaman."

"But you're the eldest, our first born." Walker's mother pointed out. "So, by

tradition it's your responsibility."

"That's not fair," blurted Walker. "I didn't ask to be born first. Healers need to take care of sick people and other people's blood makes me sick to my stomach. Little Hawk wants to be a Healer, and he's better at remembering which flowers do what. He should be the next Shaman; flowers all look the same to me."

"Your tenderness at the sight of other people's blood shows you are sensitive. That is a good trait for a healer. Your aversion will grow weaker with time. And, maybe if you paid more attention to your lessons," admonished Walker's mother, "instead of throwing sticks and chipping rocks with your uncle, you could remember them, too."?

"Can Hairy pick flowers, too?" asked Walker hopefully. Hairy looked up from his examination of one of Mom's poultice jars at the sound of his name. "Then I can knap knives afterward?"

"Don't drag little Hairy into this," warned Walker's mother sternly. "Gathering herbs is your responsibility."

"Well what good is a flower going to do me?" asked Walker arrogantly. "I can't kill a bear with one."

"No?" asked his mother. Then, looking around, she retrieved a bundle of pink and white flowers from a high shelf. "This is crown vetch, and you could certainly use it to kill a bear."

Walker examined the flower dubiously.

"And what if you're injured fighting the bear?" continued his mother smugly, for Walker had mistakenly steered the argument into her area of expertise; "Elder, chamomile, comfrey and pineapple weed will speed the healing process and meadowsweet and willow bark will ease your pain."

"Maybe I won't get injured," retorted Walker stubbornly, jutting out his lower lip.

"I've treated your uncle more times than I can remember," Replied Walker's mother compassionately. "Hunting is hazardous work."

"So, just how am I supposed to kill a bear with a flower?" Walker asked, realizing he was on the verge of losing this argument too. "Wait till he opens his mouth to bite me and shove it down his throat?"

"That sounds like something a hunter would say," replied his mother. "But I believe a wise Shaman would use his intellect and devise a more effective strategy for dealing with a bear."

Once again, Walker's mom scored the final point and won the game.

*

As he traversed the clearing, Walker bent, casually reached out his hand and plucked a spray of the flowers. The relaxed movement still caught Ryszard's attention, but Walker simply smiled and pretended to sniff the bouquet before tucking it into the brim of his cap. Ryszard promptly dismissed Walker's gesture and resumed playing with his new spear.

CHAPTER SEVEN

As they followed the trail through the night, the river wound back and forth, like a great noisy snake. Walker was ready to collapse, Hairy didn't look much better. Yet Ryszard and the other trolls were unrelenting.

It seemed that the troll's camp was at the upper end of the valley. As they rounded a bend in the river, Walker was treated to an astonishing sight—an enormous stone arch—a natural bridge—white in the moonlight and spanning the wide river. He'd never seen anything like it. It was so big that scraggily trees grew on the rock, high above the river. Passing below they picked their way along a narrow beach. Here, the river slowed, moving sluggishly as the moon reflected from its surface.

Well, Walker had wanted an adventure and he had to admit he was getting it.

The light of the rising sun provided Walker with an opportunity to get a look at the rest of his chaperones. The other trolls were typical of their people. A little shorter than the average Hurrian, they were more heavyset, pale and hairy. Their heads were long, and their hands were rough with thick fingers and knuckles. They had thick brows, wide noses and big teeth giving them a feral look.

Ryszard was certainly an exception for his kind. He was more than a head taller than his brethren and would have been tall even for a Hurrian.

Combined with his bulk, he rather looked like a giant.

Walker thought that loincloths and animal furs were standard troll attire. But these guys wore sewn deer (or maybe auroch) skins. They carried stone axes, which weren't very good for hunting, but made good weapons. Combined with the trolls' strength they'd be deadly in combat.

Walker noticed one of the trolls was carrying a large pack on his back. He wondered just what it was these guys had been doing out in the woods, last night.

It was mid-morning by the time they reached their destination. It seemed Ryszard's people were encamped in caves along the undercut base of the limestone cliffs. The hillside was pockmarked with caves. But the trolls Walker had heard about were supposed to be nomadic, small family groups that never stayed in one place too long. Yet this was an established organized settlement with racks of blankets and even wooden doors covering some of the cave entrances.

Still, while the camp was big for trolls, it was small compared to the Vadi Kabile's. There were similarities, but also differences. The drying frames Walker saw were cruder—simple stick tripods and he didn't see evidence of a latrine anywhere, also there was no longhouse. Just an enormous, high-roofed cave with a palisade of logs guarding the entrance.

Osmanek hadn't mentioned any other settlements in the valley, or trolls; could it be Osmanek didn't know about these people? The valley was certainly big enough that if the trolls were careful, they could hide undetected for years.

As they continued through the camp Walker counted dozens of individuals as well as toddlers and naked babies playing in the dirt.

Everyone looked up at Ryszard's return and a crowd was gathering. Walker and Hairy were prodded forward, but Ryszard raised a hand to his tribe.

"We have returned from hunting down the great river," said Ryszard. "And have brought visitors from a far-off land." Then, with what sounded like a touch of sarcasm, "Let us make them feel welcome."

The mob of trolls pressed in to better inspect the new arrivals. If they'd never seen a Kobold before, Hairy might have just looked like an elf child—sorry, Hairy. While Walker just looked like yet another Hurrian.

Walker was wrestling with his inner self—it was his instinct to fight—to take advantage of the confusion, try to grab a stone club, smash a few shins and make a run for it. But his training stopped him from such a foolhardy act. He and Hairy were surrounded and outnumbered by creatures known for their strength and fighting skills.

Instead, and to Walker's surprise, it looked again like his mother's training—the use of mind rather than brawn—would be the better course of action. Score a couple more points for mom. Still, this would be a serious test of Walker's diplomatic skills indeed.

"I am honored by your hospitality," said Walker as loudly as he could. And then inspiration struck, and he reached up and placed a hand on the big troll leader's shoulder. "And we are grateful for Ryszard's timely aid in coming to our rescue from those barbaric village ruffians."

The effect of the words was nothing short of magical. The crowd stopped pressing forward as the trolls—men and women alike—paused. They looked almost embarrassed by their confusion. Walker noticed just the trace of a smile on Ryszard's lips.

Ryszard stepped forward and held open the curtain to the large cave. "After you."

The troll cave was in similar fashion to the Vadi Kabile's longhouse. Timber poles covered the front, and a thick, sun-bleached bearskin served as a curtain for the entrance. The interior was lit with a few smoky pine-tar torches. It was rough but tidy. This was all the more surprising as again, trolls were supposed to be nomads and not known for their home decorating skills. Trolls were thought to mostly smack things with sticks and rocks. Yet the cave, with a huge fire pit, bear furs and array of smoky torches provided a very homey feel.

Walker had heard it said that trolls were talented story-tellers—as one would expect from a race with an oral history. If one was lucky enough to encounter some sociable trolls and receive an invitation to share a meal, you might be treated to some epic tales. That is, if you didn't end up on the menu. Walker wasn't sure what to expect from his present hosts, but as no one had stuck a fork in him yet, he remained hopeful.

He'd also heard that trolls were champion campfire cooks. It was said that the troll technique for open-air braising; the roasting of meat—called barbacoa, was legendary. As it had been days since he and Hairy had had a decent full meal, Walker hoped this tale was true. If this was to be their last meal, at least he could hope for the best.

Ryszard and his men followed Walker and Hairy into the cave and then steered his guests to a pile of furs surrounding a fire pit. A big crackling campfire put out enough heat to make the cavern comfortable, if smoky. Ryszard raised a massive hand and signaled to a couple of female trolls. The women hurried over while smoothing down their animal-skin frocks.

In the Valley of the Auroch

"Walker," began Ryszard looking serious, "May I introduce Huberta and Evelina."

From what Walker remembered of the troll dialect, both Huberta and Evelina were variations of something like Beautiful, or dark and beautiful. And in the case of these two young ladies, the names were certainly appropriate. While troll women tended to be stout, these girls were actually endowed with some pretty feminine curves. They both had rather prominent eyebrows and somewhat toothsome smiles, which provided the ladies with rather intense expressions. Their arms and legs (and most other areas of exposed skin) were covered in a soft tawny fur—which Walker had to admit, wasn't unattractive—and their shoulder length hair was an intriguing dark-red hue. And while the troll girls were a tad toothier and certainly more hirsute than Walker was used to, he found them mysteriously good-looking in an exotic sort of way.

"I must say I'm thrilled to find myself in the presence of two such lovely ladies," he said, smiling and bowing extravagantly.

Ryszard raised an eyebrow at this compliment, and then continued with his introductions. "And this is Walker's companion, Hairy."

Hairy—always the ladies' man—raised a hand and waved.

"Our guests have been traveling all night," explained Ryszard. "Could you find them something to eat? And perhaps a little libation."

In response, Evelina and Huberta giggled behind their hands and hurried off. Ryszard—perhaps just making a show of being the host—waited for his guests to take their seats before he, in turn, sat. Ryszard's men draped themselves over a variety of furs and logs, but all eyes remained focused on Walker. Off in the corner, a smaller, younger-looking troll began rapping bones on a pair of drums—skins stretched over open skulls, producing a stirring melody. In a Hurrian village such an assemblage as this would be presided over by a council of elders—at least. But Walker didn't see any seniors in this group. Nor did he see anyone who looked like a shaman or medicine man—also essential in Hurrian society. Maybe trolls were just more secular than Hurrians.

"So, you say you are traders then," Ryszard asked. "Tell us more. Where are you from? Where were you headed? What have you seen?"

It occurred to Walker that this was more than a simple interrogation. Strider had also told Walker that troldfolk culture was steeped in the stories they told around the campfire. If so, was he now being invited to provide the evening's entertainment? Well, they'd come to the right guy. Walker had never been afraid of public speaking, and he was his own favorite subject.

But before Walker could open his mouth, the women were back. Evelina carried a large wicker platter laden with glistening slabs of smoked meat, and Huberta carried a pitcher and several cups. Just the sight of all the succulent steaks was enough to make Walker's head swim and his stomach growl.

Huberta handed Walker a wooden cup and proceeded to fill it with a rich golden pine-wine concoction. It was hot and strong enough to be felt all the way to his sinuses. Walker tossed back half the cup and it burned like liquid fire going down. He accepted a juicy slab of meat and sank his teeth in. It was smoky, tender and sweet and probably the best steak he'd ever eaten.

Smiling from ear to ear, Walker stood and turned to face the crowd.

"First off, my compliments to the cook," he said with utter sincerity.

Evelina fluttered her long eyelashes.

"How is everyone tonight?" Walker started off, sizing up the crowd. "It's nice to be here at this end of the valley. Thanks for inviting me."

There was a murmured response from the room and a few trolls shifted on their furs, scratched themselves. One belched loudly.

"Hairy and I hail from Aurignac," Walker said proudly, and turned to survey the room. "Anyone know Aurignac?" There was an indistinct murmur from the back. "Thank you." Walker said smiling and pointing at the murmurer. "Yes, Aurignac, the land of enchantment by the sea."

"Enchantment?" repeated one of the bigger trolls.

"See?" asked another.

"Yes, sea," explained Walker, hoping not to have to go into that explanation with this crowd too. Just keep moving, he thought. "Yes, the sea. Really, like a very, very large lake. And it's enchanting, which is a fancy word for dreamy and beautiful."

"It is a village by the water then?" asked Ryszard, helping to steer the conversation.

"Yes indeed," agreed Walker gratefully. "Thank you, Ryszard. Aurignac is a big village of mostly fishing folk."

"And you fish from this very big lake?" asked one of the hairier trolls helpfully.

In the Valley of the Auroch

"You are correct sir," replied Walker. "Though, not me personally. But friends and family do. You could say, I'm more of a fish eater than a fish catcher."

"What is this Argnak like then?" asked a burly furry guy.

"Well, it's got a lot of nice comfortable homes," explained Walker. "Timber, thatch and mud and stuff. Not like this nice cave of yours. Very rustic."

"And where is this Argnak?" asked another.

"Oh, well, it's a hike of many moons," replied Walker airily. "In the direction of the setting sun."

"You mean west?" asked a very wide guy in a mocking tone.

"Yes, west," agreed Walker, surprised by these country bumpkins' understanding of compass points. "I see we have a cartographer here. Thanks for getting all technical sir. I'll take it from here if you don't mind."

The crowd laughed at the heckler and turned their attention back to Walker.

"Are you telling us, you two hiked and camped, alone for moons on end?" asked a long-haired troll in a voice laden with suspicion. He waved a hand to indicate Walker's rather posh outfit. "Outfitted like that?"

"Hey, if I'm going to sleep in the rough, there's no law saying I can't look good doing it. Right?" replied Walker running a hand down the length of his tunic to a roomful of chuckles. "So, it might not surprise you to learn, that I'm not really an outdoorsy kind of guy."

There were outright laughs at that.

"Let's face it. Back home I slept in a comfy bed and had a nice roof over my head," continued Walker, "I had a mom that cooked me breakfast and dinner and even cleaned my clothes. But the village elders insist that on your eighteenth birthday you have to prove you're a man. You know how you do that? You're supposed to take a really long walk and sleep outside on the ground. So, to prove I'm a man I had to leave my home and take a nap somewhere that I could be eaten by a bear looking for a midnight snack. How is that a thing?"

The crowd broke up into general laughter.

"Hey, if they really wanted to know if I was a man, they could've just asked to see the hair on my balls," explained Walker. "Is the real test that grown men survive if they don't make good bear chow?"

The crowd was going wild with laughter at this point.

"Yeah, not only did I have to give up my comfy home and bed, but to sleep, I have to wrap myself in a blanket. Did you ever try to run wrapped in a blanket?" asked Walker. "That's way more convenient for the bear, don't you think?" and he mimed a hulking, toothy bear, saying; "Awe, that's awfully thoughtful, somebody wrapped dinner up for me."

The crowd was really laughing hard, with one big guy actually smacking his shorter neighbor's shoulder and sending him tumbling to the floor. Others slammed their hands together and hooted.

"Yeah, and you know what my uncle—who's supposed to be a great hunter by the way—told me to do if I ever was attacked by a bear? Play dead. Yes, that's actually what he said. That was his advice to me, just play dead. Stop and lay down on the ground and don't move. Where did he come up with that brilliant idea? The bears maybe? What would his advice be if I was attacked by a lion? Smear myself in fish oil, lay down and twitch like a trout? You think maybe my uncle doesn't really like me?"

Ryszard laughed so hard at this that he fell sideways off his log.

"Hunting and camping outdoors are sacred traditions," yelled a heckler.

"You're right, camping was a sacred tradition in my family too," replied Walker, "until someone invented houses."

The crowd was really going wild.

"You know what's a sacred tradition in my family now?" asked Walker. "Roofs. Roofs to keep the rain and snow off. And doors are nice too; they help keep the wolves out. I mean seriously, why do people think sleeping outdoors would prove you're a man? You know who else sleeps outdoors? Animals. What do they do to prove their animalhood? Sleep indoors?"

The crowd was practically rolling on the floor by this point.

"Maybe a better rite of passage would be to ask me to build a house," explained Walker.

"Okay, okay," said Ryszard standing up and waving to the crowd. "This has all been very entertaining, but perhaps someone has a serious question for our guests? Anyone?"

"Sure. So, what do you eat on the trail then?" asked a particularly heavy-set gent trying to look serious.

In the Valley of the Auroch

"Well, Hairy and I are what you call vegetarians," explained Walker.

"What does vegetarian mean?" asked the heavy guy.

"Well, vegetarian is another name for bad hunter," explained Walker to a new round of laughter and a stern look from Ryszard. "But seriously, Hairy and I do a lot of fishing. It turns out we're pretty good fisherman. It's less dangerous and a lot less work. The last fish I caught was this big." He spread his hands apart. "Hey, do you guys know the difference between a hunter and a fisherman? Anyone? A hunter lies in wait. A fisherman waits and lies."

Even Ryszard couldn't help but laugh at that.

"Okay, okay," said Walker trying to suppress a grin. "Ryszard's right. Let's get serious. Anyone have a serious question?"

"You started by saying you have hiked for moons," remarked a tall troll in a voice full of skepticism. "How many?"

Displaying the knots along his belt, Walker answered, "Three."

"What's that?" asked the tall troll.

"My way of marking the days," explained Walker seriously.

While the trolls understood the concept of counting, using knots as a sort of calendar—on a belt—was new to them, and several came forward for a closer look.

"You have been on the trail for so long," began a long-haired brute, "What do you miss most about your village?"

"That warm bed to sleep in?" suggested someone giggling.

"Hot pine-wine?" suggested another to general laughs.

"Women!" said Walker with a big grin and a wink to Huberta. The whole crowd burst out laughing again. "Though after a couple of months on the trail, some of those deer out there start to look pretty good," Walker added.

Howls, knee slaps and guffaws. Walker caught Huberta fluttering her eyelashes as she pushed out her chest and ran her fingers through her hair.

"Have you had any trouble with wolves or tigers?" asked another troll trying to sound serious.

"Or lions?" suggested another.

"Or bears?" suggested a third.

"Actually, the most dangerous animals are the husbands of the girls I meet in villages like this," said Walker, and pointing to a particularly good-looking troll added, "this guy knows what I'm talking about."

Caught in the middle of a drink, the good-looking troll did a pine-wine spit-take.

"Have you hunted mammoth?" asked another guy.

"Actually, I thought I was seeing one earlier tonight." replied Walker and pointing to Ryszard. Beaver-coat slapped Ryszard hard on the shoulder.

"One bit of helpful advice I can give you from my experience—if you're drunk enough, bugs leave you alone." explained Walker. "I guess the little suckers just can't handle the hard stuff." He said raising his pine-wine while the crowd erupted anew in laughter.

"This is good stuff by the way," Walker said holding up his drink, "I like a beverage I can use to start a campfire."

There were hoots of agreement and more laughs.

"Which one of you cooks on the trail?" asked a big heavy-faced gentleman trying to look stern.

"Hairy and I take turns." explained Walker, "I personally like cooking with wine. Hairy cooks with bugs."

More big laughs—Walker had these guys eating out of his hand.

"Have you had any close calls on your travels?" asked the red-haired guy.

"Sure, every time it's Hairy's turn to cook," replied Walker.

The crowd guffawed.

"You know, when it's Hairy's turn to cook," added Walker, "I don't brush my teeth after I eat; I count them."

Beaver-coat laughed and snorted.

"I don't want to imply Hairy's a bad cook, but the last possum he cooked made a better pair of boots," explained Walker while pointing to his feet.

Shrieks of laughter.

"You know how some meals taste better the day after? With Hairy's it's

In the Valley of the Auroch

usually the day before."

The crowd was again teary-eyed with laughter and the mood in the room was pretty congenial. Walker guessed it was time and he should quit while he was ahead.

"But seriously folks, it's great being here among the Tal Stamm," said Walker as the laughter subsided, "And I'm relieved, because when Ryszard asked us to dinner, I didn't know if he was asking us as guests or the main course."

Red hair laughed so hard he fell backwards off his stump

CHAPTER EIGHT

More than a day had passed without a word from Osman or Tarmaz. Osmanek—who had been suspicious of Walker from the start, called a meeting of his top aides.

Taichi, Baghadur, Bahadir, Cengiz and Hosmunt gathered in the longhouse to consider the matter. Taichi spook first.

"I told you all it was a mistake to trust those two," he said.

"We don't know what has happened," remarked Osmanek, "The elves may have just moved their camp farther than the strangers suggested."

"So, you actually believe the stranger's story that the elves took Aygul?" asked Baghadur.

"I believe it's possible," replied Osmanek. "The stranger is right; we haven't seen track or spoor of a lion. We know elves sometimes hunt in the valley. The stranger said that he saw the elves leading an auroch, and we have lost several of our herd."

"Or the stranger was weaving a tale of lies to mislead us," suggested Cengiz. "It's just too great a coincidence that those two shows up and Taichi's daughter goes missing."

"A tale of lies," mused Osmanek, "about elves and aurochs. I think that would be as great a coincidence as any. No, I trust that Osman and Tarmaz can handle those two themselves. If they return empty handed, we can deal with the strangers then."

"And what if the strangers have friends?" asked Cengiz. "Perhaps his plan was to lead Osman and Tarmaz into a trap."

In the Valley of the Auroch

"Agreed. We should have sent more men." added Baghadur. "It may already be too late."

Cengiz's argument was gaining support. Osmanek could sense his authority slipping away. He knew that the men required action to sooth their restless souls.

"If you all feel this strongly, then what would you suggest?"

"Let us get to the bottom of this," explained Baghadur, pointing to Taichi, Bahadir, Cengiz and Hosmunt. "If we start off at dawn, with the daylight we should be able to pick up their trail."

Osmanek considered the suggestion. Succeed or not, at least the activity would mollify this group of complainers.

"Alright," he said standing to attention. "Everyone but Taichi. You should remain in the settlement in case Aygul returns on her own."

The search party started off before dawn and reached the clearing where the strangers had been camped by first light. They found the strangers' trail—and those of Osman and Tamraz, and followed it up towards the cliffs, in the direction that the stranger had said the elf camp was. Continuing up the trail, they soon found a loamy patch with many confusing prints—not elf but human and heavier, broader prints—trolls!

"Are you certain?" asked Hosmunt, leaning over Cengiz to get a better look. The tales of feral primitives were legend; wild men, bone-crackers, cannibals with the strength of great apes.

"Just look at the splay of the toes," explained Cengiz pointing to one particularly large footprint. "And the size of these marks. There can be no doubt."

"Here? In our valley?" asked Bahadir visibly shaken. "What are they doing here?"

"Trolls are cannibals," exclaimed Hosmunt, "perhaps they've taken Aygul."

"Then it is good that Taichi isn't here to see this," remarked Bahadir.

"True. And there is blood over here." Baghadur pointed to a dark patch covered in ants. "There was a battle."

Hosmunt, beating the bush for further tracks, stepped back as he made a disturbing discovery.

"Oh, great spirits," he declared and turned away.

Baghadur and Cengiz hurried over to investigate.

The forest floor was black with congealed blood. The air was thick with flies.

"So much blood. Someone died here," declared Baghadur. "But without a body we don't know who it was."

Cengiz, examining the turned-up ground and blood, stood. "It was Osman and Tarmaz. It must have been. They must have been taken by surprise. If they were still alive, they would have been back by now."

"What makes you say that?" asked Baghadur. "There are no bodies."

"So much blood. No one could have survived."

"Where are the bodies then?"

"Taken," said Cengiz through gritted teeth. "This was the work of trolls."

"Could the strangers have done this?" asked Hosmunt. "Could they have been working with the trolls?"

"Why not?" asked Bahadir, seething with renewed hatred. "The one who calls himself Walker travels with an ape doesn't he? He could be in league with cannibals as well."

"So, you think he led Osman and Tamraz into a trap?

"Osmanek should never have agreed to such a small party," said Bahadir, shaking with rage.

"The tracks lead off toward the river," explained Cengiz, standing up and pointing in that direction.

"Then you think the trolls mean to attack the village?"

"No, not this group. It's too small. More likely they've returned to their camp, wherever that is. Perhaps for reinforcements."

"Either way, we must warn Osmanek," replied Baghadur.

"But we need to follow these tracks," argued Hosmunt, "If we wait and it rains, the trail will be lost, and we'll never find the strangers. We can't let them escape. They must pay for what they've done!"

"We don't really know what they've done," argued Bahadir. "You don't know whose blood this is."

"Yes, we do." Said Baghadur. "If Osman and Tarmaz were still alive, they would have returned to warn us by now."

"If what you say is true, we must find the strangers and make them pay," stated Bahadir.

"And don't forget Aygul," added Cengiz, "They must answer for taking her, too."

"Then its settled. Cengiz and I will follow the strangers," declared Baghadur. "Hosmunt, you and Bahadir go back to the village and tell Osmanek what we've found."

"We have to stick together," exclaimed Hosmunt. "What can just the two of you do?"

"We will follow the trail and track the stranger," explained Baghadur. "Now that we know about the trolls, Cengiz and I won't be taken by surprise. You two head back to the village."

And at that, Baghadur and Cengiz picked up their spears, nodded an oath to each other, and set off to follow the trail. It wouldn't be hard; such a large group couldn't hide their passage.

"The savages turned here," said Cengiz, pointing off through the trees. "They headed into the forest and paralleled the river."

"Yes, they were trying to remain under cover," added Baghadur. "They attempted to avoid leaving tracks in the open ground and river sand."

But while the trail might be easy to follow, neither Baghadur nor Cengiz were under the illusion that they would find their quarry quickly. The trolls had a long head start and by nightfall Baghadur and Cengiz had ventured farther from the village than they had in several seasons. As the day grew dark, they decided it was best to camp for the night. Traveling at night they risked running into the trolls. They decided to sleep in the trees to avoid prowling wolves.

By dawn, Baghadur and Cengiz were back on the trail.

The path led upriver, and by afternoon it became obvious that the trolls hadn't stopped; they seemed tireless.

Just as Baghadur and Cengiz rounded a bend in the river they were stopped dead in their tracks.

Before them stood an enormous natural bridge, a great arch bigger than the tallest trees and spanned the river. It looked to be the work of giants.

This was the arch that Tabib had warned them about. The gate between this world and the next. Cengiz had never believed Tabib's stories, but standing here, Cengiz could now imagine it had to be a gate built by nothing less than great spirits.

Was the arch a warning to prevent hunters from venturing further into the great spirit's domain? But the savages' tracks in the sand led under the gate and beyond.

"Perhaps the trolls we chase are demons," said Baghadur, awed by the sight. "And now they've returned to their lair. Tabib warned us against venturing further."

"The stranger isn't a demon," said Cengiz. But now he was feeling less sure of himself.

"Who else but gods could have made such a thing?" asked Baghadur. "Perhaps the trolls are servants of the spirits. Maybe they have taken the strangers back to the spirit realm for punishment."

"So, what do we do?" asked Cengiz, feeling fear for the first time in days.

"The stranger continued on," replied Baghadur, pointing to the tracks in the sand. "If he could travel this path then so can we."

But it was getting late, and the shadows were growing longer. The forest would again be plunged into darkness. Baghadur and Cengiz agreed to camp early for the night and decide whether to continue in the morning. They selected a stout tree not far from the river, climbed and tied themselves to boughs several spans up.

In the Valley of the Auroch

By that afternoon, Hosmunt and Bahadir were back in the settlement. There was much anguish at their news and this time, Osmanek blamed himself for letting the smooth-taking stranger talk him into sending his men into what now like an obvious trap. He vowed revenge.

When the stranger had suggested elves had taken Aygul, Osmanek had been skeptical, but he'd allowed himself to be persuaded. But why would the strangers be working with trolls, wondered Osmanek? He'd long suspected that there might be troldfolk, somewhere in the hills. But trolls had never been a problem in the valley before.

But Hosmunt said that they all agreed, the tracks they found were definitely trolls. The very idea made his blood run cold.

There were stories of trolls—ogres, some people called them—raiding Hurrian campsites—killing and cannibalizing their victims. The idea that trolls might be responsible for Aygul's disappearance now made more sense. Had the stranger tried to cast suspicion on the elves because he was in league with the trolls? Why would the stranger—a Hurrian—be working with such monster-men? What was the stranger's game? Could it have something to do with his Kobold, the little ape-man?

Walker and that ape—the creature looked like a short elf. The elves lived rough and while they competed for the Hurrian's game, they were rarely more than a nuisance. Osmanek knew even less about Kobolds.

The more Osmanek thought about it, the more concerned he was.

"We should send another party after them," advised Volkan.

"And find my daughter," added Taichi. "We need to do something."

"Baghadur and Cengiz are already tracking the strangers," replied Osmanek. "We should wait until we hear back from them."

"What if they run into the trolls?" asked Bahadir. "They could need our help."

"If there are primitives in the valley, we need to send a war party and kill them all," declared Tabib, "especially if they killed Osman and Tarmaz."

"Trolls in our valley?" declared Taichi. "Where would they be hiding?"

"Perhaps they are from the great forest," said Hosmund. "Maybe this is the first time they have entered the valley."

"Or they are from up-river, beyond the great arch," suggested Osmanek. "We haven't explored the area in many years. If there are trolls anywhere, that's where they would be."

"We've avoided that territory for a reason," declared Tabib.

"Why do you keep saying we need to fear the arch, Tabib?" asked Volkan.

"When our tribe first scouted the valley, many brave souls were lost," answered Tabib. "Men who ventured up the river and never returned. The gate is a warning."

"Perhaps the trolls were there even then," said Taichi. "Maybe they've always been there."

"But what would the stranger have to do with any of this?" asked Volkan, "Why would he be a scout for those primitives?"

"Perhaps he's a troll slave," replied Osmanek. "Maybe he was sent to scout out our village, and to assess our defenses. A troll couldn't sit in our longhouse, but a Hurrian could. And now he's returned to his masters with whatever knowledge he's gained."

"So, the trolls killed Osman and Tarmaz because they were with the stranger," said Volkan. "They were probably meeting for a rendezvous."

"And Osman and Tarmaz were in the way," declared Taichi. "Then we need to kill all the trolls before they kill us."

"But it's a very big valley, even beyond the arch, and we don't know exactly where they are," advised Osmanek. "That is why we must wait for Baghadur and Cengiz. To know where to go and not run off leaving the village unprotected."

CHAPTER NINE

Walker awoke to find a rather furry, rather feminine arm draped across his face. The arm's owner—Huberta— was snoring softly beside him, her face hidden beneath a mass of auburn curls. Lifting the rabbit-fur coverlet, he saw that they were both naked. Also, the auburn continued all the way down. Light from the rising sun was just peeking through holes in the curtain over the cave's entrance. From the taste in his mouth and the pounding in his head Walker figured he must have had a pretty good time last night. And, surprisingly, he was still alive—that was a good sign—he hoped the same could be said for Hairy.

Walker carefully eased himself out from under the covers and quietly gathered his clothes—picking through feminine and masculine articles and being careful not to wake his still sleeping beauty. Pulling on his leggings, Walker quietly backed out of the cave. Finding a half-frozen bucket of water, Walker dunked his head to wake himself up. Giving his hair a good shake, Walker slipped his tunic over his head, tied a new knot in the fringe on his belt and then dug a licorice stick out to scrub his teeth. It was early— a fine cool morning mist still hung in the air—and the camp had yet begun to stir. Still, Walker was upset and mentally kicked himself for oversleeping. His plan had been to wake up even earlier, grab Hairy and sneak out well before anyone was up. Well, he probably blew that.

"Good morning storyteller."

Bescumber.

Ryszard stepped out from behind a tree, a steaming mug in a massive hand.

"Ryszard," Walker replied. "You're up early."

"Ah," the big guy shrugged. "You know what they say, the early troll gets the worm."

"Worms for breakfast are more Hairy's thing," replied Walker, as he realized that Ryszard had been a step ahead of him the whole time. That also meant that Walker's original plan wouldn't have worked, and it would've just given Ryszard an excuse not to trust him.

"That was quite a performance you gave last night," continued Ryszard and changing the subject. "I thought my men were on the verge of appointing you the new headman."

"I was just trying to be a good campfire storyteller, and repay you for your hospitality," responded Walker carefully.

"Yes, very… entertaining," replied Ryszard. "Though I would have liked to hear more about your home, this Aurignac. And what really brought you to this valley."

"As I said, trade," Walker replied and wondering just how much trouble he and Hairy were really in. Did Ryszard believe him? The trolls seemed pretty casual about killing Osman and Tarmaz. Were they like that with everyone or just the Vadi Kabile? Walker would have to be very careful with what he said to this guy. "But go ahead, ask me anything." he continued as they entered the cave and took their seats around the morning fire.

"Yes, trade, replied Ryszard. "Were you trading with the villagers?"

Walker realized the question could be a trap.

"No, though Hairy and I did visit the village to introduce ourselves the previous day," he replied. "But they were very rude and chased us off. Then, those two ambushed us the other night. I suppose they were after my obsidian."

"Is that what you call that beautiful material?" asked Ryszard smiling, "I've never seen anything so sharp before. And my men were quite intrigued by your weapons as well. But surely you can't carry enough to supply my whole tribe."

"No, you're absolutely right," replied Walker trying to sound like the traders he'd observed pass through Aurignac. "For instance, that spear and knife I was carrying? The rest of the stones in my pack? Those are samples. If you're really interested, I can return home and make everything to order."

In the Valley of the Auroch

"Return home?" replied Ryszard.

"Yes," said Walker and actually beginning to warm to the lie. "That's where my workshop is. Back home in Aurignac. As you pointed out I couldn't possibly carry enough with me to trade. How could I know how much my customers wanted?"

"Yes, of course," replied Ryszard.

"So, if you like what you see, I can go home, make everything you need and return when I'm finished."

"And how long would that take?" asked Ryszard.

"Oh, not long at all." Walker smiled.

"If I like what I see?" mused Ryszard thoughtfully.

"Yes and judging by the way you took a shine to that spear, I can tell you're a man of your refinement and tastes."

"Walker, you flatter me."

"No, seriously," Walker continued, smiling. "And I'm not just saying that because you intimidate me."

"You know, you seem to be quite an eloquent speaker for a trader."

"Well, you need to be to get the best deals," replied Walker, amazed at how easily this total fabrication was coming together. He couldn't have planned it better.

"Of course." agreed Ryszard. "Anyway, I thought as host it my duty to be up before my guests. The womenfolk are preparing breakfast as we speak. By the way, did you sleep well?"

Walker felt a blush rise to his cheeks and hoped his beard was thick enough to hide it.

"Yes, thanks," said Walker wanting to change the subject and cover his nervousness. "The lovely Huberta and I spent most of the night."

"Really?" said Ryszard raising his big eyebrows. "That does not sound like her at all. Huberta, while passionate, is a woman of few words."

"Oh?" replied Walker, "I wouldn't have guessed."

"No matter," replied Ryszard smiling, "So, back to why you're here."

"Yes, my trade," said Walker. "Aurignac is a village of artisans. And my specialty is obsidian cutlery. Are you interested? I see that your men carry stone axes. But obsidian is the latest thing, everyone wants obsidian these days."

"Ha!" laughed the big guy. "Well, I must be honest Walker, I find you to be a stimulating companion as well."

"Say," said Walker starting to get un uncomfortable feeling and changing the subject, "You wouldn't happen to know where Hairy spent the night?" he asked, hoping Hairy wasn't on the breakfast menu.

"I believe he slept with the children last night," mused Ryszard. He pointed to a cave with a heavy wooden door. "They seem to have taken a fancy to him."

"Yes, well, Hairy's always been a kid at heart," replied Walker and breathing a silent sigh of relief.

"Speaking of your friend Hairy," replied Ryszard. "Just what is your relationship to him? If you do not mind my asking."

"No, not at all," replied Walker and wondering just how much he should say. He wanted to stress Hairy's importance, make him sound harmless and yet not let Ryszard think he could use Hairy to control Walker. It was a tricky dilemma. "He's a close friend of the family. Sort of like my cousin, on my father's side. And he's the best guide I know."

"Interesting," said Ryszard seeming to digest that bit of information. "But he is not a Hurrian. And you are not an elf, or whatever Hairy is."

"Kobold, I think," explained Walker, "Yeah, it's complicated."

"How so?" Ryszard pressed.

"Hairy's real family were nomads, like you troldfolk or the elves." explained Walker. "But apparently, he was abandoned as a baby. We don't know anything about his people. My uncle was on a hunting expedition and found Hairy up in a tree. He brought him home and raised Hairy as his son."

"Hmm," mused Ryszard, with a faraway look in his eye. "Yes, very curious indeed."

"Anyway, enough about me," said Walker, wanting to change the subject. "What about you? I thought your people were all nomads. I didn't know you made settlements."

"We do not as a rule," agreed Ryszard, "But you see, I have had a similar experience to your friend Hairy."

In the Valley of the Auroch

"Really?" responded Walker, honestly curious. "How so?"

"I too, was orphaned when I was very young," replied Ryszard. "I have no memories of that time. I probably would have died, if it had not been for a Hurrian hunting party. They found me and took me back to their village. The medicine man of the village raised me and tutored me for a time."

"Really?" exclaimed Walker intrigued by Ryszard's tale.

"You were raised by a medicine man?" asked Walker and he couldn't help himself adding, "My parents are healers too."

"Indeed?" Ryszard responded with raised eyebrows, "And yet you are not? Would about your birthright? Have you rejected your true calling to go off trading?"

"Pfft, I have a brother. He's welcomed to it." replied Walker.

"So, your brother is a healer then?" asked Ryszard.

"No, not really," responded Walker, getting tangled up in the truth. "Actually, he's an artist. You know, paintings of animals, hunters, sculpting figures out of clay. That sort of thing. Lately he's mostly been doing the inside of houses and caves," replied Walker, remembering his brother's new 'experimental period'. "But honestly, the village is probably better off without me. I was never serious enough to study. No; with me out of the way, dad will probably just tell my brother he's the next shaman. Hawk can probably do that and be an artist too."

"I feel sad for you," sighed Ryszard.

"Why?" asked Walker touched by Ryszard's tone. "I'd rather be an artisan and trader. Honest." He was being honest too.

"Well, because for me, I would have cherished the opportunity to be a medicine man," said Ryszard.

"Well, why aren't you?" asked Walker. "You said you were raised by one."

"Yes," replied Ryszard, "But, I am not a Hurrian. The medicine man raised me, but never treated me like a son. I was merely a servant, he taught me just enough to do the chores competently. And when I grew too big, he sent me away."

"I'm sorry Ryszard," Walker said. And he really was. It sounded like a sad and lonely childhood. "Well, you never know, if my brother doesn't

111

work out there may still be an opening back in Aurignac."

"You jest, but I am serious," laughed Ryszard.

A stern-looking troll woman appeared carrying more tea. She regarded Walker with a leer which made him uncomfortable.

"Sorry, I didn't mean to make light of your situation," said Walker accepting a mug of his own. "But you told me that the other guy…Rolf, is your brother?"

"In the same way you and Hairy are," corrected Ryszard. "When I left my master, I wandered and eventually found this tribe. The clan accepted me and I was taken in by Rolf's family. That was years ago, and Rolf's parents—my parents—are gone."

"And they made you the headman," added Walker wondering. Surely it would have been Rolf's birthright. "Well, I guess that's not surprising, considering your size."

"Yes," Replied Ryszard, "I was given this honor solely because I am big. I suppose that does count for something."

"And are you the one that convinced your tribe to settle down here in this valley?" asked Walker, now honestly, curious.

"It seemed like a good idea at the time." explained Ryszard. "When they found me, the tribe were indeed nomads. Something I had no experience of. They followed the herds of bison, deer and elk. When times were good, we ate, when times were lean, we went hungry. They were superstitious and frightened of everything. But with my knowledge of Hurrian ways, I was able to help. We found this valley and I convinced them to settle here, like the Hurrians that raised me. For the first time that they could remember, they knew where their next meal was coming from. They were so grateful they that I was made chief when the old headman died."

"Well, it sounds like you earned it," replied Walker genuinely impressed.

"Yes, and it helps that I am tall," replied Ryszard with a smile.

"It was the education you got from the medicine man that saved the tribe. It sounds like fate."

"Oh?" responded Ryszard. "You do not strike me as someone who believes in fate."

"Don't I?" replied Walker wonderingly. "No, I suppose I don't. I think the future is what you make it."

"I agree." replied Ryszard. "You know Walker, I admire that about you. You changed your own fate when you decided to become a trader."

"Yeah? Well, the truth is, I get queasy at the sight of other people's blood." laughed Walker, "Not animals, but for some reason other people. Sort of an impediment to a good medicine man."

It occurred to Walker that Ryszard was giving him a lot of answers and hadn't even had breakfast yet. Who was interrogating who here? Walker wondered if Ryszard was aware of the Hurrian's herd. If so, like the elves, he probably wanted some of the aurochs for himself. This explained so much.

"Say, you folks have much of a lion problem around here?" asked Walker.

"No," replied Ryszard frowning, "the Hurrians killed them off long ago."

It was almost noon and the whole tribe, young and old, had gathered for Walker's obsidian napping, knife-making demonstration. And Walker was feeling the pressure. After all, he knew that the trolls knew how to nap stones to make tools, but they'd never seen anyone shape obsidian into works of art. They all expected to see a master in action. Yeah, no pressure.

Despite killing Osman and Tarmaz, Ryszard, the chief was turning out to be a genial host. Still, it was a good idea to play along and see where this led.

Walker considered his situation. Ryszard made it seem like Hairy and he were guests. It wasn't like they were tied up. Walker had lost the crown vetch, though he suspected the flowers were probably in Huberta's cave. The poisonous flower had seemed like a good idea at the time—Ryszard had just disarmed him—but did he really need a weapon? If the situation took a turn for the worst, Walker doubted he'd be able to defend himself, unarmed, against Ryszard and his men. If it came to that he'd have to slip the crown vetch into the troll's food and that would take time. But maybe there was nothing to worry about.

The place set aside for Walker's tool making demonstration was in the center of the settlement, near the big cave. The ground was hard but covered in a soft dark-brown bearskin rug. Several burly trolls dragged logs over for everyone to sit on while the women were serving baskets of millet biscuits and spelt crackers.

Ryszard, Rolf, Huberta and Evelina took up positions near the front from which they could best observe. At a nod from Ryszard, Walker began.

114

In the Valley of the Auroch

From his pack Walker produced a bundle of soft leather. This he carefully unrolled to reveal several pieces of shiny, multi-colored obsidian. The crowd gasped; the trolls had never seen pieces of stone so pretty before. Each piece was a different example of obsidian, snowflake, rainbow, mahogany, and even a piece of the rare black glass. With the exception of the black, no piece was larger than his fist. The black shard was longer than his hand, thin and narrow and somewhat fragile.

Walker removed another leather bundle which contained his tools; an abrasive stone, a small tapered wooden mallet, two smaller pressure flakers—one of bone the other antler—and a very thick hand-held leather pad. There were also several carving knives.

Walker knelt on the bearskin rug and draped a leather blanket over his legs. Everyone moved closer—politely jostling for a better view.

Walker started with a piece of brown striped mahogany glass.

"This is obsidian," said Walker, holding the sample aloft for all to see. "Brown obsidian to be exact. A rare rock only found on the slopes of long dead volcanos." The crowd pressed even closer for a better look. "If you hold it up, you can see light through it." He demonstrated by turning the piece in the sunlight. "My teacher called obsidian, volcanic glass."

Next, Walker picked up his tapered mallet and proceeded to smack the side of the rock, breaking off a large triangular piece of stone. The crowd gasped and even Ryszard looked alarmed.

"No worries," said Walker holding up the two pieces. "This is just the process for shaping the part."

Walker set aside the parent piece and proceeded to work on what even at this early stage, appeared to be a crude knife blade. He started by using his abrasive stone to sand off the rough points, and then switched to the mallet, using a small rapping motion to knock off extraneous bits. The crowd could now see that Walker was refining the shape. Working deliberately, Walker smacked the edge of the stone at an angle—and knocked off a wide flake to thin the sample further. It was this process—alternating back and forth, between shaping and thinning—that refined the blade.

It seemed as if by magic the weapon was taking shape. The stone was turning into art as the flakes flew off. The surface—originally dusty brown, was now shiny brown with black stripes. Just when everyone thought Walker was done, his hammering hand flashed another set of short nibbling strikes, chiseling off still smaller and smaller bits. In this way, Walker was creating a smoothly curving edge.

Walker was careful to flip the piece every few raps, alternating strikes to produce an increasingly symmetrical shape. Occasionally he switched back to a thinning stroke—striking the edges below the centerline—to still further refine the edge. The crowd was on the edges of their seats, some even reaching forward to stop him—the piece looked finished already—why was Walker continuing? Surely, he should stop—leave well enough alone—but Walker kept working, supporting the piece by the edges—holding with his fingertips—lightly, to avoid snapping the stone—and knocking off ever smaller pressure points.

Walker abruptly switched tools, moving now to his pressure flaker—and at this point Ryszard almost screamed for him to stop. But Walker was now working along the wide end, notching the sides of the blade using very small nibbles which began to produce elegantly deep clefts. The crowd was holding its collective breath—fearing the piece would shatter as the clefts grew deeper. Finally, Walker set aside the pressure flaker and switched to an antler, using its rough side to sharpen the piece's edge.

And he was done.

Walker held the knife up for everyone to see.

Bright sunlight sparkled along freshly chiseled edges. Hues of yellow, gold and brown reflected from its countless polished facets. A dazzling rainbow refracted from its many long angled planes.

The crowd let out its breath in an audible sigh. It was the most beautiful thing they had ever seen.

Walker struggled to get to his feet—his legs were asleep—and several people leapt forward to help him. Walker smiled and offered the finished product to one of the admirers, to be passed around the group for inspection.

Everyone had an opportunity to handle the glittering piece of glass. It was proclaimed magnificent! —the prettiest thing they'd ever seen. Walker was an artisan. For the Tal Stamm this was the cultural event of the year. Everyone was in high spirits.

Huberta—dressed in a hip-hugging animal skin, hair pulled back, and breasts thrust outward—fondled the blade in a most suggestive way. All the while keeping her eyes on Walker.

Looking about, Walker noted Ryszard didn't seem to be paying attention to the festivities. He followed the headman's gaze. Ryszard was looking at

Hairy, who was pretending to enjoy himself playing with the troll children.

When the knife blade finally made it to him, Ryszard—smiling broadly—made a great show of admiring the piece. Turning, he caught Walker's eye and said simply.

"Continue."

Baghadur and Cengiz were up at dawn and after lowering their packs and spears, slid down from their improvised bivouac in the tree. Bending to gather his things, Cengiz froze in alarm.

"Baghadur—look," and pointed to the base of their tree. There in the soft earth was an enormous paw print. It was unmistakably that of a lion.

"May the spirits protect us," said Baghadur grabbing his spear and searching the surrounding forest. "The stranger was telling the truth. There is a lion."

"Do you think that the lion took Aygul?" asked Cengiz looking about.

"Lion or not, the Osman and Tarmaz are missing, probably dead." replied Baghadur. "And the strangers are somehow in league with trolls."

"These tracks are recent," he said, pointing to the moss. "It was made in the night."

Holding their spears at the ready and searching the forest they crouched to reconsider their situation. The lion had obviously tracked them to the tree. But lions were night hunters and for the moment, they were probably safe.

"Should we turn back?" asked Cengiz worriedly.

"We can't go back now," replied Baghadur and weighing their options. "The lion has probably moved on; I don't think it would attack us in daylight. I say we continue and stay vigilant."

Perhaps the lion guards the gate," remarked Cengiz. "Maybe the lion waits on the other side."

Baghadur examined the narrow strip of sand under the arch.

"No, the only tracks in the sand are those of the strangers and the trolls.

The lion must still be on this side of the arch. I say we go on."

They took off immediately, forgoing breakfast, chewing acorn-biscuits from their packs. The troll's path followed avoided the river, climbing the rocks into the dense forest. It followed the base of steep cliffs and rock-strewn defiles, past stands of elm, oak and hickory, through tall ferns and thick brush. The forest floor here was slippery with soft moss and fresh fallen pine needles. There seemed to be more animals on this side of the arch, and at one point they caught sight of a speckled civet, glaring down on them from a crag. There were countless birds, blue tits, jays, skylarks, warblers, owls and several woodpeckers. There were clouds of butterflies, moths and midges. There was a magical quality to this place.

The trolls had still shown no sign of stopping and Baghadur and Cengiz despaired of ever catching up to their quarry. It was possible that the trolls were now hopelessly far ahead. Still, Baghadur was determined to follow them at least to the end of the valley.

For the second half of his performance, Walker fashioned a handle from a curved piece of bone the length of his hand—he completed it with some elaborate carved filigree and fluting. Next, from his pack Walker removed a small clay vessel. It contained a combination of crushed bark-beetle and pine-tar, with which Walker proceeded to rub into the bone. The dark stain really brought out the grooves in handle. Using a rabbit-skin rag, Walker rubbed the shaft to a high sheen and fitted the blade into a notch on one end, tying it in place with a sinew lashing. Finally, Walker wrapped a leather grip midway along and cinched it tight.

Ryszard looked awestruck. If anything, this knife was even more beautiful than Walker's original. But by the time Walker was finished, his fingers were looking a bit raw, even bleeding a little around the nails. Noticing this, Ryszard became alarmed—apparently, he wasn't a slavedriver. It was past noon and he instructed Walker to rest and have something to eat. Perhaps Ryszard feared damaging his golden goose?

Relaxing back in the big cave, Walker had done some mental calculations, at his present pace, he had a two days' supply of obsidian.

Based on this logic, Walker decided it would be prudent to slow production a bit—subtly, so it wasn't obvious. It shouldn't be too hard to do, making weapons was tough work.

Walker had been disturbed when he noticed Ryszard watching Hairy. Ryszard had seemed all cordial and friendly at breakfast, but in retrospect, and remembering the casual way his men had dispatched Tarmaz and Osman, Walker wondered who was playing who? Walker also considered his newfound popularity with the clan. Would it be enough to protect him

In the Valley of the Auroch

if Ryszard decided he had no further use for him? Walker wondered if maybe finding Huberta's cave and looking for his flowers wasn't such a bad idea after all.

Walker stood to leave and noticed Rolf loitering nearby.

"Can I help you?" asked Walker in as friendly a voice as he could manage.

Rolf's moon face split in a leering smile.

"I am supposed to keep an eye on you," answered the troll.

"Wonderful," replied Walker, too exhausted to bother hiding his irritation. So, he'd acquired an escort. That was interesting. He shrugged and exited the longhouse, turning to walk in the direction of Huberta's cave—nothing suspicious about that. He didn't get far before he was intercepted by Evelina—a plate of smoked meat in her hand.

"Ryszard wanted to make sure you got something to eat," she said, smiling toothily. She steered him over to a communal eating area.

"Thank you," said Walker sitting. He proceeded to pick bits of cooked meat from the wooden plate and considered just how complicated everything was becoming. Evelina was certainly alluring; firm fur-covered breasts, lush red lips, wavy dark hair, intense eyebrows and legs like a deer. What was not to like? And as Walker ate, Evelina asked him about Aurignac and the other lands he'd seen. Evelina touched Walker's arm, her hair, his chest, her neck and his shoulders. She also batted her long lashes. He knew where this was headed. But as soon as Walker finished his meal, Rolf arrived to shepherd him back to his work station.

For his second performance, Walker selected the star obsidian, and working smoothly, magically transformed it into a handful of sparkling charms for the ladies. Walker also braided thin strips of leather into cords from which he hung the charms to make necklaces. By the time Walker had finished, the shadows were growing long and even Rolf knew Walker couldn't work in the dark.

Before retiring for the evening, Walker tidied up his work area—rolling up his tools, packing away his samples and sweeping up the debris. Back home, he would preserve every piece big enough to be useful. As Walker was tidying up, he uncovered a particularly big shard of glass. It wasn't much more than a long splinter, but Walker had an idea. Sweeping up the fragments, Walker made a show of brushing down his tunic and casually slipped the shard into his pocket.

Evelina came over to see if she could help and noticed the condition of Walker's fingers—they were starting to bleed again, from all the tiny nicks and abrasions. This was one of the consequences of working with glass. Alarmed, Evelina took Walker by the arm and steered him in the direction of her cave—with Rolf few paces behind—visibly steamed for some reason.

Evelina's cave was warm, dry and cheery, with little feminine adornments—feather wall coverings and dried flowers—here and there. Walker had decided that he had to find that crown vetch, but that would mean sneaking out of Evelina's cave and into Huberta's.

Seated on a bear-skin rug next to a small central fire, Walker leaned back and tried to relax. Evelina busied herself assembling a meal. Her back turned, Walker dropped a hand into his pocket, bringing out the shard for closer inspection. It wasn't much—he had no illusions about facing off against Ryszard with just a splinter of glass. Still, it was something. Walker had an idea. He cleared his throat to get Evelina's attention.

"You wouldn't have any pine tar, would you?" Walker asked. "I seem to have left mine back with my tools."

"Pine tar?" repeated Evelina, while still working on the meal.

"Pine sap," explained Walker. "It speeds up healing in cases like this," he said wriggling his red fingers.

Leaning down and inspecting Walker's digits, Evelina bit her lip worriedly and thought to herself.

"I do not, but there are pine trees around camp," she explained. "I could go find some."

That's what Walker hoped she'd say.

"Let me look before it gets dark," replied Evelina exiting the cave.

Walker removed the shard from his pocket and examined it. It was so small, could it really be an effective knife? He rubbed the blunt end on the floor to dull it further. Acting quickly, Walker tore off a strip of from the fringe of his jacket. He threaded the razor-sharp point through one end of the leather, creating a crude sheath. Next, Walker tied it to the inside of his forearm, up, under the sleeve. Lifting his arm and flexing his muscles, Walker made sure the little blade was secure and remained hidden. Next, Walker rolled to his feet and stuck his head through the blanket covering the mouth of the cave. Rolf was sitting a short distance away, staring malevolently back at him. So much for retrieving the crown vetch.

CHAPTER TEN

Baghadur and Cengiz had followed the stranger's trail from the morning under the great arch until sundown. But it seemed their quarry still alluded to them. While the trolls never bothered to cover their tracks, they also never stopped for a rest. If anything, the trolls were even farther out of reach. While Baghadur had vowed to track the stranger to the end of the valley, it now seemed that the valley was endless.

The trail was difficult, the forest denser. Moss-covered logs make footing treacherous at the best of times. Where the trees thinned out, waist-high brush grew thick between. Baghadur and Cengiz clambered over rocks and shouldered aside ferns. And all the while birds berated them for invading their territory.

"We're lost," said a tired Cengiz.

"Not if we just keep following the river," replied Baghadur.

"I meant we've lost," explained Cengiz. "We're not going to catch the trolls and the stranger. It's pointless; we might as well turn back."

"Not while they remain in the valley," argued Baghadur.

"This valley never ends," replied Cengiz.

Tired, frustrated and dispirited, Baghadur and Cengiz made camp early that second night. They hung their packs from a tree and made a fire. Next, they fetched water from the river to refill their sacks. But while it was important to rest and regain their strength, that was easier said than done under the circumstances. Dispirited, neither man spoke as they sat and ate. They had enough food for several more days but now they felt like they were being watched. It felt like the forest was haunted.

Cengiz tapped Baghadur on the knee to get his attention and then slowly raised a finger to his lips. He pointed into the gathering darkness. It took Baghadur a moment for his eyes to adjust, and then he saw them; eyes glowing in the darkness. Could it be the lion? Had it followed them?

"Maybe it's a wolf," said Cengiz, "Or a big cat."

"Climb the tree," said Baghadur as he picked up his spear. "Do it slowly. Get off the ground. I will cover you."

Cengiz didn't argue. Without taking his eyes off the forest, he backed up to a tall, sturdy oak and began to climb until he reached the heavy limbs. Baghadur followed, moving like a ghost. When they felt high enough to be safe, they tied themselves to the tree and tried to relax. Under the circumstances, it wasn't easy to fall asleep, tied to a tree, high off the ground worried by what might be down there. The moon rose and the forest came alive with the sounds of tree frogs and buzzing insects. It had been an exhausting day and eventually, both men fell asleep, high above the forest floor.

Evelina turned out to be a very good cook. Walker decided that if Ryszard was going to eventually kill him, at least he'd go with a full stomach—so, that was some consolation.

But that was only if the troll women of the Tal Stamm didn't kill him first. Huberta and Evelina were certainly attractive enough—in a feral, woodsy way—but being trolls, they had twice his strength. It was like getting frisky with pretty, passionate bears.

The next morning, Walker crawled out from under the animal fur blankets, feeling a bit battered and bruised—in a good way. He was comforted to see that the poultice he'd applied the previous night, had done wonders for his fingers—another point for his mother.

Evelina—naked—rose and stretched. She wriggled her downy hips into a tight-fitting tunic. Walker couldn't help noticing all the fine tight-stitching and tailoring, unusual for troll garments. Somebody around here did nice work. Dismissing it, Walker slipped on his clothes and tied a new knot into the fringe of his belt. With Evelina's back turned, he tied his new dagger on the inside of his shin this time and pulled up his leggings. Evelina excused herself and stepped outside. Walker grabbed his kit and followed, heading to the nearby stream to complete his own morning ablutions. Looking over his shoulder to make sure his ever-present shadow Rolf—visibly irritated—was faithfully at his side.

As he finished his washing up, Walker turned to address his companion.

"Something bothering you, Sunshine?" Walker asked his irascible attendant.

"Evelina is my woman," growled Rolf in response.

"Oh great, that's just perfect, thought Walker wearily.

"I am going to enjoy killing you when Ryszard is finished," continued Rolf.

"Well, then we both have something to look forward to, don't we?" Replied Walker, drying his hair and slipping into his tunic before turning back towards Evelina's cave.

On the way back, Walker saw Hairy emerge from a small cave farther along the cliff. He was surrounded by troll kids who had dressed Hairy in children's clothes. Aside from these indignities, Hairy didn't look much worse for wear. He even managed a weary smile for Walker's benefit. Then he placed his closed hand—thumb up—on top of his palm and raised it— "Help."

Walker grinned in return.

Next Hairy raised a finger to his temple and then spread his hands questioningly—"What's the plan?"

Walker responded with both hands—extending the thumb and smallest finger while holding the three middle fingers curled and pushing forward, then he put a finger to his temple, clawing down and out with two fingers— "Still working on it."

Hairy shook his head and brought the thumb and index finger of one hand together then moved his hands—held in parallel—sideways— "No plan?"

Walker drooped the fingers on one hand down and made a shooing motion with them while shaking his head— "Not yet."

"What are you two doing?" growled Rolf stepping between them.

"Oh, Hairy's just telling me what an ass I am for dragging him along on this adventure," remarked Walker airily.

Rolf regarded the smaller hominid appraisingly.

"Well, maybe he is the smart one," laughed Rolf, and shoved Walker in the direction of the big cave.

Walker's audience had yet to gather but Ryszard was already there, two mugs in hand. He passed one over to Walker, who accepted it gratefully.

In the Valley of the Auroch

They touched cups and both sipped, savoring the misty morning.

"How do you find your accommodations?" Ryszard asked.

"Exhausting," Walker replied with a hand on his back. "Another night like that and I'll need a walking stick to get around."

"You know those are my adopted sisters you are talking about," Ryszard said warningly but with a grin.

"Yes, but I don't want to appear rude and decline my hostess's hospitality." Walker replied, "Which reminds me, you could have warned me Evelina is Rolf's girl."

"Humph," mused Ryszard nodding, "I do not believe Evelina shares his opinion."

"Even better—unrequited love," Walker sighed. "So, what's on the agenda for today? Also, you wouldn't happen to know where I could find some more of this volcanic glass?"

"I have never seen this obsidian before," Ryszard replied shaking his head. "But do you have enough to fashion another of these?" he added, holding up Walker's knife. "It would go some way towards ameliorating Rolf's mood if you made one for him."

"Possibly," answered Walker. "But he'd probably just poke me with it as soon as I was done."

"Probably," agreed Ryszard laughing in response.

Walker noticed several troll women using stone knives to chop at a slab of meat.

"What are the ladies making for dinner?" asked Walker. "I thought game was scarce."

"Auroch I believe," replied Ryszard.

"Really?" replied Walker. "You and the people of the Vadi Kabile have similar tastes."

"Then you know about the animals they keep penned?" asked Ryszard, possibly probing Walker for a reaction.

"I've seen their aurochs," replied Walker. "Where did you get yours?"

"Those aurochs do not belong to the Hurrians," growled Ryszard ignoring Walker's question. "They belong to the forest."

"I agree," replied Walker. "And I think it was wrong for them to take most of the game and trap the auroch for themselves."

"Oh?" asked Ryszard genuinely interested. "You are not sympathetic? They are your people."

"The Vadi Kabile aren't my people," replied Walker. "And the aurochs are wild animals. As such, they don't belong to anyone. It's like the people of the village saying the mountains and the trees belong to them too. Aurochs, deer, bison, aurochs and boar, they don't belong to anyone. It's wrong. The animals of the forest are part of the wild world."

"Your attitude surprises me, Walker," said Ryszard smiling, "I would have thought an educated person such as yourself would find their experiment compelling."

"Well, there were a few squirrels around your camp the other night," replied Walker. "If you think it's such a good idea perhaps you could try herding them up."

"You jest," said Ryszard lowering his gaze. "But tell me, from the sound of it, you were raised in a large village. How did they feed your people?"

"They fish," answered Walker. "But here in the forest, you should keep moving. Follow the seasons, hunt and gather as you go."

"It is always difficult finding enough food for so many people," Ryszard responded. "One drought or a harsh winter and people can starve."

"That's what happens when folks have too many kids," answered Walker. "Too many mouths to feed for one place."

"But your people settled down in one place," retorted Ryszard.

"Like I said, that's different," explained Walker smugly. "My people fish and there's an endless supply of fish in the sea."

"You believe that to be so?" asked Ryszard. "Do they fish in the winter?"

"No. But my people have learned to dry and preserve fish. The store enough away in salt to last the winter," explained Walker. "And they hunt a little too, but conservatively. And they preserve that as well. My tribe have learned to prepare for the winter and nature's ups and downs."

"Do you think we could do that here?" Ryszard asked and indicated the surrounding valley. "This is a very large valley, and the river provides water year-round."

In the Valley of the Auroch

"Sure, there's water." said Walker, "but what do you do in winter? There isn't enough game for everyone. The Vadi Kabile have seen to that."

"Those are certainly challenging problems," agreed Ryszard. "But what is the alternative, starvation?"

"Move on," said Walker. "Leave the valley and follow the herds. Return to what your people do best."

"That is a hard life," replied Ryszard, "Always uncertain. But now the people of the village have possibly demonstrated another way."

"Indeed? You want to trap another herd of aurochs?"

"Soon after the Hurrians arrived in the valley all the boar, deer and the antelope were gone," explained Ryszard. "But the Villagers trapped the last of the big game, the auroch in that gorge. After that, they began rationing what they killed from that point. You see? By then even the Hurrians could see their mistake. The Hurrians were trapped, they forgot how to live like nomads. So now, instead of hunting aurochs they feed them. They even try to get them to breed. So now, if they are careful, the people of the village have enough to eat."

"And you know enough to try it for yourselves?" asked Walker.

"I believe we have to, either that or leave the valley," agreed Ryszard. "Even though we were not the ones who took most of the game."

"But you stayed," said Walker. "Because you wanted to live like the villagers? You stayed because the Vadi Kabile stayed?"

"Our old chief argued that we are nomadic people, and were not meant to live in one place," replied Ryszard. "But I was inspired by the Hurrian's solution. I knew that leaving the valley and returning to the way of the nomad would mean a hard life and no guarantee of our survival. This tribe might have starved before we regained our footing."

"So, you want to keep aurochs, too?" asked Walker. "But in the meantime, you've got to steal a few of the villager's aurochs to survive."

"Yes," said Ryszard. "The Hurrian's may work hard to keep those aurochs, but it was their own gluttony that put all of us into this situation."

"So, that's what you were doing when you killed those two villagers?" asked Walker. "Taking an auroch or two?"

"The villagers have forced our hand." replied Ryszard, "Does their killing disturb you?"

"Well, it's like I said, they aren't my people," replied Walker. "And I don't like seeing anyone killed. But I think this whole idea is bad for everyone. It's bad for the land."

"Perhaps, but why should we suffer for the Hurrian's mistakes?" asked Ryszard.

"And what about the elves?" asked Walker. "The Vadi Kabile have killed or driven off most of their game too."

"The elves are not my problem," replied Ryszard. "They can leave. They should. There is no room for them here. Remember, they are nomads too. Anyway, their tribe is too small to pose an argument."

"Well, I'm arguing," replied Walker.

"Yes, and we are all in this situation because of the people of the village," said Ryszard, "I will give the villagers credit for an inspired idea, Walker. I think this could be the future." Then turning away, Ryszard called over his shoulder, "Come, I want to show you something else."

Ryszard led Walker along a path to the cliff face where a ledge overlooked a large pit. Logs had been driven into the ground to form a half-circle around the pit. The arrangement created an intimidating barrier forming a semicircular lower pen. More aurochs? The stout timber was packed tightly together and pointed in the direction of several caves. Ryszard picked up a stick and began beating loudly on the fence, and for a moment nothing seemed to happen, but then a monster appeared, and Walker took a step back.

Something big was growling in anger.

Lumbering out of the largest cave was a bear. A creature from a nightmare. It was covered in heavy brown fur and twice as tall as Ryszard. The monster's claws were as long as Walker's fingers and its teeth were brownish daggers. The beast must be the weight of ten men. Upon reaching the barrier, the ursine giant rose and bellowed in fury, spittle flying as it shook its head and clawed the sky. Yet miraculously—to Walker's absolute amazement—the sharpened logs contained the beast. The bear dropped to all fours. There, it swayed side to side, snarling and roaring in frustration. But the bear, faced with a forest of spikes, remained at bay. Walker had never been this close to a full-grown living bear before. Under any other circumstances it would probably be fatal.

"Another guest?" asked Walker, still trying to come to grips with what he was looking at. The idea that such a monster could be trapped and kept alive by mere men was a horror to him.

"My people regard the bear as divine," explained Ryszard, shaking his head sadly. "A spirit of nature—a forest god. They worship bears as deities. Now look at this god of the forest. Imprisoned—just like the villager's aurochs. What sort of God would allow itself to be caged by its own food?"

To Walker, it appeared that the bear grew bored snarling at them. It must have endured many such performances before. The bear ceased growling and turned its attention to one of the many bones strewn about the pen. Annoying a fog of flies, it picked up the meatiest, flopped to the ground, and began to gnaw on the joint. Walker noticed there were countless piles of bear shite amid entire clouds of buzzing flies. This was hardly a fitting existence for a forest god.

"How did you manage to trap it?" asked Walker. He found himself vacillating between shock and wonder.

"This bear killed members of our tribe. But we followed it to where it slept for the winter. We made this fence around its cave while it was sleeping. Something we learned from watching the Hurrians." Ryszard tossed the stick into the pen. "Not a very dignified god, would you say?"

"What's your point?" asked Walker with a newfound sense of...blasphemy? The sight of this forest creature penned in so humiliating a fashion struck Walker as wrong. Walker certainly wasn't the religious type, but he still had respect for nature. And to him this wasn't right; it would've been better to have killed the bear, to give it a dignified death.

"My point? I have controlled nature!" said Ryszard. "I have caged a demon and prevented it from killing any more of my people. And we did it the same way the people of the village have caged the aurochs."

"You should've just killed it," replied Walker. He pointed to the fouled pen. "This is all wrong."

"Why?"

"It's disrespectful," replied Walker. "Cruel."

"Disrespectful?" repeated Ryszard. "I am surprised at you. You did not strike me as the superstitious type."

"It's not about superstition," replied Walker. "It's about nature. You're fencing in nature, the wild, the wilderness."

"Ah," Ryszard shook his head in understanding. "Your precious wilderness. But is not the wilderness just another type of God? There are plenty of wild spaces beyond this valley, Walker. I do not think my actions are going to imperil your precious natural world."

But Walker felt a sense of panic—it felt like he was suffocating—at this way of thinking—and it weighed heavily on his mind—it was as if it were smothering his soul.

"What if this idea spreads?" asked Walker. "What if everyone starts building fences around the land? The wilderness ends; that's what happens. That's the end of the frontier—the world. What's next? Would you damn up the river like the beavers, to make your own lakes? Or build fences around all of the plum trees in the forest and claim them as your own? Maybe you should start herding fish."

"You sound like the elders, mired in traditions so old he cannot remember why we did them," said Ryszard. "I would have thought you—of anyone I have met—would see the logic here. This is the solution to hunger itself. Denying nature's fickleness—its capriciousness—the souls of my starving people. Think of it, Walker! Allow your mind to use these tools. You could build a village the likes of which we cannot even imagine."

Walker did, and actually shuddered at the thought. He'd left his own village because it had begun to embrace ideas like this—he'd gone off in search of the true wilderness. The idea of an even bigger village—something two or even three times larger in size was stifling—claustrophobic—madness! But Walker couldn't seem to stop himself from thinking about it. Ryszard's ideas—the damn Vadi Kabile ideas—were infectious, inescapable—the logic perfect. Ryszard was right; this could be the end of starvation. Tribes wouldn't have to fight each other over hunting grounds. And Walker's taunts to Ryszard—of damned rivers and penned trees—weren't all that crazy either when you thought about it. What would his mother think of Ryszard's arguments?

"No!" shouted Walker, surprising even himself. "No! Why can't you people just live within your means. The land provides if you just follow the rules. It's always worked like that."

"Rules, Walker? I did not expect you to insist we start following rules," said Ryszard shaking his head. "Nature is cruel, fickle. It rains and brings game for a bountiful season, and everyone eats. Or the rain fails, and the animals die, and people die with them."

"So, you follow the game," Walker replied, gesturing with his hands. But at this point he was almost arguing for the argument's sake. "It's what your people have always done." But Ryszard was right. This was the logical way

In the Valley of the Auroch

to fight nature's capriciousness.

"Really, Walker?" asked Ryszard searchingly, "Then tell me, what brought you here? To our valley, so far from your own. You say you are a trader, but are you not really searching for knowledge, for new ideas? Well, you have found them."

CHAPTER ELEVEN

It came in the night without making a sound. The big cat had followed the scent of the men to the clearing and now to the tree in which they were both sleeping. It sniffed their cold campfire and it sniffed at their scat. The night forest was loud, a cacophony of tree frogs and insects, but the lion, with its remarkable senses, was able to focus on the sound of the men, asleep, high above.

Men weren't the great beast's usual prey, but the lion was old, and its teeth were worn. The scent of many aurochs had drawn it into the valley, but the painful memories of the lion's last meal tempered its strategy. And the lion was tired of chasing fleet-footed rabbits and the tough agile boar. Humans were easier prey for a lion past its prime.

Now it circled the tree, assessing its options and estimating the distances. The men were high—almost three times their own height—but that wasn't high by the lion's standards. The night was dark, the moon had nearly set, but there was more than enough light for a cat; it could easily make out the shape of the men, it saw their heat.

Now it tensed, selected its prey and squatted, a tightly coiled spring, tail twitching. It settled lower and lower.

In the Valley of the Auroch

Then it sprang.

The lion scaled the tree in a single jump, front claws gripping the trunk as it bounded, and it was on its victim.

Baghadur screamed as teeth ripped into his flesh. Shaking and jerking; the lion tried to tear its hapless victim from the tree. But the ropes held Baghadur in place and the lion—not an arboreal hunter—lost it footing and slipped, rear claws flailing, teeth and front claws in Baghadur's flesh—too stubborn to let go.

Cengiz was awake and reacted quickly, swinging his spear at the huge dark shape that appeared to be hanging from Baghadur. His blow did nothing but attract the monster's attention. Frustrated, the lion released its grip and dropped to the forest floor. But it coiled again and launched itself back up the tree.

Tied to his own limb, Cengiz could do no more than point his spear in Baghadur's direction as the lion returned. The spear was wrenched from Cengiz's hands and clattered to the ground.

Unexpectedly stung by the spear, the cat dropped once more and licked its shoulder. The lion circled the tree growling and roaring in anger.

Baghadur was alive, but his injuries were severe. He just managed to pull himself back but was in no condition to help and passed Baghadur his spear.

The lion came back for one last attempt, but its heart really wasn't in it. With a swipe of his spear, Cengiz was able to keep the beast at bay. Growling and hissing in frustration, the lion slunk off to the far side of the clearing to stand and glared back at its troublesome prey.

*

The next morning Ryszard was gracious enough to wait for Walker to finish his breakfast and for the sun to warm the clearing before putting him back to work.

All the tribe members—young and old—had gathered to watch Walker's next performance. The trolls had named all of the pieces he'd made the previous day. The items were now more art than device and everyone was eager to see what he would come up with today.

Walker knelt on the rug and draped the leather pad across his knees. Again, the crowd pressed forward as Walker selected this morning's sample—a colorful piece of rainbow obsidian. He'd start with something small—a simple scraper—and work up to the climax—Rolf's big knife— which Rolf would probably use to eviscerate Walker immediately afterward.

Muscle memory guided his hands—yesterday had almost been a practice exercise. Not that Walker wasn't already proficient—but it helped bring everything into focus. Strider's lessons had been long and tedious and there were times—hot summer days under the blazing sun—when young Little Fox had wished he'd taken his mother's advice and picked flowers.

In the Valley of the Auroch

"You need to practice," his uncle Strider had intoned, "practice, practice, practice. Until you know how to make the tools with your eyes closed, without you even thinking."

"But why?" asked Walker, probably taking momentarily leave of his senses due to the heat.

"Why?" asked Strider without changing expression. Walker realized it was too late to take the question back; he'd have to see where this led. "Why what, Little Fox?"

"Why do I have to work so hard to know how to make tools?" asked Walker. "I mean I suppose it's good to know how to make them sure, but couldn't someone else do it? I thought we were supposed to be hunters?" He had enjoyed yesterday's lesson well enough, making a spring-trap.

"That's a good question, Little Fox," replied Strider to Walker's complete surprise. "I suppose we could just put all our trust in the work of others. And we could hope that those tools they'd make were up to our standards."

"Yes," agreed Walker hesitantly, as he began to think his question had been a mistake and he was about to get another lesson.

"And I suppose that we could carry all the weapons we'll ever need on the trail, "continued Strider, "Because it's not like we would ever break our weapons. Or lose them through mishap or misadventure."

"No," said Walker, remembering too late that his uncle played the argument game a little differently than his mother. "I guess I do need to learn toolmaking," admitted Walker, essentially surrendering early, before it was too late.

"No!" exclaimed Strider dropping his rock and indicating that it was indeed too late to surrender. "You want to learn about weapons boy? But these are just tools," he indicated the napping equipment and freshly made spear tips. "These are nothing but sharp rocks."

"I understand," lied Walker miserably, chipping faster and faster.

"Stop!" shouted Strider, "Look at your feet."

Walker looked down; his feet were hidden, buried under shards of broken flint and obsidian.

"Find a weapon!" challenged his uncle.

Walker—eyes wide—examined the refuse pile, but nothing looked suitable. Chunks of rock, bits of glass, shards of this and that, nothing like a knife or spear tip. Walker almost burst into tears and shook his head in frustration.

Strider quickly reached down, selected an egg-sized knuckle of obsidian, and without hesitation, whipped it at a nearby tree, beaning a viper that had decided to nap in the sun amongst the roots. The viper curled over, upside down and went still.

Strider held up his prized bone-handled obsidian knife.

"This isn't a weapon," he declared. "It's just a piece of rock." Strider pointed a finger to his temple, "This is a weapon."

Walker looked over to the tree, at the little rock and the very dead viper. Yes, everything is a lesson.

In the Valley of the Auroch

Finished with the scraper and a small hand-axe, Walker went to lunch with Evelina—she'd brought a plate of cured meats and some fruit and asked Walker what the women of his village wore. He sat next to Evelina and feigned small-talk. In reality, Walker was watching Hairy playing kick-ball with a couple of oversized troll kids on the other side of camp. The children were laughing but Walker could tell that Hairy was miserable. Walker looked around the clearing—doing his best to ignore Rolf's intimidating glare—but he didn't see Ryszard anywhere. Despite whatever Ryszard said, he and Hairy were prisoners. They weren't to be left alone. He wouldn't be given the chance to escape or even have an opportunity to sneak into Huberta's cave.

Finished with lunch, Walker decided he might as well just return to the work area and finish the demonstration. At least Rolf seemed to enjoy the demonstrations as much as the rest of the troll tribe. Maybe he could win Rolf over? Maybe he could become an ally for he and Hairy?

Just as Walker settled down to begin, Ryszard appeared out of nowhere.

For Walker's final act, he would make a long knife.

The truth was obsidian was a terrible choice for a long knife. Obsidian might be beautiful, and it certainly had the sharpest edge of any material, but it was brittle and was easily cracked if twisted. As a serious weapon, obsidian was mostly ornamental—like the vanity piece he'd given Ryszard. It was one thing to use obsidian for spear-tips and cooking utensils, but for hand-to-hand, Walker preferred a bone-knife sharpened to a respectable point. Nevertheless, obsidian was truly beautiful and like many pretty things, everyone wanted some.

Walker's hands moved in a steady blur and once again, the blade seemed to magically emerge from the rough stone. Walker switched back and forth between tools as needed. The rough gray rock melted away to a shiny striped, brown cinnamon sheen. Nipping and napping produces finer and finer edges and notching produces elegant flutes. For a handle Walker selected a white and brown antler. He polished the barrel and notched a slot into one end. Finally, he fitted the blade into the slot and bound it tight with sinew.

Walker stopped and held up the finished knife.

The crowd gasped in awe.

It was magnificent.

Long and dark and deadly looking. The rainbow obsidian blade glittered and gleamed and split the sun into countless colors.

Even Walker had to admit it was a remarkable piece. Possibly his best work.

Strong hands helped him to stand on his shaking legs. Bowing, he presented the knife to Ryszard, who—in turn—inclined his head in thanks and turned to present the knife to Rolf who—despite his gruff demeanor—couldn't stifle a smile from ear to ear.

Ryszard—now beaming—clapped Walker on the shoulder, almost knocking him to the ground.

"In honor of our craftsman, I propose a feast!"

Walker meekly accepted the tribe's enthusiastic approbation—everyone came forward to clap him on the back.

So, was this it? wondered Walker. Was he really an honored guest or a boar fattened for dinner? Judging by the mixed messages of his hosts, he still wasn't sure.

"What the heck," he thought. "We might as well enjoy a good last meal.

In the Valley of the Auroch

The sun rose and the lion was nowhere to be seen. Baghadur was in a bad way. He was bleeding from numerous wounds and without aid, Cengiz was certain he would soon die. There was nothing else to do. After untying themselves from the tree, Cengiz used the ropes to lower Baghadur to the ground. Cengiz examined the clearing floor—there were numerous lion prints, but it was difficult to determine in which direction it had gone.

Cengiz had no illusions of them either making it back to the settlement before nightfall. That meant they could probably expect another visit tonight.

There was no time to spare.

Cengiz dressed his friend's wounds as best he could—Baghadur bravely attempting to brush off any assistance.

"Leave me, Cengiz," Baghadur pleaded weakly. "You can't save us both."

"We will be ready for the lion tonight," replied Cengiz, more confidently then he felt. "Or perhaps the beast will seek easier prey."

They drank their fill from the river, topped up their water sacks and started home as fast as they could manage. By now they could follow their own fresh tracks—and they practically ran. But Baghadur's injuries were taking their toll and by noon he was barely able to stand. Cengiz forced his friend to rest, and Baghadur once again demanded Cengiz leave him.

By afternoon Baghadur was once again dragging. Cengiz decided they could use the extra time and selected a tall stout tree for the night. Still, it would be an arduous endeavor, assisting his wounded friend up the tree. Cengiz tied loops along the length of the line. He then climbed high up the tree, tied off the rope and lowered the free end back to the ground. Once back down, Cengiz rigged a harness around Baghadur, and tied him onto his back. Finally, using all the strength he had, Cengiz climbed the rope, using the loops as footholds, with Baghadur holding on and trying to assist.

When they reached the safety of the heavier limbs, Cengiz tied Baghadur to one stout tree limb and himself to another.

Tonight, they would try to rest, though neither expected to get any sleep.

The lion appeared in the night. One moment the clearing was empty, the next it was there, like a ghost materializing out of thin air. It circled the tree over and over before sitting back and staring up at the two men high above.

With a snap, the lion launched itself halfway up the tree in a single bound. High up, the tree was willowy and swayed under the big cat's weight, which apparently unnerved it enough to let go and drop back to the ground. There, the big striped cat growled its annoyance and retreated to the edge of the clearing.

Cengiz found that he'd been holding his breath the whole time. Baghadur was tracking the big cat with the end of his spear.

All at once the lion turned and bounded up the tree.

In the Valley of the Auroch

The trolls laid out a veritable feast in Walker's honor.

There were heaped platters of roasted flesh, stone-fried onions and mushrooms, hazelnut bread, plum pies, and flagons of fermented sloe juice.

Everyone was there, all wanting to praise Walker for his handiwork. Maybe things were going to work out after all. The cavern was crowded, and the aroma of smoked meats masked the musky scent of warm unbathed bodies.

A young drummer was accompanied by men banging bones against rocks and others blowing pipes of hollowed bone. There was even a fellow plucking cords stretched across an open auroch skull.

Walker's obsidian spear points and knife blades were laid out for all to admire.

The merriment was infectious, and everyone appeared to be in a fine fettle. Ryszard presided as host and even Rolf seemed to be enjoying himself.

Hairy was in attendance; a couple of little troll girls taking turns feeding him like a baby.

Huberta—squeezed into her slinkiest deerskin tunic—leaving essentially nothing to the imagination—slipped up alongside Walker and delivered a bone-crushing hug. The musky scented woman remained firmly attached to Walker for the rest of the afternoon, much to Evelina's chagrin.

The platters of food were emptied and refilled while flagons of sloe juice flowed like river water. As the revelry wore on, revelers collapsed into friendly drunken heaps. Most were stuffed and/or intoxicated to the point of paralysis. Some, occasionally regaining consciousness long enough to raise another flagon to whatever came to mind, before passing out again. Trolls knew how to throw a party.

Walker was shocked stupid at finding himself not only still alive but apparently the most popular person in camp. As the party wound down, Huberta tossed back a flagon and turned her big brown eyes on Walker. She threw him over her shoulder and was in the act of carrying him off for a celebration of a different sort when Evelina stepped between them.

"Ladies, please," he said.

Walker suspected he was in danger of being torn apart by the aggressive females. But then Ryszard appeared, stepping between the girls and speaking directly into Walker's ear.

"We need to talk," he said, forcibly separating Walker from Huberta and Evelina.

Ryszard took Walker by the arm and shoved him towards the door.

Walker nodded accession, and allowed himself to be ushered outside while inconspicuously confirming that his little dagger was still strapped to his arm.

It was now dark outside night having fully descended during the celebration. The racket from the party was considerably reduced. Ryszard motioned to a couple of rocks and gestured for Walker to sit. What now? Walker wondered, totally confused.

"Sorry for interrupting, but I wanted to speak in private," said Ryszard.

"Don't think about it. You probably saved my hide."

"I wanted to ask you to consider staying with us," explained Ryszard, surprising Walker completely.

Walker shook his head. He'd tried to avoid drinking too much, in case the opportunity to escape presented itself. He hadn't expected whatever this was.

"What?"

"I have come to admire you, Walker," admitted Ryszard, and sounding like he was speaking seriously. "Your intelligence and humor, not to mention your skill as an artisan."

"I don't understand. What?"

In the Valley of the Auroch

"I know you and I have our differences. But, philosophically speaking—we also share ideas. I know—for example—that whether you admit it or not, you empathize with us. I would like you to stay and help me lead the tribe."

"You want my help?"

"Yes," said Ryszard trying not to laugh. "What did you think this was about? That I was going to kill you?"

"That idea had crossed my mind," admitted Walker. "I noticed you didn't ask those two villagers for help before your men killed them."

"That was Rolf. I am afraid he is overly enthusiastic. And you must remember, you caught us in the act! We were there to steal their aurochs. Remember?"

Walker didn't remember it quite that way.

"Yeah," agreed Walker for the sake of diplomacy. "But you have to admit I'm more like one of the villagers than one of your people."

"I thought we were above that sort of thing Walker. The differences do not seem to bother Evelina and Huberta very much. I think we should be able to overlook your shortcomings as well."

"You're too kind," replied Walker. "You know, think I've been getting some mixed messages lately."

"Well, to be fair, some members of the tribe have had reservations. But you have more than redeemed yourself."

"Is Rolf one of those members?"

"Ha!" laughed Ryszard, "As I said, Rolf is enthusiastic. I think if you just avoid Huberta you will be fine."

"What if I say no?"

"But why would you refuse? We make a good team, you and I. We think so much alike."

"I don't know," responded Walker honestly, "I left my village to see the world."

"Perhaps it was not the world you were seeking, but your situation you were rebelling against. You felt trapped. That your future had been preordained. You wanted to choose your own destiny. I understand that. You and I are more alike than you know—we are both idealists."

"You think I was running away?"

"I think you are running from someone else's destiny," answered Ryszard.

"I don't think running a tribe is what I had in mind though," replied Walker.

"I am offering you a challenge. Is that not really what you have been looking for? Staying here would provide that challenge."

"I left to have an adventure."

"Yes, an adventure. To explore exotic lands. Have I not proposed an adventure? Is this valley not exotic enough for you?"

Was this some game Ryszard was playing? If he was really asking Walker to stay, would he be allowed to reject Ryszard's offer, like he had his parents'?

"Are you reluctant because we are trolls?" asked Ryszard.

"Don't call yourself that," said Walker feeling a twinge of guilt.

"Oh? Why not?"

"I just don't like that name."

"Really? The villagers you were with called us ogres. Is that any better?"

"No, that's not right either. You're the Tal Stamm."

"That is the name of our tribe."

"Well, what do you call yourselves? Or others like you?"

"We do not call ourselves anything. And we have no name for others like us. Whenever encounter another tribe, we just call them people. It seems Hurrians are the only ones who require names for everyone."

"I suppose because they see everyone else as different."

"Oh, why is that?"

"Probably out of fear. Objectify what frightens you and you diminish its power."

"Maybe. You have to admit we are different," replied Ryszard.

"Yeah, you Tal Stamm are strong."

"And you Hurrians are nimble and dexterous."

"But you guys make tools too."

"But we are not so dexterous," said Ryszard holding up a thick fingered hand. "None of us could have made those knives."

"It's just a skill. Acquired through lots of practice."

"Not for us," explained Ryszard. "We are not nimble enough. But you, see? That is why we would make a good pair. Each with their own strengths and weaknesses."

"Even though I'm not Tal Stamm."

"The tribe has great affection for you, Walker. And my people celebrate the joining of two-spirits," explained Ryszard. "Relationships such as ours are useful to bind societies, like the relationship you and I have been cultivating."

Uh-oh.

"I think I might have given you the wrong impression."

"I felt from our conversations, that you were a kindred spirit."

"Uh, look, you seem like a nice guy Ryszard, but I don't really have those kinds of feelings myself."

"I just thought, we have much in common. But if it is that I intimidate you, I must apologize."

"Oh, no. Look, I am flattered, I truly am. But I'm more of a lady's man."

"Indeed?" replied Ryszard, "But perhaps it is the novelty of my suggestion that has made you uncomfortable."

"No, no. I know others like you…I mean, who feel like you. Not about me, I mean, just…in general I mean," Walker couldn't shut himself up.

"That is alright," replied Ryszard. "Do not give it another thought. But, perhaps, with time, you will change your mind."

"Sure."

"But, consider my offer, will you?"

"Alright, but what makes you think I could even help anyway?"

"I think you could do whatever you put your mind to. When we first met, rather than try to fight, or beg for your life you…tried to talk your way out."

"Yeah, but that didn't work out so well. I'm still you're prisoner, right?"

"No. Not a prisoner. If anything, whatever you did, worked too well."

Ryszard took a step back.

"I will admit that it had been Rolf's intention to kill you that very night. But you convinced me to spare your lives. You did so by fabricating that absurd story about the villagers attacking you and being a trader. It was most entertaining. And a mesmerizing performance. I had to see more. That was the reason I kept you with us."

"You mean, you didn't believe me? I didn't really have to make all those knives?"

"Of course, they helped to endear you to the tribe."

"Look, maybe I can introduce you to the villagers. You never know, maybe they'd be willing to help you."

"I doubt they would be so inclined. Not after learning the fate of the two villagers, you were with when we first met."

"Yeah, but mistakes happen. Maybe they'll understand." replied Walker, though he doubted it.

"I doubt we would get any help from the Hurrians Walker. That is why I would like your help."

"Well, do you need my answer now? can I think about this?"

"Of course," replied Ryszard. "I have confidence that you will come to the right decision."

CHAPTER TWELVE

Walker returned to the cave. The celebration had quieted down considerably—the musicians had retired to their huts and many of the revelers were asleep, overcome with drink and good cheer. Trolls were sprawled over every soft surface. Walker found Huberta, curled up on a beaver-skin coat and snoring loudly. Walker took the opportunity to head back to Huberta's cave. He found Hairy waiting.

"Hairy!" Walker exclaimed and hugged his diminutive friend. "I see you've escaped the clutches of those terrible toddlers."

Hairy, for his part, didn't appear to be amused. A disposition underscored by his dress—flowers and a beaded necklace. Hairy gave Walker a questioning look and tossed his hand up while shaking his head— "What gives?"

"I think it's all over," replied Walker beaming. "I think we're free. Ryszard's not going to kill us after all."

Hairy's questioning look grew more intense; he put a hand to his head, brought it down, extending the thumb and smallest finger while holding the three middle fingers curled and thumbed his chin— "Why not?"

"Well, it's complicated," replied Walker, embarrassed by the details and unsure how much to tell Hairy. "Basically, he wants me to stay and help run the tribe."

Hairy raised his hand to his head and holding the little finger upright closed the rest of his fingers twice— "Why?"

"Well, for one thing, I guess he likes me," explained Walker. "Which makes things uncomfortable. But he also likes the way I think. He's looking

149

for help herding animals and so on. Did you know they have a bear? Anyway, he wants help—so his people can survive the next winter instead of going back to being nomads."

Hairy repeated the "why" gesture.

"Because his people were starving. Because the Hurrians took most of the game. Ryszard has seen what the Hurrians are doing, and he wants to try herding aurochs too. You know, I think they could build a pen, here by the river. They'd have access to all the water they needed. If it worked out the Tal Stamm would have plenty to eat, maybe we can even get help from the villagers."

Hairy held up his hands, then curled a finger in front of his mouth and then passed it under his outstretched palm— "The Tal Stamm?"

"Yeah, the trolls, I'll explain…"

Without waiting, Hairy launched into another complicated series of hand gestures— "Why didn't they just leave the valley when the game became scarce? They're nomads, right?"

"I don't know. Maybe they didn't have enough food to make the journey."

"So, what have they been eating?" signed Hairy.

"I don't know; maybe they managed to get a few aurochs before the villagers herded them all up. Or maybe they took some of the villager's animals."

Hairy pointed at Walker and made the "why" gesture again.

"Why what?" asked Walker, "Why ask me to stay? Ryszard thinks that since I'm Hurrian, this stuff should come naturally to me. He thinks we could help these people."

Hairy pointed to his right breast then to his left— "We?"

"Ryszard and me," answered Walker, and realizing his goof even as it left his mouth, added, "And you too Hairy, I made it clear we're a team."

Hairy held each index finger up, then pointed to his chest and then motioned back and forth with his index fingers— "What am I going to do?"

"What do you mean? You can help too."

Hairy held his hands together like he was choking someone and spread them apart— "How much?"

"I don't know," replied Walker, tired of Hairy's questions. "We'll figure it out. You know, I thought you'd just be happy learning we aren't on the menu anymore."

Hairy pointed at his jaw and flicked his fingers forward. Then he pointed to his right breast and then to his left, jabbed a finger to his chest, twirled a finger around at his temple and then waved his cupped hands in front of his face— "What the hell, I thought we were exploring."

"We will be," replied Walker defensively. "This is part of the adventure, too. Look, I haven't given him an answer yet."

Hairy, pinching the air, moved his hand back and forth, finger to forehead and flicked it out. Next, he pointed at his chest and then waved his hands around about his waist— "Nothing for me here."

"Look, I said didn't say I wanted to stay," replied Walker. He left out the part about Ryszard being sweet on him. "Look, maybe we can take some time, relax and think about our next move. We're brothers, Hairy— we're in this together."

Hairy raised a hand, then laid two fingers over the back of his hand and held up both palms, moving them back and forth questioningly— "What is your name?"

"What? You know my name."

Hairy repeated the gesture.

"Walker, I know, I get it."

Walker was annoyed that Hairy was even arguing with him about this. Hairy hadn't talked to Ryszard like Walker had.

"Look, let's talk about this tomorrow after my head clears and I can explain everything to you."

But instead of agreeing, Hairy changed the topic. He held up his palm, and then mimed patting a kid's head— "What about the kid?"

"Kid?" asked Walker, confused. "What kid?"

At this, Hairy pointed to the dress the troll kids had dressed him in. Specifically, careful stitching around the shoulders and down the sleeves. He then pointed to Huberta's garments, draped around the cave.

It took a moment for it to sink in.

"Hmm, no way a troll did this."

It was just a fact; trolls just didn't have the dexterity for this kind of detailed work.

Hairy pointed forward and brought one hand down on top of the other— "Correct."

"The missing girl. What was her name? You think she made these?"

But Walker already knew the answer. Hurrian girls were taught how to sew at a young age.

"Huh."

Hairy just nodded.

"Well, shite," said Walker, "So, you're saying the trolls have her?"

Of course, Hairy's senses were so much better than his. If she was in the camp, he'd probably know it.

"But where is she? We've been here for days, and I haven't seen her."

Hairy pointed to his chest, tapped his ear and moved two fingers in front of his mouth several times— "I heard voices."

"Voices?" repeated Walker, "Whose voices? When? Where?"

Hairy pointed to the top of the back of his hand and then one hand over the other— "At night." Then two fists together, thumbs up and then hopping one away— "Next door."

Walker poked his head outside. Just past the children's cave where Hairy had spent the last couple of nights, was another, larger cavern. Just then, Evelina exited the cavern carrying an armload of garments. She walked off towards the big cave. Walker watched for a little while longer and then turned back to Hairy.

"Well, let's see if you're right."

Hairy poked Walker in the ribs and handed him a bunch of dried flowers—it was all the crown vetch.

"What?" Walker was shocked, "Where did you get that?"

Hairy just shrugged and pointed out the door to Evelina's cave.

"Well, I'm not sure we need it anymore," said Walker, crumpling the flowers up and stuffing them in his pocket. "But I'll hang onto it just in case."

Hairy and Walker

In the Valley of the Auroch

They left Huberta's cave, and crept through the darkness, to the larger cavern. The opening was covered by planks of wood, but it wasn't barred. With Hairy beside him, Walker entered the cave. They both came up short. Sitting cross-legged, on a rug was a girl. She was busy at work sewing something. Just behind her sat an adolescent troll boy. He was carving animal-head beads, but on seeing Hairy and Walker his eyes opened very wide. Walker stepped inside the cave and began to open his mouth to speak but was immediately seized in a brutally strong grip. Twisting about, Walker saw Hairy caught as well, in the grip of the troll Dolphus. Walker tried squirming loose—futilely. He was in the clutches of the big troll named Cael.

Rolf was glaring down at Walker, a vicious look on his big ugly face.

Walker smiled back in as friendly a manner as possible. It was a little difficult considering the way he was bound, hands behind his back and forced to kneel on a rug. Hairy was tied up in a similar fashion a few arm lengths away. The kids had been removed.

"Is there a problem here Rolf?" Walker asked the big ogre in his most innocent voice. "I mean, I thought we were friends now."

Instead of answering, Rolf walked to the other side of the cave and examined the girls' handiwork—several rabbit-skin cloaks and a bear-fur.

"Where's the girl?" asked Walker. "And that boy?"

"Dolphus took them to Evelina's cave. Not that it is any concern of yours," Rolf replied. "You think you are so smart," growled Rolf in the troll's falsetto, "You may have Ryszard wrapped around your finger, but not me."

Walker opened his mouth to speak but Rolf cut him off with a backhanded slap that left Walker seeing double.

"Shut up!" barked Rolf, "I do not need to hear any more of your talk. You are not one of us—one of my people. You are not of this tribe. You are just another Hurrian."

"What is your problem with me?" asked Walker.

"Everything," snarled Rolf, "Every word out of your mouth is a lie. You may have Ryszard and Huberta all turned around, but I know the truth. You are just a sneaky no-good Hurrian, and I am going to kill you like all the others—like we should have done the night we found you."

"Really?" Walker said, expressing surprise, "Don't you think Ryszard will have something to say about that?"

To Walker's genuine surprise, for the first time Rolf smiled.

"Ryszard does not tell me what to do. It is I who tell him what to do."

"You're saying you're the headman, not Ryszard?" asked Walker.

Rolf actually laughed out loud.

"Ryszard is the pretty one, the one with ideas. But he does not have the backbone to do what needs to be done."

"So, you're the real brains here? And Ryszard's your minion?"

Rolf started to open his mouth but paused. A look of confusion on his big ugly face.

"What is a minion?" asked Rolf genuinely curious despite the situation.

"Minion's a lackey," explained Walker. "The guy who takes the beating if things go wrong."

"Humph. Yes, I like that. Ryszard is my minion. Not that anything will go wrong. My tribe likes to eat and they like sleeping in the same place every night. No, the tribe is not complaining. And they like Ryszard enough to do whatever he says."

This was bad. Walker had to keep Rolf talking to buy time. To try to think of a way out of this.

"So, you're keeping the girl around just to do your sewing?"

"You know nothing, Hurrian."

"No? So, tell me, why have you kept her around?""

"She is good at sewing and the tribe likes nice things. She is like you in that way. As long as she keeps sewing, maybe I will keep her around."

"Was it your idea to steal the villager's aurochs?"

"Ha! You think this is about the aurochs? You are an idiot. You have no idea what is really going on. Those damn Hurrians showed up and took most of the game. And then they have the arrogance to take the only animals left to keep that for themselves. Well, no matter. We troldfolk will have plenty to eat from now on. Not aurochs. But men! We will take the people of the village. Let them herd their aurochs. We hunt the Hurrians."

So, the trolls were cannibals after all.

And just like that Walker realized that he was, indeed, an idiot. It all made sense. All the stories Walker had heard growing up. And what the trolls were really doing in the forest that night. Not to mention the callous way they dispatched Tamraz and Osman. Walker remembered the big sack one of the trolls had carried back to their camp.

"By the way, what did you think of your dinner last night?" asked Rolf.

"I thought it tasted familiar," replied Walker to cover his sudden nausea.

"Would you like to guess what we will be eating tonight?" asked Rolf.

"May I be excused?" asked Walker, "I think I lost my appetite."

"Oh, no," replied Rolf. "You are the guest of honor."

"What about the girl?" asked Walker, stalling for time.

"Oh, we were going to eat her too, but Ryszard argued that would be a waste. Considering her talents."

"And what about that boy?" asked Walker. "How does he fit into all this?"

"My nephew? He was my idea," explained Rolf smiling at his own ingenuity. "We used him to learn her language. And to lure the girl away from her village so that we could take her."

"The villagers will be looking for her," Remarked Walker.

"I hope so," replied Rolf. "My plan is to draw them farther upriver, one small search party at a time. We used to hunt the elves, but they have become too wary."

"But if the people of the village start to go missing, they'll send larger parties," answered Walker.

"Not at first," explained Rolf. "Somebody told them the elves were stealing their aurochs. You convinced them the elves took the girl. The Hurrians will be chasing the elves and we will pick off the stragglers."

"And you think that will work? At some point the villagers will discover the elves had nothing to do with the missing girl and they'll come looking for you. What are you going to do then?"

"It will take them some time to find us. They fear this end of the valley. For good reason! And when they come looking for us, we will be waiting." replied Rolf.

"But they outnumber you three to one." said Walker.

"They will send small scouting parties. And we know this forest better than they do. We will take them on the trail, one by one. You see, we know more about them than they know about us. Did you know their shaman tells them the river is haunted by spirits, angry at their greed? The villagers are superstitious and will be on the lookout for ghosts. We will lie in wait like the spirits of their nightmares."

"It sounds like a good plan," admitted Walker.

"Yes, I thought so too," laughed Rolf.

Walker was at a loss. Everything Ryszard told him had been a lie. Of course, this was what trolls did, they were cannibals, not settlers, why was he surprised?

"This is justice, Walker, even you have to admit that. The people of the village took most of the game for themselves. Now they will be hunted. But worry not; we would not eat them all at once. We learned from their mistake."

Walker was angry at himself. Ryszard was big and scary, but he had only been a distraction. Rolf was the one Walker should have kept his eye on. And Rolf might be right—the Vadi Kabile would be lost in this forest. It sounded like Rolf's plan could work.

But should Walker even care? The Vadi Kabile weren't his people. And it was their own gluttony that had gotten them into this.

"Look Rolf, this isn't any of our business. It's not even our land."

"I do not worry about you," replied Rolf. "I just do not like you."

"Hey, if this is about Evelina," replied Walker, "you should know, there's nothing between us."

"I know Walker," said Rolf, enjoying himself. "Evelina likes the taste of Hurrian flesh; she's looking forward to having you for dinner."

This was just getting better and better.

"Rolf, what about that knife I made for you?" asked Walker. "Don't I get some goodwill for that?"

"Yes, thank you for this," replied Rolf and flourished the beautiful weapon. "I shall use it to carve the flesh from your bones."

"Well, as long as you're putting it to good use," Walker grumbled.

But Rolf wasn't listening anymore. He turned to Cael.

"Ryszard should be here for this. I will go get him," said Rolf. "I do not need Ryszard finding out about this later and weeping all over camp. Watch these two. That one," he pointed to Walker, "is a trickster. Do not listen to him. We will kill them both when I get back."

Rolf turned back to face Walker and smiled evilly, "Then we will have ourselves another feast."

In the Valley of the Auroch

This time the lion focused all of its attention on Baghadur. It sank its teeth into the scout's thigh. Then, griping the warrior in its huge jaws it gave a savage tug, and tore him from his perch. It all happened so fast, Cengiz hadn't time to react.

Releasing its grip on the tree, the monster cat dropped to the ground and trotted off into the forest, Baghadur's screams echoing in the night. A few moments later, the screaming stopped.

Cengiz clung to the tree limb, paralyzed with fear. His hands shaking uncontrollably. There was nothing he could have done. The lion was an unstoppable monster, focused on its prey and not to be deterred by the pathetic actions of a mere mortal.

Now, Cengiz was alone, with nothing but his fears.

Walker's head was spinning. Was Rolf really telling the truth? Had the trolls been eating people this whole time? Rolf was a monster. As bad as any lion or bear. And Ryszard had just been pretending to be the headman. Walker had been ignoring Rolf—even made fun of him—and played it up for Ryszard. Walker even thought he had been playing Ryszard for a fool. But it was Rolf who had played him.

So why had Ryszard asked Walker for help if they were going to kill him anyway? A troll's idea of fun?

And poor Hairy was tied up in this too. Rolf had said he was going to kill him as well.

"Sorry about all this Hairy," Walker said to his little friend, on the other side of the cave.

Hairy, always the better man, just smiled and shrugged.

Well, Walker thought, they weren't dead yet.

No sense feeling sorry for himself and giving up. No. He was determined to at least get Hairy out of this… somehow.

The first step in getting away was to deal with their guard, the ogre Cael. This was a problematic situation, but Walker still had a trick up his sleeve— literally.

Walker had to get his hands on that sliver of obsidian he'd strapped to his forearm, but his arms were tied behind his back. Walker concentrated and began twisting his wrist and working his fingertips up to reach the little blade. Unfortunately, his squirming attracted Cael's attention.

In the Valley of the Auroch

"What are you doing?" growled Cael and squatting down for a better look.

"Sorry," said an embarrassed looking Walker. He even managed a little fart. "Gas."

Cael wrinkled his face in disgust and stepped back.

"Hey."

Walker and Cael both looked up at the peculiar sound, a strange whispery voice.

"Hey,"

Cael —a look of astonishment on his face—turned to look at Hairy.

"What did it say?" asked the troll. He'd never heard an ape speak before. He took a step closer to inspect the pint-sized prisoner.

"Hey Cael!" exclaimed Walker, drawing Cael's attention back to him.

"What?" asked the henchman. "What do you two think you are doing?"

"Hairy said, hey," explained Walker louder and drawing it out.

The henchman squatted back down to Walker and lent in close to his face.

"Say that again," dared the heavy troll.

"Hey," whispered Hairy, momentarily distracting Cael one last time.

Walker's right hand flashed forward and slashed Cael's throat. Yanking the shard clear produced a fountain of blood, soaking Walker's tunic.

Cael—eyes wide and both hands on his neck, jumped to his feet, followed quickly by Walker. Walker shoved the troll backwards. Cael crashed to the ground in an ever-growing pool of blood. Even more blood gushed from his silently gasping mouth. Walker waited anxiously for Cael to stop twitching.

As the blood stopped flowing and the light faded from the big troll's eyes, Walker turned, dropped to his knees and proceeded to retch up his dinner. He'd never actually killed anyone before, though it absolutely had to be done. It was either Cael or them—still, the act of killing Cael, made Walker go weak in the knees.

"Give me a moment," raising one finger to Hairy, the other hand on his stomach.

Walker took a couple of slow deep breaths and then pulled himself together—if they were extremely lucky, there would be time for this later. Now he had to move. Walker stood and dropped the bloody knife into a pocket, then turned to untie Hairy.

"About time you found your voice," said Walker. "They're monsters, Hairy."

They both got to their feet.

"They're all monsters. How could I have been such an idiot?"

Hairy patted Walker on the shoulder consolingly and pointed at the door.

"You're right," replied Walker, "I can beat myself later. Let's just get out of here."

Hairy stuck his head out of the cave—it was pretty dark, but the coast was clear—and they started to make their way for the trees—just as Rolf and Dolphus stepped out of Huberta's cave, directly into their path.

"Run!" said Walker, and he and Hairy turned to sprint off in the opposite direction.

"Do not let them get away!" ordered Rolf, waving for Dolphus to cut them off.

Walker was faster than the heavy trolls, but Hairy's short legs limited his speed. Walker reached out for Hairy, but Rolf beat him to it, snatching him right out of Walker's hands. Rolf must have realized he wouldn't be able to catch Walker, so he turned and—to Walker's horror—tossed Hairy over the fence and inside the bear pen.

Walker reacted quickly. He didn't see the bear—it was probably asleep in a cave—and he dove headfirst between the closely packed sharpened logs. Walker just managed to avoid Rolf's grasp and continued to wriggle through the cold, rough timber to Hairy's side.

"You are both bear food now!" bellowed Rolf. He then picked up a stick and began beating loudly on the logs, "Bear food!"

Walker bent to examine Hairy in the dim moonlight. An enormous pile of bear shite had broken his fall. Hairy was stunned and smelly, but still conscious. Something else caught Walker's eye. A jawbone lay next to the fetid pile. A Hurrian jawbone. And this one had a small pointy beard.

Osman.

In the Valley of the Auroch

Turning his attention back to Hairy and ignoring Rolf, Walker said, "Can you stand?"

Hairy nodded and picked himself up just in time to hear an angry growl echoing from the biggest cave.

Hairy and Walker weighed their options—Rolf and his henchman on one side of the barrier, and the cave bear on the other. At least the bear was still out of sight. Nodding to each other, they ran for the smallest cave they could squeeze into. Hopefully it would be too small for the bear. They squirmed in headfirst and made their way back.

All the racket Rolf was making had worked. The bear—angry at having its rest disturbed—bounded out into the open and stood to survey its surroundings, wrinkling its nose as it sampled the air.

Walker was drenched in Cael's blood, and bears have an excellent sense of smell. The bellowing giant followed its nose directly to their cave. The entrance was indeed too small for the bear to fit, but it immediately began digging its way in. The mighty bruin tore away at the hard-packed clay and limestone, sending dirt flying.

The cave wasn't very deep and ended in a shallow hole, into which both Hairy and Walker had fallen. They were safely out of reach of the bear's claws— at least for the moment. Pulling themselves up, Hairy and Walker peered over the edge of the hole, but in the dark cave, even Hairy was blind. But from the sound of it, the bear was digging furiously to reach them.

"Well, this is a tight spot," confessed Walker in a classic understatement.

Outside, Rolf watched the proceedings with gleeful satisfaction. It was the best of all outcomes for him. Turning, he gave his minion Dolphus instructions.

"Keep an eye on them, in case they manage to slip out somehow," Rolf turned to go. "I am going to find Ryszard. I will be back."

CHAPTER THIRTEEN

It was as black as pitch inside the cave. The bear completely blocked any moonlight from entering. But Walker could hear the beast—digging noisily for all its worth—with increasing anxiety. The cave walls were hardened with clay and stone, but it was only a matter of time before the bear managed to dig its way to them.

Had Strider taught him anything that could help them now? Thinking furiously, Walker dug into his pocket to retrieve the improvised obsidian knife, now covered in sticky troll blood. Walker pulled himself up out of the hole. Working entirely by touch, and taking extreme care to avoid the savage claws, Walker felt around for a tight crevice just out of reach of the determined bear.

Walker jammed the shard into the crack in the rock floor, wiggling it back and forth until it wouldn't move. Only the sharp edge protruded. Walker jammed a few pebbles into the crack for good measure, and then dropped back into the hole with Hairy.

"Now we wait," he said. "And hope this works."

In the Valley of the Auroch

In the dark, Walker Hairy poked him in the side questioningly.

"It's something Strider told me. I've never had an opportunity to try it before."

Rolf returned shortly to find the bear still at work digging. Disappointed—Rolf had hoped to find Walker screaming in agony—he turned to Dolphus.

"Ryszard will not come out. No heart for this sort of thing."

They leaned on the fence and watched the proceedings for a while. But all they could see was the bear's shaggy butt, its rear claws straining to push further inside the hole. This was obviously going to take a while, and Rolf was getting bored. He turned to Dolphus.

"This could take all night. Call me when it gets interesting."

And with that Rolf turned and slumped back towards Evelina's cave.

Hairy and Walker

In the Valley of the Auroch

In contrast, from the perspective inside the cave, things were already about as interesting as they could get. Though Hairy and Walker could see nothing, they could still hear and nauseatingly, smell the bear. Its breath was hot in the small cave and loose pebbles rained down on their heads. But then, after what seemed like a very long time, the noise abruptly changed. The sound of digging was replaced by a low snuffling, and then a grunting whimper. Whatever it was sounded like something in pain. The whimpering changed into a plaintive groaning, and then by a sucking-slurping sound.

The grunting, groaning and sucking slurping continued for what seemed like forever, but even that tapered off to a tired, wheezing and then, silence.

Still, Walker waited—impatiently. Finally, he mustered up his courage, fully expecting a claw in the face, and peeked over the edge.

It was still too dark to see. The bear was still wedged into the cave entrance. Finally, neither of them could stand it anymore. The bear was as quiet as death.

Walker tossed a pebble. When that brought no response, he tried another, and then a fist-sized rock, but the bear never stirred.

"Huh. I guess it worked."

Hairy poked Walker questioningly.

"That shard is very, very sharp," Walker explained. "The bear smelled the blood on the knife and started licking it, slicing its tongue to ribbons. The bear drowned in its own blood."

Hairy patted Walker's arm gratefully.

Walker summoned up his courage once again.

167

"Okay, let's go," he said and climbed out of the hole. Carefully feeling around in the dark, Walker retrieved his knife from the crevice. It was next to the bear's still warm mouth, and a most unnerving experience.

The very dead and smelly bear was firmly wedged into the cave entrance. That meant that Walker and Hairy had to wriggle their way out, practically swimming through the thick, dirt-encrusted fur. Reaching the entrance, they slowly poked their heads outside. The moonlight was bright after the pitch-black cave. They could hear someone snoring, apparently Rolf had left a guard who had gotten bored, fallen asleep and missed the action. The troll's back against the barrier. As quietly as they could manage, Hairy and Walker wriggled the rest of the way out past the bear and then— as soundlessly as possible—slunk their way to the barrier. Locating the guard, Walker squirmed his way through the logs and up behind the sleeping troll. Reaching out through the posts with his knife and taking a deep breath, Walker slashed the guard's throat ear to ear. The troll opened his mouth in a wordless scream and then slumped face-forward into the dirt, bleeding out. Walker felt a shudder run through him but didn't heave. It disturbed him how quickly he was getting used to this sort of thing. After waiting until they were sure the troll was dead, Walker turned to Hairy.

"Hairy, the next time I tell you I want an adventure…" said Walker, "slap me. Now let's get out of here, I've had it with this valley."

Hairy signaled— "Girl."

"I knew you were going to say that" replied a weary Walker. But he couldn't just walk away. As much as he wanted to leave, he felt some responsibility for the innocent child. No one else knew she was here.

"Fine. Who knows? Maybe we'll even get the chance to settle the score with Rolf."

Hairy and Walker

In the Valley of the Auroch

The trolls had retired for the night, worn out by their celebration. Now the camp was quiet, aside from the buzzing night insects, the gurgling of the nearby river and the hoots of a lonely owl.

Hairy and Walker crept along the base of the cliff, moving as silently as possible. The moon was fully up and bathed the camp an eerie white light. Slinking on their stomachs from cave to cave, and being careful to stay in the shadows, they made their way, slithering from entrance to entrance. They inspected each cave, doing their best not to wake the occupants. It wasn't until they reached the big cave that they heard voices—Ryszard's and Rolf's among others.

Hairy signaled to Walker and pointed to a smaller cave further along the cliff. Walker picked his way over to join Hairy, who pointed to the cave and mimed someone sleeping.

Holding his breath, Walker lifted the corner of the entrance blanket and peeked inside. The big troll Arick was sitting on the floor an arm's length inside, arms crossed and mostly asleep. The girl, clutching a blanket around herself, was huddled against the far wall.

Walker had no illusions of taking on the oversized ogre armed only with an obsidian flake. They needed a plan.

Hairy was hidden some distance away, behind an old log. Walker picked his way back to join him. Walker pointed to his eyes, waved at the rest of the camp and pantomimed stabbing and using a spear.

Hairy scrunched up his face in confusion.

"We need to find some weapons," whispered Walker.

Hairy's face brightened, and he held up a finger. He untied his belt and held it up for Walker to see. Hairy's belt was also a sling. A length of braided cord, with a finger loop at one end and a pouch at the mid-point. The sling had been a favorite of Hairy's since they were kids.

"Seriously?" whispered Walker. "This isn't a rabbit we're taking about, it's a full-grown troll."

But Hairy gave Walker a double thumbs-up and began to search the ground for suitable ammunition.

"Okay little brother, but we still have to lure the ogre out of the cave," explained Walker. "And we need to do it quietly and without attracting attention."

Hairy just smiled and pointed at Walker.

"Great."

Walker bent down and proceeded to crawl back to the cave entrance. Once there, he picked up a twig and began quietly scratching the rock at the mouth of the cave. Presently he heard the sound of movement from inside the cave. Walker scratched a few more times. This time it sounded like someone heavy was getting to his feet. Walker dropped the twig and scrambled back to Hairy's position as quickly and quietly as he could manage.

A gnarled hand emerged from the cave and swept aside the entrance blanket. Arick emerged, his bulk framed in the aperture. He yawned and peered out into the dark.

Hairy stood, swung the sling around over his head and let go. The stone flew slightly wide and ricocheted off the limestone over Arick's head. Walker's heart almost stopped.

The sling had been nearly silent, with the exception of the ricochet. Arick made the mistake of looking up for the sound at the cliff face. By the time he turned back, Hairy had another stone and was swinging the sling. Arick opened his mouth but was interrupted by a stone striking between his eyes. It hit with enough force to cause the troll's eyes to cross. Arick collapsed into a silent heap.

Hairy stood motionless for several breaths, the shock of his success not yet registering. Walker stood and picked up his friend in a bear-hug. Returning to the present, they hustled over to the dead troll. Walker took a deep breath and slit Arick's throat for good measure.

"I'm never going to get used to doing that," he whispered.

Hairy patted him on the arm.

Examining Arick's body, Walker found the brown striped mahogany knife he'd made a few days earlier. He slipped it into his belt and felt their odds had improved by a significant amount.

"We're certainly diminishing the troll population tonight," whispered Walker.

Hairy kept a lookout while Walker slipped into the cave. He crept over to the girl and, waking her, placed a hand over her mouth to keep her from screaming.

"My name is Walker, and that's Hairy," he said pointing to his buddy. "We're friends from your village and we're here to take you home."

CHAPTER FOURTEEN

With the sunrise, Cengiz was able to see well enough to try climbing higher up the tree. The bark was slippery with dew, crows and magpies cawed their annoyance at the early morning disturbance. Cengiz tied a line around his spear and then climbed until the limbs grew too thin to support his weight. He tied himself to the stoutest branch he could find, surely the lion couldn't reach him here. Now Cengiz retrieved his spear but doubted it would do him much good against the cat.

Cengiz was consumed with guilt. He had tried everything he could. And still he had failed. He was sorry Baghadur was dead. but what could he have done? The worst part was that it had been Baghadur and not him. He felt guilty, because he was glad to be alive.

As the sun rose higher, shafts of light pierced the canopy, and bathed the clearing in bright yellow and green. Morning birds sang and insects buzzed. Steam rose from the mossy earth as the day warmed the forest floor.

Cengiz realized he had forgotten his pack, but now that the sun was fully up, he was afraid to move.

Stupid, he thought. The lion was a night hunter. He was probably safe now. And yet he still couldn't bring himself to climb down.

Cengiz searched the bushes for any sign of movement. But aside from a few birds flitting between the trees, the forest seemed deserted.

Silly birds thought Cengiz. Graced with the power of flight, the birds didn't fear the lion. They chattered, tweeted and whistled without a care in the world. Oblivious to the danger Cengiz was in.

And after a time, even Cengiz started to relax.

A breeze ruffled through the foliage.

Cengiz heard a twig snap. Turning, he saw the huge lion slink out of the green and pause directly below.

The lion sniffed the ground at the base of the tree. Stopping to urinate and mark its territory. Cengiz knew that included him. The lion was telling any other predator that the man in this tree was his dinner.

He felt trapped, tied to the thin branch by circumstances beyond his control.

Then the lion heaved itself upright and gave the tree a violent shake. Then it dropped back on all fours, found a patch of sunlight, laid down in the warmth, yawned while twitching its tail.

Cengiz shuddered. He knew now that he would probably not see his home again.

"We have to go back for Nefin," said Aygul, stopping at the edge of the forest.

Hairy and Walker stopped midstride and turned to face the girl.

Just a few moments earlier, they'd hustled her out of the cave, as quietly as possible. Aygul had been upset at the sight of the dead troll. But before she could speak, Walker hushed her with a finger to her lips. Hairy and Walker practically carried Aygul the rest of the way. They'd only set her down when they felt they'd managed a safe distance. This was Aygul's first opportunity to speak and it wasn't what Walker had been expecting.

"What?"

"We have to go back for Nefin," repeated Aygul.

"That's what I thought you said," replied Walker. "Who's Nefin?"

"He's the boy I was with," she said.

"You mean that troll boy?"

"Yes, we need to go back for him."

"Are you crazy? He's the one who got you into this."

But in response, Aygul took a step back, in the direction of the troll camp.

"Whoa, whoa, whoa," replied Walker eloquently. "What are you doing?"

"I'm not leaving without Nefin, he's the reason I'm here."

"Could we please continue this discussion later?" pleaded Walker, "preferably somewhere far away from the trolls?"

In the Valley of the Auroch

Aygul took another step back and folded her arms across her chest.

Hairy stared at the girl in utter disbelief, and then turned to Walker and threw up his hands.

"This was your idea, remember?" replied Walker to his silent friend. Then turning back to the girl, "seriously? Did you happen to notice the dead body you had to step over on your way out of the cave? Don't you think your new troll friends are going to be a little upset about that?"

Aygul jutted out her chin.

"That was you," she said. "I didn't ask you to kill anyone for me."

"Well how else were we going to get you out of there?"

"Who asked you to do that?"

"Oh? Well, excuse us for rescuing you," replied Walker.

"Hey, I didn't ask to be rescued," she said. "And who are you anyway? I've never seen you before. And what's wrong with your friend? Doesn't he say anything?"

"Too much. Look, I told you before," replied Walker. "This is Hairy and I'm Walker. We're friends of your father."

"Really? Well, I don't know you. And, I didn't ask to be rescued," repeated Aygul.

This time it was Walker who threw up his hands. He took Aygul by the arm and ushered her behind a tree and out of sight of the caves.

"Do you mind?" she said shaking off his hand.

"I'd just rather continue this conversation out of sight of the bad guys if you don't mind." replied Walker. "So, are you saying you liked being tied to a post while they worked your fingers to the bone?"

"How's that any different from how I'm treated back home?" asked Aygul.

Walker opened his mouth to answer, then shut it and turned to Hairy.

"Is there anything you want to say here?"

In response, Hairy made a face and growled while doing a clawing motion with his hands.

"Good point." Then turning back to Aygul, Walker pointed back towards the camp. "Your friends; Rolf and Dolphus? They threw Hairy into a bear pit. I had to go in and rescue him. We almost died."

"Humph," said Aygul under her breath. "Boy stuff."

"What?" spluttered Walker. He was almost too dumbfounded to put together a coherent response. Then, pulling himself back together; "Didn't you hear me? I said they tried to kill us!"

"You both look fine to me," Aygul replied stubbornly.

"Oh really? I'm covered in blood and Hairy's covered in bear shite."

"Seems about right."

"Wha…, Okay, how about this? The trolls also plan to kill—and eat—everyone in your village. What do you think about that?"

For the first time, Aygul hesitated before answering.

"Nefin wouldn't be a part of anything like that."

"Oh? Well, maybe Nefin wouldn't," admitted Walker, "But believe me, the rest of his family definitely has plans. Dinner plans."

"But that doesn't mean Nefin is involved," said a visibly more subdued Aygul. "Nefin and I love each other."

"Love?" exclaimed Walker. "Oh, well of course you do. That takes care of everything."

"We're going to live together, me and Nefin," responded Aygul.

"Live together?" said Walker. "Is that what he told you?"

"Yes, more or less."

"What does that mean?"

"We're still getting to know each other. I'm just learning to speak troll."

"So, you two can't even talk?" asked Walker. "Hey, they used Nefin as bait to lure you out. And now they want to use you as bait to lure your people into a trap. This isn't about you two making googly eyes at each other. This is serious."

"Well, maybe Rolf was using Nefin too," Replied Aygul. "Did you think of that? Maybe Rolf is using both of us."

"Rolf told me it was his idea to use his nephew to lure you away from the village."

"That doesn't mean Nefin knew anything about that. I think if Nefin knew the truth he would come with me," replied Aygul.

"And you know that from the deep conversations you two have had. Look, Nefin is a cannibal. They're all cannibals."

"That's stupid, they have plenty to eat."

"Yeah, plenty of people. Your people."

"I don't know you and I don't believe anything you say. I'm not going anywhere with you unless we go back and get Nefin." Insisted Aygul and stomping her foot. "I'm not leaving without him."

Walker stared at the girl, silently assessing his next move.

"And you're willing to bet our lives, and the lives of everyone in your village on that?

"It doesn't matter what you say, I'm not going anywhere without him," replied Aygul.

Walker regarded the young—maybe not really so young—girl for several breaths. He felt defeated and said, "Fine." Then turning to Hairy, he said, "Let's go."

They'd only taken a few steps, when Aygul said, "Wait! Where are you going?"

"Away from here," said Walker from over his shoulder.

"Wait!" implored the girl. "You can't just leave me out here."

Walker spun on his heels.

"Oh really? Why not?"

Aygul didn't say anything.

"Look, just how do you propose we get Nefin to go with us anyway? Do you even know where is? How would we find him without waking up the whole camp? At the moment Rolf may not know we've escaped. But that could change at any moment. And that means that we may still have a head start. And we're going to need it since the trolls know these woods and we don't."

But Aygul just continued to stand there—arms crossed, dark eyes wide and on the edge of tears. After a moment, Walker looked at Hairy, who in turn just shrugged and shook his head.

"Okay." said Walker, his shoulders slumping in defeat. "Think about this; Rolf probably isn't going to hurt Nefin, is he? I mean, they're family, right? So Nefin is safe here, right?"

It took a few moments, but Aygul nodded yes.

"Fine. So how about the three of us go back to your village. You and Nefin can get back together later. After you've talked to your parents about this.

At the mention of her parents, Aygul's eyes got wide.

"I mean, if you and Nefin are meant to be, then maybe your families can arrange for you two to get together."

Aygul biting her lower lip, stood in stoic silence for a handful of breaths. Then she turned and looked back at the troll camp. Aygul bobbed her head and turned back to face Walker.

"Alright. But only if you promise you'll talk to my parents with me."

Walker's eyes went wide, but he managed to keep a straight face. Inside he was seriously considering just going back, killing a few more trolls and dragging Nefin back to the village with them.

Shite

"Fine."

"Really?" Aygul beamed; "Okay then."

Walker turned back to Hairy,

"Okay little brother, lead the way."

Somewhere out in the forest, Walker could hear a jackal laughing.

Hairy and Walker

In the Valley of the Auroch

Hairy picked his way through the dark forest.

Ryszard had led them along some unseen trail on the way to the troll camp. But Walker figured all they had to do was follow the river. That would lead them back to Aygul's village. But Hairy was avoiding the beach, undoubtedly because they were less likely to be spotted under the cover of the forest itself.

"We could climb out of the valley," said Walker. "Maybe it would be faster overland?"

Hairy looked up at the tall white cliffs and the broken ridges beyond and shook his head.

"Okay, the river it is then."

Back in the cavern, Rolf knelt to examine the bodies in the light of the flickering torches. Cael, Dolphus and Arick's throats had been cut, but Arick also had a deep red dent in his forehead.

"What do you make of this?" Rolf asked, fingering the dent.

"I do not know," replied the troll standing nearby.

Rolf turned his head and growled to the troll standing over him,

"Bernt, you, Horst, Hagan, Babak and Gino. Find those Hurrians before they reach the village. You have been to the village. These three should not be hard to catch, traveling in the dark, they will not be able to hide their tracks."

Rolf turned to the younger troll standing to the side,

"Go with Cadmael."

"I understand," said the thick-set youth.

"The girl trusts you. Use that. And do not be deceived by their size," added Rolf. "They are more dangerous than they look."

Rolf turned back to Horst. "How did this happen? How could they kill the bear?"

"It is a mystery," said the older troll. "We pulled the bear from the cave but there are no wounds on the body. Nothing but blood."

"Such a thing should not be possible," replied Rolf. Then, turning to address a larger troll sitting by the fire, "You, see? This is your fault. I told you we should have killed those two the first night in the woods."

"You could not have known this would happen," replied Ryszard. "And it is your fault that our men are dead."

"Me? How do you figure that?"

"Walker was not a problem until you made him one. He was eating out of my hand. And I could have explained to the girl. After all, she seemed happy enough being with Nefin. It was your overreaction that caused this problem."

"That is ridiculous. Walker was nothing but trouble. If he was so smart, sooner or later he would have become suspicious. But no, you had to have your little pet. Though I could see you wanted more. Now look where we are."

"Because you were so eager to frighten Walker you had to tie him up and tell him you were going to kill him. You even bragged about your plans. What did you expect him to do? Of course, he would try to escape."

"My only mistake was not killing him in the first place. Like I did all the others. No, my mistake was letting you talk me into letting him live."

"You underestimated Walker because you thought he was weaker than you. You always think brute force is the answer and cannot imagine how a weaker opponent could beat you. Well, I suppose now we shall see. It is your strength against his intuition, and he has a head start."

"And that girl to slow him down. Walker does not know these woods. We have hunted Hurrians before. I will have them before they reach the arch."

"No, you are still underestimating him. I am sure there will be more surprises before this is finished."

Hairy, Walker and Aygul hiked through the night. Even with Hairy's better night vision, the heavy forest was making it difficult for him to divine the trail. The morning sun provided welcome warmth. Early birds chittered at the trio's passing.

Aygul explained to Walker how she came to end up in the troll camp. Walker rolled his eyes at her story. It seemed that just when he thought he knew what was going on, something even stranger popped up.

So, the missing girl and the troll-boy were sweethearts.

"You just met him in the forest?" asked Walker.

"I was doing errands for my mother and ran into Nefin on the trail," explained Aygul, not wanting to get into it with this stranger.

"And that didn't strike you as strange?"

"I didn't know where he lived," she said. "And he was the first stranger I ever met. He wasn't just another boy from my tribe. It was fun."

"Fun."

"You weren't there. Don't judge me."

Hairy took Aygul's arm and helped her over a fallen tree in the path.

"Well, a little advice for the future, don't talk to strangers. At least not when you're alone."

"Well, I don't know you two. Maybe I shouldn't be talking to you. Anyway, when are we going to stop? I'm tired. We've been walking all night."

"Oh, we're not stopping. When the trolls find all the bodies Hairy and I left, you can be sure they aren't going to be stopping either."

"Ugh! I'm not like you guys—I don't usually spend my nights on forced marches through the woods."

"Well, when we get back to the village you can put your feet up. Until then, we keep moving."

Aygul was quiet for a while, then,

"How do you even know we're going in the right direction?"

Without breaking stride, Walker lifted his left arm and pointed through the trees.

"Hear that? It's the river. If we keep that on our left, sooner or later we'll reach your village."

It was midday when Hairy raised a hand and brought them to a halt. He then crept forward and crouched. After a moment he turned and signaled for Walker to join him.

As Walker started forward, Hairy raised his hand again. He sniffed the air. Walker followed suit.

"Yep, lion pee," Walker whispered.

Aygul walked up and stood next to them to see what was going on.

"What are you two doing?"

"Shush!" said Walker grabbing her hand and pulling her down to a crouch. "There's a lion around," He whispered.

In unison, the three began duck-walking back the way they came.

"Oh," squeaked Aygul as she kicked something heavy.

Turning, they all saw a disembodied head staring up at them.

"Bagmurmumph…," Aygul managed to say before Walker's hand cut her off. She bit him and wrenched the hand away.

"Do you mind?" she whispered, "I wasn't going to scream. How stupid do you think I am?"

"Sorry, I don't know how stupid you are," replied Walker shaking his fingers. "But we've got to get out of here—now."

Just then, Hairy elbowed Walker in the ribs and pointed.

A dozen spans away, on the upwind side of a slight clearing, a familiar character emerged. The big striped cat from the river was sniffing through the bushes. Being that they were downwind, and the lion hadn't caught scent of them—yet.

Walker tapped his companions on the shoulder, pointed upwards. He was motioning towards a tall sycamore only an arm's length away. Moving slowly, and without taking their eyes off the cat, they all began climbing the narrow trunk. A stiff breeze ruffled the leaves, and they all froze. The lion looked up, but in the opposite direction.

Hairy scrambled up out of sight. Walker, hand on her butt, half-pushed Aygul from below. She swatted his hand away, turned and shined up into the canopy. Walker paused to watch as the lion began scratching its big ass against the rough bark of an old oak, then he turned and pulled himself up after the others.

"Well, now what?" said Aygul as soon as Walker emerged through the leaves. They were easily ten heights from the ground.

"Now we wait—quietly—for the lion to get bored and leave," answered Walker, looking to Hairy for confirmation. "Hopefully it shouldn't take too long. It's had a meal and peed on everything. So, unless we get its attention, it should just move on."

"Hey!" came a shatteringly loud call.

"Bugger," exclaimed Walker.

"Hey!" repeated the call—too loudly. "You people in the tree!"

"Shut up, shut up, shut up," whispered Walker. "That fopdoodle is going to get us all killed."

"Hey!" repeated the loud disembodied voice. "Over here!"

"Cengiz?" whispered Aygul and brushing the intervening vegetation away. "That's Cengiz. From my tribe."

"Well, that explains why the lion is still around," said Walker.

Hairy tapped Walker on the shoulder and pointed a finger down.

The lion was sniffing around the surrounding trees.

"Nobody…make…a…sound," whispered Walker.

"Hey!" yelled Cengiz. He followed that up with a stick thrown in their direction. "Who is that? You over there in that tree! I can see you! Why don't you answer?"

"Think you could hit that guy with your sling?" Walker whispered to Hairy.

In the Valley of the Auroch

Aygul punched Walker in the arm.

"I was kidding," whispered Walker. "You know that lion is never going to leave with your buddy making all that noise."

"Well, what can we do about it?"

"I don't know."

"Won't the lion just get tired and leave?" asked Aygul.

"Why should it go off hunting if it already knows where its next meal is? Especially since your people ate everything else in this valley. We're the meal left. By the way, your boyfriend and his family want to eat you, too."

Aygul smacked Walker in the arm. Then she looked at the narrow branches, green foliage and the small birds flitting about.

"Well, we can't stay here forever. There's nothing to eat or drink."

Walker tore a leaf off a nearby branch and offered it to her.

"Funny."

"Hey, it's not my fault we're in this predicament."

"Oh, no? I didn't see any lions back at Nefin's camp. I was perfectly safe until you two dragged me away from there."

"Define safe. That camp was nothing but lions. Rolf told me the only reason they hadn't already eaten you is because you were handy with a needle and thread. With Hairy and I taking ourselves off the menu, I'm pretty sure they would have been happy to substitute you instead."

"Hey, what's wrong with you people?" yelled Cengiz, interrupting their conversation, "Don't you hear me?"

Walker glanced down at the lion. It was sniffing around the next tree over. He turned and quietly pushed aside the leaves blocking his view of Aygul's friend.

The moment Cengiz saw Walker's face, he began to open his mouth. Walker angrily shushed him with a finger to the lips and another finger across the throat.

Walker then pointed down to the lion and shook his head whiles silently shushing.

"What?" asked Cengiz in confusion. "The lion already knows I'm up here.

Walker's expression went blank. Instead, he pointed to himself and the rest of his party.

"Oh," replied Cengiz "Sorry."

Just then the tree began to shake, which caused the surrounding trees to rustle noisily together.

Hairy, Aygul and Walker responded by wrapping their legs around the tree limbs and tightening their grips.

Peeking down, Walker saw the lion staring back up. It was now standing and shaking the tree. After a few moments, it gave up and dropped back to the ground.

"Well, I guess the lion knows we're here now," said Aygul.

"Probably," agreed Walker. "But we should keep quiet anyway. We don't want to get it anymore excited then it already is."

As day turned into afternoon and then to dusk, Aygul poked Walker in the arm.

"Yes?" he whispered back.

"Not that I think there's any chance I could sleep up here," she began, "but just in case I did, what's to keep me from falling out of the tree?"

"Well, Hairy and I usually just tie ourselves in for the night," replied Walker. "But what with escaping from the trolls and saving you, we seem to have lost our rope."

"So, then what do we do now?"

Walker looked around, then turned his attention to their garments.

"We could tear strips off our outfits and tie ourselves in place with those."

"I guess that's better than nothing," agreed Aygul. She promptly set about removing her skirt without falling out of the tree. Her tunic was long enough to cover her to the knee. "I don't need this, and it should be enough for the three of us," continued Aygul. She started trying to tear the leather, but it soon became apparent that it was too tough.

"Here," whispered Walker handing Aygul the obsidian shard still sticky with dried blood.

Hairy reached over, tapped Walker on the arm and pointed down. Peering through the foliage, Walker could see someone moving through the clearing.

Trolls.

"Its Nefin!" exclaimed Aygul a little louder than Walker would've liked.

"Quiet," hissed Walker.

"Nefin!" Called out Aygul waving a hand. "Up here!"

"What is wrong with you?" asked Walker.

But Aygul's call had already produced a response. Nefin stopped and looked up into the trees. Another, bigger troll carrying a club, emerged from the forest to join him.

"Nefin!" called out Aygul while brushing off Walker's attempt to quiet her.

On the ground, the two trolls marched across the clearing, in their direction.

"What's going on over there?" called Cengiz, unable to see from his vantage position.

In a flash, a giant gray cat exploded from the bush, grabbed the bigger troll in its jaws and bounded back into the forest.

It happened so fast Nefin hadn't time to react. The youth looked around for his companion, and then back up into the trees.

"Nefin!" screamed Aygul. "There's a lion!"

The screams of the vanished troll ended abruptly.

With a dawning awareness, Nefin leapt to the closest tree and began to scramble upward.

"Nefin!" screamed Aygul, "Nefin climb faster!"

"What's going on?" repeated Cengiz. "Aygul, is that you? Who is Nefin?"

Walker certainly had no love for the trolls, but even he was soundlessly urging the boy to move. "Go on kid," he hissed through gritted teeth.

Nearby, even Hairy was shaking the tree in sympathetic desperation.

Nefin was strong, but also a troll, and heavy. He climbed with impressive speed. But the lion bounded back into the clearing, turned, and went tearing for the tree.

"No!" Aygul and Walker screamed.

"Over here!" yelled Walker, banging on the branch. "Over here!"

Nefin hauled himself up and it looked like he would make it, but then the lion hit the dirt and bounded upwards to grab Nefin by the foot and yank him free.

"No!" screamed Aygul, nearly tearing herself from the tree.

But it was too late. Nefin crashed heavily to the ground followed by the massive feline monster.

Before the boy could move a muscle, the lion clamped his jaws around his head, and padded back into the forest with his prize.

For a moment everything was still. And then.

"No!" screamed Aygul in a long, loud wail. "No! No!" She yelled again and again, as the full realization of what had happened overwhelmed her, Aygul lowered her head to the branch and began to cry.

"Nefin."

Walker looked at Hairy and they both looked at Aygul.

Hairy laid a hand on her back.

After a moment, Walker stretched across the canopy and placed a hand on Aygul's shoulder too.

"Could someone tell me what's going on?" called out Cengiz.

In the Valley of the Auroch

Aygul was spent. She'd cried until the sunset, looked up briefly, then put her head down and cried some more. Eventually, she lifted her head again and looked around. She felt like someone waking from a nightmare.

"Cengiz?" she called.

There was no answer.

"Cengiz?" she called again.

"Aygul?" he answered, sounding very concerned. "Are you alright?"

"No. No, I'm not," she replied, and then looked at Hairy and Walker. "But I'm safe."

Hairy and Walker had been keeping concerned eyes on the girl. They'd had cut the leather skirt into strips and knotted them together. Hairy had crawled over to Aygul and tied her in place on her branch. His efforts didn't seem to disturb her. Finally, they tied themselves to the tree.

Walker felt sorry for Aygul. But at the same time, he couldn't help being glad the trolls were dead.

The lion was certainly a problem. But the trolls had been two problems and they could climb trees too. And Walker hadn't shared Aygul's faith in her friendship with Nefin. He figured that if the trolls had lived, he'd be dealing with them now too.

No, the lion had done them a favor.

"Aygul, who is that with you?" asked Cengiz.

"Friends," said Aygul.

"Friends? I don't understand."

"It's Walker. And my friend Hairy."

"Walker?" replied Cengiz. "You mean the stranger? Aygul, what are you doing with him?"

"And what are you doing here?" asked Walker. "How did you come to be up it that tree?"

"We were tracking you," replied Cengiz. "Baghadur and I. But the lion attacked us. It came in the night and Baghadur was injured. Then it returned the following night and took Baghadur."

But the lion had stayed. Evidently, it liked to keep an eye on its prizes.

"You still haven't told me what you're doing here," said Cengiz.

Walker shook his head in frustration.

"Hairy and I rescued Aygul from the trolls."

"Trolls?" exclaimed Cengiz. "You told us she was abducted by elves."

"My mistake."

"Where is Osman? And Tarmaz? "Why aren't they with you?"

"They're dead," replied Walker. "They were killed by the trolls. We were ambushed not long after we started out."

"Dead!" exclaimed Cengiz. "And yet you lived? And now you have Aygul?"

"Yeah. It turns out the trolls took Aygul. They did it to lure you villagers upriver and into an ambush."

"And yet you are alive," repeated Cengiz. "Why were you spared?"

"I guess the trolls were saving us for later," said Walker, hoping to avoid a lengthy explanation.

"But before, you said that elves…"

"Yeah, I was wrong. The elves were a diversion. The elves took your auroch, but it was the trolls that had Aygul."

Everyone was quiet for a time as Cengiz digested this information.

"Aygul?" called Cengiz. "Aygul, is any of this true?"

Aygul lifted her head from the branch and considered Hairy and Walker through red-rimmed eyes.

"I don't know," she answered wearily. "Maybe. I don't really know anymore."

Cengiz was quiet for a much longer span.

"Who was this Nefin then? What was he doing here? And who was the other troll down there with him?"

Aygul looked at Walker. Walker wagged a finger and Aygul put her head back down.

"Nefin was a friend of Aygul's," answered Walker. "He was keeping Aygul safe back at their camp. I don't know who the other troll was."

"Aygul's friend?" said Cengiz. "And just what makes you think the trolls took Aygul to lure us into an ambush?"

"Because they told me," Replied Walker. "With your people killing or driving off most of the game, the trolls got hungry, and they blame you. So, they decided they'd eat you folks instead."

"Why would the trolls tell you, their plan?"

"I think the chief was just bragging," answered Walker. "He was going to kill Hairy and I anyway, I guess he wanted to let us know how smart he was."

"But you managed to escape? I find this all hard to believe."

"I don't blame you," replied Walker.

"So, you escape. And you rescue Aygul. And this Nefin and the other troll were pursuing you? To try to stop you from returning Aygul and warning us?"

Walker looked over at Aygul, lying quietly with her eyes closed.

"I think that's about right."

"If this Nefin was Aygul's friend, why was he pursuing you?"

"I don't know," lied Walker. "You would have to ask him."

"So, what now? I haven't seen the lion for a while. Do you think it's safe?"

Walker had been considering that very question. There'd been no sign of the lion since it had taken Nefin. But that didn't mean it had gone very far.

According to Cengiz, the lion had taken Baghadur a couple days ago, and it took Nefin and his friend this morning. You would think that would be enough even for a starving lion.

"The lion may be sated," added Cengiz. "If we move very slowly, to not to provoke it, maybe we can get away."

"No," replied Walker.

"We might make it to the ground and even get out of the clearing," continued Walker. "But remember, there's not much big game in this valley. I'm guessing the lion knows that. That's why it's been hanging around. The lion might let us get down, but it'll just follow us. Then it will take us when we're not expecting it. This lion knows what it's doing."

"Then what do we do? We can't remain here forever."

"No." agreed Walker. "We're going to have to kill that lion."

In the Valley of the Auroch

"You've slept like this?" asked Aygul, already sore from laying on the hard, narrow branch.

She'd been silent, Hairy and Walker had tried to give her what little privacy they could, all tied close together in a tree. It wasn't much, but she had some time to grieve. Apparently, she was ready.

"Oh yeah, we sleep in trees all the time. Safest place to be in a forest full of monsters. Providing you're tied in, so you don't fall out of course. Mind you, we're usually better prepared."

"Prepared?"

"Yeah, provisions and water and such," replied Walker. "And Hairy's better at this than I am."

Walker nodded towards Hairy. His diminutive friend was in the act of plucking a caterpillar off a leaf. Looking up, he smiled and offered the bug to Aygul.

"No thank you," she said, managing to smile back.

Turning back to Walker she said,

"So, how are you going to kill the lion?"

Walker lay forward on his branch, fingers locked under his chin and chewing a twig.

"I've got an idea, but I'm now sure how to carry my plan out. I need some meat."

"What?" asked Aygul. "Meat?"

"Yeah, meat," said Walker. "But I don't think I can catch any of these birds," he said indicating the chatty little finches flitting about, staying well out of reach.

Aygul turned to look at Hairy.

"Bugs won't do," said Walker.

"What's going on over there?" asked Cengiz.

"Walker has a plan to kill the lion," replied Aygul. "But he needs meat!"

Hairy tapped Walker on the arm and pointed at Baghadur's head, resting in a pile of leaves on the forest floor. Walker pouted his lips and shook his head no.

"Meat?" asked Cengiz. "What for?"

"Bait," replied Walker.

"Well, I've got some jerky in my pack," replied Cengiz.

"Really?" called out Walker, surprised. "That would do!"

"Only one problem," said Cengiz. "My pack is tied to a branch five spans down."

Walker, Aygul and Hairy peered down through the foliage to the pack, tied to Cengiz's tree. It was perilously close to the ground and therefore, within reach of the lion.

"Well, that could be a problem," replied Walker. "Anyone see our furry friend lately?"

"No."

"No."

"Neither have I," continued Walker. "But that doesn't mean he isn't down there watching us."

"I could climb down and retrieve it," offered Cengiz. "Then climb back up and throw it to you."

Walker considered the distance and elevation between their relative perches. Not too far to throw, but there were plenty of leafy obstacles in their way.

"I appreciate your very brave offer," answered Walker. "But there's no way you could throw it through the trees."

Hairy tapped on Walker's arm, tugged on the fabric strips holding him to the tree and pointed towards Cengiz.

"Hairy's got an idea," Walker called out. "You wouldn't be using a rope to tie yourself to that tree, would you?"

"Yes," answered Cengiz. "Oh! You think I could swing it over?"

Aygul patted Hairy on the arm.

"It's better than climbing down to the ground and walking it over," replied Walker. "But that would still mean climbing down and get the pack."

For a while no one but the chatty little birds made a sound.

"How certain are you that your idea will work?" asked Cengiz, considering the situation.

Walker looked at Aygul and Hairy with a strained expression.

"Pretty sure," he answered honestly. "I've never actually tried it, but I think it should work."

Aygul rolled her eyes and Hairy shook his head in exasperation.

"What?" asked Walker. "It was my mother's idea. She's a medicine woman."

"Alright," replied Cengiz. "I'll do it. Let me just untie myself."

Cengiz descended the tree at a snail's pace. Aygul, Hairy and Walker held their breath and watched. Walker was gripping the handle of his knife hard enough for his knuckles to turn white. Everyone kept an eye on the surrounding forest for any sign of the lion, but so far so good.

Just as Cengiz reached the branch the pack was tied to; the forest went quiet, and the bushes stirred.

The lion sauntered out.

Cengiz froze.

The lion glanced up, apparently aware of Cengiz's position but the big cat just stood there, gently swishing its tail back and forth.

Everyone waited. Cengiz, hanging from the side of the tree.

After what seemed like forever, the lion yawned again, turned its head and lay down at the edge of the clearing, seemingly content to watch.

Everyone relaxed a bit, but no one, especially Cengiz, moved.

Once again, the birds resumed chattering.

Finally, after what seemed like an eternity, Cengiz slowly lowered himself down onto the limb. After taking a pause, and with his arms wrapped around the branch, Cengiz began sliding forward. When he reached his target, he began to untie the pack.

The lion turned its head, seeming to lose interest and twitched an ear.

Pack over his shoulder, Cengiz scooched back up to the tree trunk, then ever so slowly stood up and began to climb. It wasn't until he was safely back in the canopy, that everyone was able to breathe normally again.

"I certainly hope this plan of yours was worth this," observed Cengiz, and collapsing onto the branch exhausted.

In the Valley of the Auroch

"Trust me, this should work," called Walker. "But retrieving that bag might have been the easy part."

Cengiz lowered the bag slowly down through the canopy. This got the lion's attention. When he thought the bag was low enough, Cengiz began to swing it, back and forth. The lion was completely captivated, eyes following the swinging bag.

"He's not going to be able to swing it far enough," said Walker, gauging the distance.

Cengiz was half hanging off his perch, swinging the rope while clinging to the branch, legs wrapped tightly around the bough. His position looked precarious. The bag swung farther and farther.

"I think he's going to make it," argued Aygul. "Come on Cengiz!"

Cengiz, putting his shoulders into the swing. was too busy to reply. As the bag soared, it brushed past increasingly denser foliage, which hampered its progress.

Far below, the lion watched, twitching its tail and shifting its weight.

"This isn't going to work," said Walker. "And that lion is getting ready to move."

But Cengiz was persistent. Twisting his body with an extra, muscle-bulging effort, he swung the bag still farther. But the bag bounced off a branch which sent it spinning off course.

The lion tucked its rear legs under in what looked to Walker like it was preparing to spring.

"Stop it Cengiz," Walker called out. "The lion is getting too excited."

"Just a little more," replied Cengiz, straining to get the words out. "I think I can do it."

Far below, the lion got to its feet and took a step forward, eyes on the swinging bag.

"Cengiz," Aygul called out, her fingers cramping from gripping her branch in sympathetic strain. "The lion is starting to move!"

In an explosion of gray, the lion sprang into the trees and flew. It twisted and clawed at the swinging bag, and it only missed by a hair before dropping back to the ground.

"Shite!" exclaimed both Walker and Aygul.

Cengiz scrambled to haul himself back up onto the branch. He then quickly pulled the rope up after him, removing the bag from the lion's reach.

"Sheesh!" exclaimed Walker and collapsing from pent up stress. The lion, having landed on its feet, now turned and loped off to await further developments.

Hairy threw a twig to get Walker's attention. When that didn't work, he followed it up with a handful of crumpled leaves.

"What? Oh! Good idea, Hairy," replied Walker.

"What?" asked Aygul looking back and forth between the two.

"Cengiz!" called out Walker and ignoring Aygul. "Try tying the other end of the rope around a heavy stick. Then throw that over instead."

"What?" asked an exhausted Cengiz. Then, "Oh, good idea."

The lion followed Cengiz's attempts to throw the stick with some interest. But it eventually yawned, to demonstrate its boredom.

After several attempts it soon became apparent that while throwing the stick was easier, it wasn't heavy enough to carry the rope through the trees.

On the sixth attempt the rope became almost hopelessly tangled in the tree.

"Well, this day just keeps getting better and better," observed Walker.

Cengiz pulled and pulled, violently shaking the two trees, but it was obvious that he wasn't making any progress. If anything, the rope had become even more thoroughly entangled in the greenery.

At least the lion seemed to be entertained.

"It's no use," called out Cengiz dispiritedly. "The rope is too firmly twisted."

Hairy raised a hand.

"No." said Walker firmly. "Not a chance."

"What?" asked Aygul, perplexed by their strange, one-sided conversation.

"Hairy," replied Walker, as if that was enough of an answer.

But in response to Aygul's further questioning look, Walker added, "He thinks he can climb out and untangle the rope."

Aygul's eyes opened wide at the prospect. The rope was twisted in the leaves at the far end of the limb below. The branch was much, much thinner than the one she was sharing with Hairy, essentially just a collection of twigs and leaves.

"Oh, no," Aygul blurted out at the mere thought of it.

Hairy smacked Walker's arm and began to sign.

"Stop it," said Walker sternly. "You're not doing it."

"What is he saying?" asked Aygul, frustrated and curious.

"Hairy says he's sure he can do it," paraphrased Walker, leaving out the part where Hairy said he would swing through the trees like a monkey.

Aygul turned to reexamine the task again. A climb like that would be utterly beyond her skill, but she wasn't Hairy, and neither was Walker. Turning back, she asked as delicately as she could, "Could he?"

"No," replied Walker firmly.

Aygul considered the situation for a bit and turned back to Walker.

"Is there any alternative?" she asked. "Is there anything else you can use? I mean, are you even sure this idea of yours would work?"

Walker was silent, staring down at the lion. Hairy reached over and punched him in the arm.

"I'm pretty sure it would. And, no, I can't think of anything else."

Aygul turned to Hairy. The face that looked back was completely alien to her experience. Dark, small and gnarled, with a low forehead, heavy brows and a wide nose. Yet the eyes were intent, intelligent and full of questions. Why hadn't she noticed that before? Aygul was overcome with the desire to be able to speak whatever language Hairy and Walker shared.

"Hairy," she said. "It looks impossible to me. Are you really sure you can do this?"

In response, Hairy smiled, reached out a hand and patted Aygul's arm.

Aygul smiled back and took a deep breath.

"Walker, I think you should let Hairy try."

The lion watched Hairy's like a cat stalking a bird. Hairy was hanging legs wrapped around the branch, climbing hand over hand and pulling himself along. The bough had sagged from his weight, but Hairy continued undeterred.

Walker had suggested tying their bindings together into a harness for Hairy, but he brushed the idea aside with a shake of the head, acting insulted. Now that Walker watched Hairy's progress, he admitted to himself that the safety harness would probably have just gotten tangled in the branches and twigs Hairy had to crawl through.

"Come on Hairy," muttered Walker. "Take it slow."

In response, Hairy turned his head and smiled up at him.

"Is he always this reckless?" asked Aygul. She was gripping her section of tree limb hard and shaking slightly.

"Yes."

"I think I see him," called out Cengiz. "Yes, I see him now."

Hairy was halfway along the branch, but still more than two full body lengths from the end. The tree limb curved downwards from his weight—arrested only by the now taut rope, pulling the leafy end up, towards Cengiz's tree.

With a smooth display of strength, Hairy—legs wrapped around the branch—released his grip and swung over and down, now upside-down to grab the thinner end of the limb and facing the tangle.

"Shite," whispered Aygul.

In the Valley of the Auroch

Hairy scooted closer to the tangle and reached out a hand. Suddenly the leaves tore loose and Hairy was left suspended over the clearing, gripping the end of the rope in one hand and the branch in the other.

"No!" said Walker lurching forward and reaching out.

"Hairy!" yelled Aygul.

The lion was on its feet, completely focused on Hairy. It took a tentative step forward, the muscles under its fur rippling in anticipation.

Walker put his knife between his teeth, and frantically began to untie himself.

"I'm going to kill that buggering lion."

"No, wait!" exclaimed Aygul, reaching out to stop him.

Cengiz, meanwhile was untying his end of the rope, in an attempt to feed out slack to take the strain off Hairy. As he let out the line, Hairy pulled the rope back towards his branch, until with a final effort, he pulled his arms together and wrapped himself safely around the limb.

"That guy's going to kill me one day," sighed Walker and shaking his head.

Moving slowly and with great care, Hairy transferred the rope to his mouth. Gripping the line in his strong teeth, he began climbing back up the branch until he was directly below Aygul. Using the utmost caution, Hairy raised himself to a standing position, grabbed a handful of leaves, and handed the rope to Aygul. Then he relaxed back down onto his new perch.

Everyone let out their breath.

As Aygul passed the line Walker shook his head wearily.

"He's been doing stuff like that since we were kids."

Aygul and Walker chewed the jerky into pulp and mashed and rolled the meat into half a dozen, egg-sized balls. Each, held together with a leather ribbon. Each meaty nugget contained the leaves, stems and flowers of the crown vetch. It was a reasonably quantity, but Walker had no idea how effective this amount of poison would be on a creature as large as the lion.

"I've been told the seeds are very bitter," remarked Walker as they worked. "Though deer seem to like it well enough."

"How is it going?" called out Cengiz.

"I think we're ready," Walker called back.

Peering down through the leaves, they could see the lion, its head down, perhaps asleep.

"Hey!" yelled Walker, trying to get the lion's attention. "Hey, pussycat!"

But the lion didn't stir. After all the activity, maybe the lion was taking a nap.

"Maybe it's lost interest, offered Aygul.

"No such luck," replied Walker. "Hey fur ball!"

Nothing.

"We could just drop the meat and hope for the best," said Aygul.

But Hairy had a better idea and started climbing down the tree.

"Hairy!" yelled Walker. "Get back up here!"

But down on the ground, the Lion raised its head.

Hairy descended to the next branch.

"Damn it Hairy! Get back up here!"

Now the lion was on its feet, tail twitching.

"I would say Hairy's got the lion's attention for you," called Cengiz.

"Fine," grumbled Walker. "Hairy, that's far enough, we're dropping the bait."

Walker and Aygul leaned out as far as they felt safe and tossed the poisoned nuggets down towards the lion.

The first actually bounced off the big cat's head. Startled, the lion blinked, sniffed the meatball and then slurped it up without further hesitation.

"That's one!" squealed Aygul and clapping her hands.

The rest of the meatballs landed in the clearing in front of the lion. The cat eagerly ate the free meals, and then turned to look back to the humans in expectation of more.

"It worked!" cried Cengiz, "The lion ate them all! Now what?"

Walker stared at the gray monster in the clearing below. The cat lowered its head and sniffed about and looked at the humans again.

"This could take a while. I think we just have to wait and see."

"Hairy," called Aygul, "Climb back up here and tie yourself in."

CHAPTER FIFTEEN

It was dark when they heard the first groan.

It was low and sounded uncomfortable, and only lasted a moment, but it was an unmistakable sound.

And then silence.

"Walker?" whispered Aygul in the dark.

"What?"

"Nothing."

The night was dark, chilly, damp and uncomfortable. None of them had eaten or had anything to drink and they were all sore from lying on the narrow tree branches. Walker figured Cengiz must be in even worse shape as this was his third or fourth night aloft.

Crickets chirped and birds called to each other in the dark. A breeze caused the branches to sway, rustling the leaves. In the dark, even tied to the tree, it was an unnerving feeling. And then, it started to rain.

Aygul couldn't sleep. She was frightened. Her elbows and knees were sore from clinging onto the branch, and her bare legs were cold.

After what felt like an eternity, the first light of the morning sun illuminated the leaves in the tops of the trees.

Early morning mists appeared, floating over the forest floor like ephemeral ghosts making their way between the trees.

The silence was finally shattered by the early birds tweeting and chirping to announce the new day. As if released from some cursed spell, Aygul— cold and stiff—began to move and turned to Walker.

"Now what?" she asked.

Walker turned to the girl, tied to the branch. Dew dripped from Aygul's dark hair, and her eyes were rimmed red from the lack of sleep. Lines were etched in the dirt on her pretty face, making her look older than her years. Nevertheless, she had not complained even once, exhibiting a strength that surprised Walker.

"Good question," he said, looking down to the forest floor; there was no sign of the lion. "I don't see our friend, but that doesn't mean it's gone."

Aygul rubbed her face and opened her eyes extra wide to join the search.

"Walker?"

"Hmm?"

"What if we try dangling the pack again? The lion couldn't resist it before."

"Hmm," mused Walker. "That's a good idea."

With everyone watching, Walker lowered the pack down through the leaves. He stopped when it was only a few heights above the forest floor and tried to swing it back and forth. When that didn't work, he switched to jerking the line to bounce the pack up and down. The action made enough noise that if the cat was anywhere nearby, it should certainly have gotten its attention.

When the lion failed to appear, Walker dropped the bag still further, until finally it was on the ground. But still no cat.

"Perhaps the lion's gone," suggested Cengiz. "Or maybe it's gone to the river for water."

"Maybe it's off looking for an easier meal," added Aygul, her own stomach growling.

"Or…" said Walker, "it's dead or dying somewhere out of sight."

"So, what do we do?" asked Cengiz.

Hairy pantomimed climbing down the tree and running away.

"I think we should at least wait until the sun is higher and see if the lion shows up," replied Walker. "I say if there's no sign by noon, we climb down and take our chances."

Noon arrived with no sign of the lion. They were all stiff from their time spent clinging to the tree. Nevertheless, they climbed halfway down, pausing to watch the forest. After what felt like a forever, they climbed down halfway again. Walker tried yanking the pack back and forth but still the lion failed to materialize. Finally, with a unanimous nod of agreement, they climbed the rest of way to the ground.

Cengiz's first act was to recover his spear. He handed Baghadur's spear to Walker.

While Cengiz was clearly relieved to finally have a substantial weapon in his hands, Walker passed Baghadur's spear to Aygul.

Hairy and Walker beat the bushes until Hairy found a heavy stick that he was comfortable with and Walker a long, straight branch. Stripping off the leaves, Walker used his knife to carve a notch into one end and. With a flourish, he produced a glittering obsidian arrowhead. Walker always kept one hidden in the collar of his jacket. Then, with a thin strip of leather, Walker secured the barb to the tip of his new spear.

Watching Walker's performance Cengiz shook his head and remarked, "You don't trust our spears?"

"I mean no offense, but I'm more comfortable with my own tools."

"Well, I thank the spirits that guided your path, Walker. I don't know how much longer I could have lasted."

"I don't know about giving the spirits any credit," Walker replied though trying to tamp down the cynicism. "We were just following the best trail. But I'm glad we were able to help."

"So, you are not a believer," said Cengiz. "But you cannot deny that something guided your path, for that, and the inspiration that showed you the means to deal with the lion, I am grateful."

Cengiz was on the verge of complete collapse from exhaustion and exposure. And Walker himself was dead tired. Under the circumstances he decided to let the subject drop.

Hairy examined the clearing and pointed off in the direction he thought the lion had taken, which was up the hill. With a nod, the group set off in the opposite direction, which happily was towards the river nearby.

In the Valley of the Auroch

Hairy still reeked from the bear shite and Walker was covered in the blood of several trolls. And after their time spent in the tree, Aygul and Cengiz were in need of a good bath as well.

They found a tree-shrouded spot; a small waterfall emptying into a crystal-blue pool. Walker kept watch while the others bathed, before taking his turn. Though the water was shockingly cold, it was a luxury after the previous night.

Still, the experience left Walker uncomfortable. He'd reluctantly become protective of Aygul, and keeping watch meant just that. Nevertheless, her water-soaked garments left little to the imagination, and Aygul was mature for her years.

"If the lion still lives it could still be stalking us even now," said Cengiz. "We should follow the river. The bank open and wide enough to aid us in spotting the cat before it attacks."

"I think that plan is as good as any," agreed Walker, Hairy shrugging to concur.

They picked their way along the gravel bank, avoiding trees or shrubbery that could afford a predator concealment. At several points the bank narrowed. The group had to navigate between the sheep cliff wall and the river. There were stretches where the trees grew right down to the water. The steep and rocky surfaces, punctuated by trees, made the endeavor taxing.

Cengiz kept close to Aygul, offering her his hand around the worst obstacles.

Aygul was comfortable to be in her tribe member's company. He was familiar. She couldn't help but feel some resentment towards Walker for dragging her from Nefin, maybe even getting him killed. Cengiz firm grip was reassuring, and it wasn't the first time she'd noticed his rugged good looks.

Taking his hand to climb around a hanging tree, Aygul took the opportunity to speak to the scout.

"I am sorry for Baghadur," she said. "But I'm grateful you're here."

"Everyone was worried for you Aygul. Your father and mother especially."

"I'm sorry for the trouble I've caused."

"It's not your fault, you were taken by the trolls, but how did you come to gain the protection of that troll boy... Nefin?"

Walker's ears pricked up at that, but Aygul answered before he could stop her.

"Nefin was the reason I was there," she said.

"I don't understand," Cengiz replied, a look of confusion on his face.

"The trolls lured Aygul out of the village," Walker added. "That was their plan."

"Lured Aygul out? How?"

"I met Nefin in the woods near our village," explained Aygul not taking Walker's cue. "When I was doing the washing up and gathering water."

"When was this?" asked Cengiz, his tone serious.

"Several weeks ago," replied Aygul, misinterpreting the alarm in Cengiz's tone.

"Weeks ago?" exclaimed Cengiz. "And you told no one about it?"

"She's young..." remarked Walker.

"Aygul!" said Cengiz ignoring Walker. "You discovered there were trolls in the valley and said nothing? Why didn't you tell someone? Why didn't you warn us?"

"Nefin was just a boy. He was nice and gentle. He just wanted to get to know me."

"Look, in her defense..." Walker started to explain, but Cengiz cut him off.

"How can you even defend her?" Cengiz demanded. And turning to Aygul; "Great spirits, we all could have been killed in our homes! And you knew about the troll for weeks. And you consorted with these troldfolk? You were in their camp? Did you go willingly?"

"It wasn't like that!" exclaimed Aygul, alarmed at the direction the conversation had taken.

"Cengiz," Walker said "Lower your voice. The lion could still be tracking us."

"What?" replied Cengiz, turning on Walker. But remembering their circumstances, spoke no further.

"Look, the trolls were using Aygul," continued Walker. "They took advantage of her youth and trusting nature."

"Again, how can you defend her?" asked Cengiz. His tone became suspicious. "But then, you aren't one of us, are you? No. You are just a stranger here, too."

"Cengiz…" began Aygul.

"It doesn't matter," snapped Cengiz. "Osmanek and the elders will decide what should be done."

"…with you." Walker imagined Cengiz had meant.

"Look, why don't we worry about this later. We still have to make it back to your village. And remember, it's not just the lion we have to worry about, the trolls are probably on our trail too."

"Yes? And who's fault is that?" asked Cengiz, glaring at the girl.

"You wouldn't even know about the trolls if it wasn't for her," explained Walker. "And you should thank Hairy and me. And the lion. Because of us, you now have five less trolls to deal with."

From the look on Cengiz's face, Walker didn't think he'd been swayed by Walker's argument. Aygul on the other hand, walked with her head down dragging her spear.

Hairy poked Walker with his stick and rolled his eyes in Cengiz's direction. Walker exhaled and shook his head.

The constant switchbacks made their journey frustrating. Sometimes the river twisted back almost on top of itself. Not for the first time they had to climb over a downed tree.

"What about lashing some of these logs together to make a raft?" Cengiz said, breaking his silence. "Floating would offer some protection from the lion."

"But we would be exposed to anyone looking for us from the bank," replied Walker. "And from what I've seen, there are many stretches too shallow for a raft to pass."

And then they reached the arch.

"I would say this is a good sign," said Walker.

"Yes, Tabib was right. We should have listened," said Cengiz. "This is surely a cursed place."

"I don't mind the place," replied Walker. "It's some of the people I have a problem with. The valley itself is beautiful."

Hairy held up a hand, calling for attention. He knelt to examine the beach under the arch. He pointed to the various tracks, left in the sand.

"Trolls," agreed Walker. "a lot of them. These tracks are fresh and head downriver. Well, it seems Rolf and his boys beat us through the gate. That figures, they didn't waste the night hiding in a tree. I wonder how they got around the lion?"

"They're ahead of us," said Cengiz. "How can that be if they're following you? What do they want?"

"I'm sure Rolf wants revenge for killing his men." answered Walker. "But more than that, they want to stop us from reaching the village and warning your people. I would guess that Rolf took a party ahead to block our path while Nefin and that other troll tracked us."

"If that's so, what do we do?" asked Cengiz. "How do we make it to the village if the trolls are ahead of us?"

"We try to spot them first," replied Walker. "Hairy will be on the look-out for their tracks but this trail following the river is narrow, perfect for an ambush. But there are deer-paths up the canyon walls. We should be able to avoid the trolls if we get to higher ground."

Hairy pointed along the river trail and shook his head—they shouldn't continue in that direction. Walker nodded, it would be safer to climb the nearby rocks and climb to the shelving ledges overhead. Once aloft, it would be easier to spot trouble from above.

The troupe made its way up the hill. As they passed from the emerald, green shadows, the footing became more unstable. Gnarled, twisted roots snaked across the path to trip up the travelers and slow their progress. But while the limestone cliffs looked intimidating, the boulders of the rocky defiles were manageable. In short order they had reached a ledge level with the treetops. Hairy pointed out several narrow deer-paths leading to even higher ground. This approach led to an even narrower ledge, traversing a sheer clean slab and finally emerging onto a broad shelf just below the crest of the cliff. From their new height they had a commanding view down into the forest. Hairy and Walker paused to confer about the safest route to continue. Aygul stuck close and was now avoiding Cengiz's company.

The path they had been following narrowed and around a rock tower, weathered from countless years of run-off. As they transited the ledge, a flock of doves exploded from the rocks, disturbed by the troop's arrival.

Walker felt more comfortable, now that they were high above the valley floor. His instinct told him the trolls were fixated by the river and hence, the valley. By leaving the gorge they were now on a safer route.

"You know, we would be better off if we just left the valley altogether. Let's just finish our journey overland."

"The uplands are mountainous with deep ravines," replied Cengiz. "It would take days longer trying to find our way home that way. And I don't know the best route."

Still, it would be safer," replied Walker. "The trolls would never find us in those hills. We could even hike to the mouth of the river and backtrack. The trolls would never be able to cover both ends of the valley. How far are we from your village do you think?"

"If we followed the river, we should reach the village this night," said Cengiz.

Walker looked at Hairy who shook his head.

"We shouldn't be on the trail in the dark. I say we try to reach the hills, or baring that, to find shelter for the night."

"We have been walking all day and I have yet to see a troll," challenged Cengiz. "What makes you so sure you're still being hunted?"

"You saw the trolls taken by the lion."

"Yes, and those are dead."

"And what about the tracks? The ones under the arch. You saw them yourself."

"They could have been left days ago. I haven't seen any sign of these trolls you speak of. If there were anymore, they've probably returned to their camp by now."

"We haven't seen them because we've been trying to avoid them. Look, I know you're anxious to get back to your village, but that doesn't mean we should do anything rash.

"Again, I remind you I have only your word for any of this. And I think it would be a waste of time to spend another night in the woods when we're so close. Unless there is some other reason you are reluctant to return to the village."

"What does that mean?"

"Perhaps there are trolls, perhaps they even took Aygul. But you make them sound like demonic spirits. Your tale of killing many trolls? It sounds like a tale. Perhaps there aren't any trolls searching for us."

"Why would I lie about such things?"

"I don't really know. But then, I don't know you either. Even you have to admit your tale is hard to believe."

"This from the man who spent the last few days in a tree."

"Yes, hunted by a lion that followed you into our valley."

"This again. You know there were lions in the forest before we showed up. Are we responsible for the bears too? The tigers, wolves?"

"I know that Osmanek thought you might be responsible for Aygul's disappearance. And now here you are, with her."

"He didn't have anything…" began Aygul.

"I am speaking to this man," snapped Cengiz. "I do not know why you say the things you are saying. You ran off with trolls? How more likely you were with a fine-looking stranger."

"You seriously think I took Aygul?"

"Osmanek may have been right. Perhaps you are a young man on a bachelor quest. Maybe you were bringing home a wife."

Walker shook his head in frustration but didn't want to argue anymore.

"I suppose the only way to prove my virtue is to find the trolls and make introductions. But to be honest, I don't really care. Believe what you want. We're leaving the valley and heading overland. But just so we're clear, I'm touched you think I'm fine-looking."

"And I say, it's a waste of time to leave the valley."

"Well, nobody's forcing you to go with us. Hairy and I are going to return Aygul to her village taking the safest route."

Cengiz looked to Aygul and then back at Walker.

"Aygul is a daughter of our village. I'm not leaving her alone in your company."

"Good, it's settled then. Let's keep moving, we can look for shelter along the way."

"No. I'm leaving and Aygul is coming with me."

Walker counted to ten before he answered.

"We rescued you once already. But if you really want to try to make your village tonight, go ahead. But Hairy and I are taking Aygul and heading for higher ground. We'll finish the rest of the trip in the in the hills in daylight."

Aygul smiled sheepishly and lowered her head. Cengiz, however, looked furious.

"This isn't any of your business and I'm not asking your permission," replied Cengiz reaching out to take Aygul's hand.

"What? No! I'm sure the trolls would like to get his hands on Aygul almost as much as me. You're not dragging her through the forest in the dark."

"Get out of my way or I'll kill you," growled Cengiz.

Cengiz never saw Walker's fist move. It hit him square on the jaw, the next thing he knew, he was on his back.

"I'm not letting you get Aygul killed because you're too impatient to take precautions. And at this point, I don't care whether you believe me or not. You're not taking Aygul anywhere."

Cengiz sprang to his feet. He threw himself at Walker like a wild man. But Cengiz wasn't a trained fighter, while Walker had spent his youth learning fighting techniques from his uncle.

Walker tried not to hurt the older scout as Cengiz attempted to grapple. Cengiz flailed his arms attempting to strike, but the blows landed harmlessly on Walker's shoulders.

Exhausted, as well as humiliated, Cengiz staggered back in defeat. Though from the look on his face, his attitude hadn't changed.

"Are you finished?" asked Walker, feeling better now that everything was out in the open. "Just take a few breaths. If I'd wanted to hurt you I would've. That should tell you something. Now just trust me and Hairy and I will guide the both of you back to your village."

Cengiz didn't reply, ignoring Walker's remark and staggering off.

Aygul wasn't sure if she should say anything. Walker was a stranger and young too. But Cengiz was a member of her tribe, family and tradition. She didn't feel comfortable disagreeing with him.

"Fine, I will go with you," said Cengiz.

"Fine," said Walker.

"Whatever," answered Walker. Then, turning to Aygul, "How are you doing?"

Aygul shrugged and looked down and then backed up a bit bashfully.

They continued to follow the trail up the side of the cliff. Hairy pointing out a pack of wolves making their way across a clearing far below. The wolves looked to be trying to flush a ground squirrel from a bush, out into the open.

"Well, looks like somebody's going to eat today," said Walker and putting a hand to his growling stomach.

The path broadened onto a wide terrace. The cliff face, gray-striped stains from years of rain was pocked with caves.

It was late afternoon and Walker called a halt and surveyed the forest below.

Hairy pointed to a wisp of dust at a bend farther down the river.

"Who knows what that is—could be more wolves, or Rolf and friends." agreed Walker.

Cengiz pointed ahead. The trees were thinning out and the deer path looked pretty exposed. "Won't that make us easy to spot from below?"

"You could be right," agreed Walker. He looked at the path up and over the crest. They still had some distance to go, and it would be dark soon. "Why don't we take a rest here for a bit."

Aygul cleared her throat and held up the edge of her skirt, it was full of elderberries.

"Anyone hungry?" she asked. "I found these bushes growing all along the path up here."

Walker selected a berry from the cluster and held it up to the light.

"These aren't completely ripe," he remarked. "Don't eat very many or you'll get sick."

"What?" exclaimed Aygul, both skeptical and disappointed. She scrutinized a berry for herself. "How many is too many?"

Walker popped the purple fruit into his mouth and made a face.

"They're still a little sour. They won't kill you, but they will give you a stomach ache."

Aygul held up a berry, sniffed it, dropped it in her mouth and chewed. Then squeezed her eyes shut and coughed.

"Okay, they're not ripe," she admitted. "But I'm so hungry I could eat a dead mouse."

"That doesn't surprise me considering the meal we had back in your village," replied Walker.

"What's that supposed to mean?"

"Just that you folks could take some cooking lessons from the trolls," said Walker. "You know, I think I see some gooseberries on the ledge below. Those would be safer to eat, and that bush is probably full since your village ate all the deer, goats and elk. There's also some knotgrass in the rocks back along the trail. You can eat as much of that as you want, just avoid the seeds, they're poisonous."

Aygul tried another elderberry, made another face and tossed the rest aside.

"You know a lot about gathering herbs for a hunter."

"And yet you don't seem to know enough for a frontier girl."

"I'm more of a seamstress than a cook."

Aygul lifted her skirt and scrambled down to the gooseberry bush.

"Say, where did Hairy go?" she called from the ledge below.

Walker looked around and spotted Hairy near a dried out fallen tree.

"Hairy has a more sophisticated palate," explained Walker.

Later, after a meal of gooseberries, knotgrass and grubs, the quartet set off on the path, back down into the woods.

"It will take us another half-day at least to reach the hills," said Cengiz as he surveyed the path upward.

"That's if we don't run into trouble," agreed Walker. "We should find a place to camp for the night and continue in the morning."

"Another tree?" asked Aygul.

"No, I think we're safe enough up here," said Walker. "How about a cave?"

There were numerous hollows farther along the cliff face.

They explored the entrances to several caves. Walker and Hairy took turns throwing rocks and sticks into the entrances to flush out any napping bears or lions.

The cave's entrance was hidden by trees. It also had multiple openings allowing for a hasty escape if needed. The floor was dry, a combination of rock and sand. Part of the roof was open to the sky, which for the time being, filled the cave with light.

Walker climbed down to one of the ledges below and turned to look for the cave. Satisfied that their shelter afforded enough concealment, Walker climbed back to rejoin the party.

"Do we chance a fire?" asked Cengiz, in anticipation of another uncomfortable night.

"I think it should be safe enough," announced Walker on reentering the cave. "But we should wait until dark to hide the smoke."

"Look at these!" called Aygul, pointing to drawings on the cave wall. They were the color of charcoal and ochre.

There were drawings of animals. There were deer sporting huge racks, rhinoceroses, aurochs, wolves and spotted leopards. Hairy pointed to a series of lions.

"See?" said Walker. "Our lion wasn't the first in the valley."

"Who made these?" asked Aygul.

"Whoever it was, they were done back when all these animals were still around," pinned Walker.

"These were not made by my people," remarked Cengiz. "We only use such images for ceremonies."

"Yeah, well, they're pretty common where I come from," explained Walker. "Folks even paint them on the inside walls of plaster huts. My brother's well known for it."

"These are beautiful," remarked Aygul. "I really like lion heads. Why do you think they made so many?"

"Practice?" answered Walker. "Maybe they were bored. They were probably taking shelter in here too. Maybe getting in out of the rain."

Hairy, farther back in the cave, held up a big bone. He used it to rap on a skull laying in the dirt.

"This one's elk," said Walker on close examination. He spotted a few more off to the side. "And these others are deer bones. And this looks like an old fire pit. I guess this was someone's home."

"Where are they now do you think?" asked Aygul.

"No way of knowing," replied Walker. "These bones are old. This might have been someone's winter shelter and when spring came, they moved on."

"What makes you think winter?" asked Aygul and examining the old fire pit.

Hairy held up one of the deer skulls and pointed to where the antlers should be. Deer loses their antlers in winter.

"Ah," she said.

Hairy and Aygul went off to do a little foraging before the sun began to set. Walker collected a sizable quantity of dry wood while Cengiz used a broken bone to dig the fire pit out before surrounding it with stones.

Walker arranged the wood in the pit and packed in a generous quantity of dry leaves and kindling.

"Look what we found!" squealed Aygul, practically dancing back into the cave. She held up the forward of her skirt which was almost overflowing with brambleberries. "They're ripe and delicious too!" she exclaimed excitedly and threw a handful at Walker.

Hairy—a big grin on his face—produced a couple of handfuls of big, pink grubs.

"Well done you two." Though Walker stuck out his tongue at Hairy. "I'm just waiting for it to get a little darker to try to start the fire."

But that turned out to be easier said than done in the dark. But eventually, between Cengiz twirling sticks and Walker striking rocks they finally got a small fire going.

Everyone huddled around the little blaze and from the looks on their faces, the morale of the party rose considerably.

As everyone ate and snuggled up to the fire, Walker busied himself building a clock. He started by filling the elk skull with sand. The sand drained out of a hole onto the end of a hollow thighbone set on the edge of a large rock. When enough sand filled the open end of the bone—it took a

219

while—the bone tipped up and off the rock to clatter onto a collection of bones below. He experimented with the precise balance point for the thighbone. The rest of the party watched the proceedings in silence.

"Do we really need that?" asked Cengiz.

"I just want to be fair," explained Walker, finally satisfied with his toy. "Any volunteers to take the first watch?"

"I'll do it," replied Aygul yawning. "I'm awake and enjoying the fire. You big guys probably need your rest more anyway."

Walker wasn't going to argue though it was obvious Aygul could hardly keep her eyes open. The girl's attitude had improved significantly from earlier in the day. Apparently, enjoying her forest adventure.

Hairy nodded, which could mean anything.

"I will take over for Aygul," said Cengiz.

"I'm a pretty light sleeper. If anyone gets tired, just let me know, I'll take over," added Walker. "Otherwise, I'll take the watch after you."

In the Valley of the Auroch

At this elevation, the night outside the cave was full of distant sounds. Birds called and insects buzzed down in the forest.

Hairy, Walker and Cengiz were asleep in the darkened cave. Aygul pinched herself to stay awake. She thought about how many changes in circumstances she'd been through in the last few days. It was pleasant to be able to truly relax, for what seemed like the first time in a long while.

By now her Aygul was impelled by a more prosaic motivation. Leaving the cave and stepping to the far corner of the ledge, she crouched and answered the call of nature. Standing, Aygul felt a hand fasten across her mouth.

Hairy shook Walker awake.

"I'm up," he said before seeing the look on Hairy's face. "What?"

Aygul and Cengiz were gone.

In the Valley of the Auroch

"Fine," said Walker. "We did everything we could, but if they want to take their chances with the trolls, that's not our fault. Good riddance. Let's get out of this valley and put all this behind us."

Walker picked up his spear and started up the trail. He stopped when he realized Hairy wasn't with him.

"Are you coming or what?"

Hairy wasn't coming. He was crouched by the edge of the path leading down back down the hill.

"What are you doing?"

Hairy ignored Walker's question, intent on the examination of the ground off to the side of the trail.

"Fine, you can catch up to me when you're done playing tracker." And Walker turned to resume his escape.

Hairy hit him in the back with his rabbit-stick.

"Ow!" exclaimed Walker. "Damn it Hairy. What do you want from me? If she wanted to go with that idiot that's her choice."

In response, Hairy pointed to the ground.

There, in the soft earth was a damp spot, bracketed by a pair of small footprints. And scuffed turf that indicated a struggle. There were drag marks, and a single set of larger footprints leading off down the trail.

"Huh."

Hairy raised his hands questioningly.

"Alright, you've convinced me."

In the Valley of the Auroch

The deer path Cengiz followed angled down towards the river. The moon was up, providing enough light for him to see the trail through the sparse brush. But, even heading downhill, it was slow going carrying the struggling girl. When he could carry her no farther, Cengiz set Aygul down, but his hand remained fastened across her mouth.

"Make a sound and I will push you off this hill."

Aygul worked her sore jaw and rubbed her arms where Cengiz had held her. Cengiz unshipped his spear from his back.

"Why are you doing this?" she whispered back.

"I am taking you home. I don't trust that stranger or his ape and I wasn't going to leave you in their company."

"Why do you care? You obviously aren't happy with me."

Cengiz, using his spear, prodded him farther down the trail.

"This is not about you. This is about the honor of our tribe, your family."

"Our honor? Have I embarrassed you? Brought shame on my family?"

"I will let Osmanek and Taichi decide for themselves. But do not test me."

Morning dawned and Walker yawned.

He and Hairy had been following the trail as quickly as safety allowed in the relative dark. They didn't know how much of a head start Cengiz had, but a reluctant Aygul would surely slow him down.

As they reached the river Walker knelt to dunk his head in the water.

Hairy elbowed him and pointed to the crystal-clear water. A catfish the size of a baby auroch was feeling its way along the rocks.

"Sheesh," Walker said. "If I hooked that thing, I'd throw away my fishing pole and make a run for it. I guess the villagers missed a few."

The path they were following wound its way through towers of rock and trees. By noon, Walker figured they had to be closing in, but then they came to a fork in the trail and had to make a decision.

"Any idea?"

The path was rocky and the soil dry. Half buried stones bore scuff marks but nothing conclusive.

Hairy shook his head.

"So, it's one or the other. Want to choose?"

Hairy shook his head again.

"Fine," Walker pointed to the right. "If they're following the river, we may have a better chance of spotting them from above."

Hairy nodded agreement.

"But the lower path follows the river and may be faster to the village."

Hairy nodded again and shrugged.

"But the higher path may bypass the river's switchbacks and could be faster still."

Hairy socked Walker in the arm.

"What? The last time we were on this trail it was night, and I was distracted by trolls."

Hairy pointed to the upper path.

"Good choice."

But by noon the path ended abruptly at a sheer cliff face. Hairy and Walker were forced to backtrack and follow the river trail anyway.

"I shouldn't have left Aygul to keep watch," grumbled Walker, "If Cengiz hurts her, I'm going to kill the idiot."

Hairy stopped Walker and they crouched down together. Hairy pointed to a depression in the river-bank sand.

"Cengiz? Aygul?" asked Walker, but Hairy was shaking his head.

"Great."

CHAPTER SIXTEEN

It had been a forced march. Night had fallen by the time they reached the edge of a clearing. Hairy signaled for them to stop.

The moon was up, providing enough light for Walker to be able to see. It looked and smelled familiar.

The Aurochs.

The trail had brought Hairy Walker to the same meadow the villagers were using to pen the aurochs.

"This could work out," Walker whispered. "If they're still guarding the herd, that means reinforcements. They might be safe here."

He could see several dozen aurochs silently clustered together in the middle of the field. They stood in a rough circle, with their horns facing outward.

Hairy shook his head and pointed.

"What?"

But even as he asked Walker could see that the villagers were absent from their posts.

"Maybe they just don't stand watch at night."

Hairy pointed across the field. Something was moving in the trees.

"The villagers?"

Hairy shook his head.

"Shite."

A bulky figure emerged from the trees. He stood, silently surveying the field.

Rolf.

"Maybe Cengiz and Aygul made it to through to the village," suggested Walker, trying to stay positive.

Hairy pointed to a dark area in the trees behind Rolf. Several heavyset figures were moving in the shadows. There may have been several others on the ground.

Hairy pointed to Rolf and mimed slitting his throat.

"I appreciate your confidence Hairy, but I doubt the trolls are going to let me pull that trick again."

More figures emerged from the trees—three trolls Walker recognized but couldn't name. At Rolf's direction they lifted the far end of the log barrier.

"Hairy, can you sling a stone into the trees behind them without drawing attention to yourself?"

Hairy climbed to his feet and took a couple steps back. He removed his belt and produced a couple of stones from his tunic pocket.

Meanwhile, the trolls had set the log on the ground and were walking towards the end nearest Hairy and Walker's location.

Hairy loaded his sling with a knuckle-sized stone and twirled it over his head. Then he released it in the direction of the trees behind Rolf.

Crack!

The report of the rock smacking a tree was followed by the sound of it ricocheting off into the brush.

The trolls spun on their heels. They ran into the woods, in the direction of the noise.

In the Valley of the Auroch

Walker snatched up his spear and took off in a crouching run. But he got no farther than the near end of the log when Rolf reemerged from the forest. Walker froze, crouched down by the rock cairn holding up the end of the gate. He held his breath. For a few moments, nothing happened.

Crack!

Another stone, farther down field.

Rolf turned and disappeared into the woods.

Walker got to his feet.

Rolf stepped out of the trees.

"I've got him!" yelled the big troll launching himself in Walker's direction.

Walker got to his feet and hurled his spear.

Rolf stopped halfway and watched the missile fly, then at the last moment, casually knocked it aside.

The other trolls emerged from the forest behind Rolf.

"Now you are dead, Hurrian! I am going to kill you!"

Walker grabbed his knife and prepared to fight.

But Rolf hadn't taken a step when he was brought up short by a commotion.

It was the sound of a stick, banging on rocks, and the screaming of a demon.

The aurochs—startled by the pandemonium—turned and bolted, stampeding out of the pen.

Walker dropped his knife and heaved the log off the cairn then jumped for the rocks.

The three trolls barely escaped the worst of the charging monsters.

But Rolf had time to react.

Throwing up his arms and screaming, Rolf was bashed by a pair of enormous bulls. A third beast skewered him and threw him high into the air. Hitting the ground, Rolf was trampled under heavy hooves.

Bellowing in rage, the aurochs charged off into the night.

Walker stood, retrieving his knife.

The remaining trolls got to their feet. They looked battered, probably having sustained broken limbs.

Rolf's twisted body lay in the turned-up earth.

The trolls looked at Walker, moonlight reflecting from his obsidian blade and then at what remained of Rolf. Dropping their weapons, they backed into the darkness and shambled off into the forest as fast as their injuries allowed.

Hairy trotted up, battered rabbit-stick over his shoulder.

"Thanks, Hairy. That was pretty quick thinking. You probably saved my life."

There were several bodies laid out in the darkness, under the trees. Hairy and Walker rushed over. Moonlight filtered down through the forest canopy, enough so they could see that Aygul and Cengiz weren't among the dead. These were probably sentries the villagers had posted to watch the herd. Blows to the head by stone axes.

Hairy looked up then off to a nearby clearing and a couple darker shapes. He and Walker rushed over to take a look.

They found Aygul and Cengiz in the shadowed clearing, bound hand and foot. Aygul appeared to be unhurt, but Cengiz had taken a beating.

"Well, this is something," said Walker as he untied the leather straps binding Aygul. "Rolf must have been saving you two for something special."

"Where are they?" she asked, searching the dark woods.

"Gone." he said, giving her a hug.

Then addressing Cengiz; "And you. Don't go springing to your feet, these wounds look serious."

Though Walker had been murderously angry at Cengiz, seeing the beaten scout, he figured he'd probably been through enough.

"I owe you our lives," wheezed Cengiz. "I am in your debt."

"Again," replied Walker. Then looking back to the nearby corpses, added; "Anyway you two are safe enough. But you're in no shape to be going anywhere. Let me see what I can do about the bleeding." Turning to Aygul. "You know, my mother always wanted me to be a medicine man."

"No, I am fine," lied Cengiz. "We should leave in case they return."

"I don't think that will be a problem."

Walker set to work binding Cengiz wounds, seemingly on instinct. He instructed Aygul to gather green moss to staunch Cengiz's wounds and sent Hairy to gather jewelweed for ointment and dandelion for a poultice. Mixing them into a thick paste, he gave Cengiz a piece of willow bark to chew while he dressed his wounds.

Finally, Walker applied the poultice and covered the wounds in the moss. He bound the bandages with fibers pulled from Hairy's rope.

Standing back to regard his handiwork. Walker had to admit, he'd learned more of the healing arts than he'd care to admit.

"What?" asked Aygul, noticing the look of concern on Walker's face.

"Mother knows best," replied Walker, shaking his head.

He then crouched down in front of his patient.

"So, how are you feeling?"

"I will live."

"You think so?" asked Walker looking Cengiz in the eye. "Then when you speak to Osmanek, leave out the troll boy. I think Aygul's been through enough already."

"I will do as you ask," promised Cengiz. "You have my word."

"Alright, let's go."

As they emerged from the forest, Walker saw a familiar face.

Ryszard.

Ryszard stood in the now vacant field, looking down at Rolf's mangled form. Walker's old obsidian knife in Ryszard's hand. At the sight of Walker, the big troll put his hands up.

"What are you doing here?" asked Walker.

"Rolf forced me to accompany him, to look for you and the girl."

"Why would he do that?"

"He was very angry at you, and me. He thought it was all my fault that you were able to cause so much trouble for him and the tribe."

Walker waved towards the empty field. "I didn't see you during all the commotion."

"No, he just brought me along just to embarrass me."

"So, you're saying you weren't involved in all this? Killing the villagers here or catching the girl?"

"No. Walker, you know me better than that."

"Do I? Rolf told me you and all the other trolls are cannibals. And he said you knew about the girl and his plans to kill the villagers."

"And you believed him? I learned of Rolf's plans only after he discovered you with the girl. I was trying to talk him out of hurting you. As for the girl, I admit, I knew he had taken her, but I was able to convince him to keep her alive instead of killing her."

Walker noticed his spear on the ground, where it landed after Rolf had deflected it.

"And what about eating people? I notice you didn't start by denying that."

"How can you think I could be a part of that? I was after the villager's aurochs, remember?"

"But you didn't try to stop him from killing those villagers or tying up the girl. And what did you think he was going to do with me?"

Ryszard shook his head.

"I could not. As I have said, I was afraid of Rolf."

But Ryszard hadn't actually denied being a cannibal.

"So, why ask me to help you lead your tribe? Or was that just to keep me from trying to escape and warn the villagers?"

"What? No. I meant everything I said. I like you, Walker. And I thought we could make everything work, and Rolf would see reason."

Hairy poked Rolf with his rabbit-stick to make sure he was dead. Walker used the distraction to retrieve his spear. Aygul and Cengiz were still back at the tree line.

"But when you discovered Rolf's plans, he became enraged. To him it was the evidence that you could not be trusted. It proved all of his arguments right, and mine wrong. I tried to reason with him, but it was too late."

"You know what I think?" said Walker, raising his knife. "I think you let Rolf think he was running things. I think that's why you're here, to be able to manipulate him, make suggestions. I think you manipulated him the way you tried to manipulate me."

Walker saw the slightest hint of a smile appear on Ryszard's face. In that moment, Walker knew the truth.

"So, what are you going to do now?" asked the troll.

Walker gauged his chances, even with his spear, against Ryszard.

"I'm going to give you a head start. Go back to your tribe. And I would suggest you get out of the valley before Osmanek, and the rest of the villagers come looking for revenge."

Ryszard regarded Walker for a moment.

"That does not seem fair."

"No, it doesn't."

Ryszard nodded and then turned and walked back into the forest.

With a motion to Hairy, Aygul and Cengiz, Walker turned and pointed off in the direction of the village.

"You speak troll?" asked Cengiz.

"Yeah," replied Walker still on guard.

"What was that all about?"

"Just insuring we make it back to your village alive. Hairy? Lead the way."

CHAPTER SEVENTEEN

The first rays of the sun were just peeking over the hills to reach the valley floor as Aygul, Cengiz, Hairy and Walker reached the village. Even so, they were soon surrounded by large men with spears and were immediately marched to the longhouse.

After walking all night through the dark forest, the smoky warmth was a welcome relief. Walker, Hairy and Aygul helped Cengiz to the fire, and the four huddled together to warm their bones.

Moments later, Osmanek, and a dozen other men and surrounded the eclectic prodigal souls. The chieftain sat opposite Walker. He looked like a man who hadn't slept in a long time. Taichi entered the longhouse and rushed forward to embrace Aygul. Volkan, Tarkan and Hosmunt appeared and descended on Cengiz. Tabib brushed them all aside and bent to examine his bandaged wounds.

Osmanek eyed Walker, then turned to address Cengiz.

"Tell me," Said Osmanek. "And where is Baghadur?" "Baghadur is dead," Cengiz said. A hush fell over the group. "We were attacked by a lion and Baghadur was killed."

Osmanek turned to Walker.

"I sent you off with Osman and Tarmaz to the elf camp. Where are my men?"

"Walker helped rescued me from the lion," said Cengiz.

Osmanek hadn't taken his eyes off Walker.

"I asked you, where are Osman and Tarmaz?"

"Dead," replied Walker.

"How?"

"We were ambushed by trolls."

A murmur ran through the group.

"Now its trolls?" asked Osmanek. "Before it was elves."

"Trolls," said Cengiz. "There are trolls upriver. They took me and Aygul."

"Trolls?" said Volkan. "Great spirits."

Cengiz turned to Taichi.

"The trolls took Aygul. And they killed our men and turned the animals loose."

Men wailed and voices were raised in anger.

Osmanek still hadn't taken his eyes off Walker. And from the look on his craggily face, he didn't believe Cengiz's account.

"So?"

For once, Walker thought he was better off keeping his mouth shut and trusting Cengiz to explain.

"The trolls tracked me through the valley, they took Aygul and me prisoner. Walker drove them off and saved us."

"You rescued Aygul from the trolls?" Taichi asked Walker. "But you said that elves had taken her."

Osmanek's eyes narrowed.

"Yeah," replied Walker. "I guess I was wrong. The elves took one of your animals, but we were attacked by the trolls."

"Why?" asked Osmanek. "How?"

"The trolls were hunting the elves," replied Walker. "I didn't know about the trolls; they were the ones who took Aygul. The elves were a distraction."

"Osman and Tarmaz?"

"They were killed while we were tracking the elves. The first night."

"And you survived," said Osmanek. "And saved Cengiz. And Aygul."

"How?" asked Volkan. "Why did the trolls let you live?"

"I suppose because they didn't know me," explained Walker. "But they had a quarrel with you. You killed off most of the game and rounded up the remaining animals for yourselves."

There was a lot of grumbling from the crowd.

"This is our valley," said Osmanek.

"The trolls disagree. They were here first, and you left them with nothing to eat. They decided to hunt you for food instead."

"What did you say?" asked Osmanek, surprised for the first time.

"The trolls took your girl as bait," answered Walker. "With your scouts chasing elves, and others guarding your aurochs, they'd ambush your men in the confusion. By the time you realized what was really happening, it would have been too late."

"What of the trolls then?" asked Tarkan.

"Some are dead, the rest will be on the run by now," replied Walker. "By now, the trolls will be heading for the hills."

"And how is it you were able to kill these trolls when our scouts couldn't?" asked Volkan.

"I had help," Walker replied, looking at Hairy.

Osmanek turned to Volkan and Tarkan.

"Take as many men as you need and try to round up as many of the animals as you can. Watch for trouble. And double the guards around the village."

Osmanek turned to Walker and glanced at Hairy. "I suppose you have done us a boon. We are in your debt."

Walker clapped a hand on Hairy's shoulder.

"I said that we'd do our best to rescue your girl," He replied. "The rest was chance. Now, can we get something to eat?"

In the Valley of the Auroch

Walker and Hairy were given several baskets of food and a warm, dry hut in which to rest. No sooner did they wolf down their meal, they collapsed and slept till dusk.

The news of the deaths of so many men cast a pall on the tribe.

Nevertheless, that the meal that evening, Osmanek toasted Walker for saving Cengiz and Aygul.

Pine-wine and sloe-berry juice and platters of what Walker would charitably call "food" were served. Osmanek limped over to Walker with a couple of mugs of juice and shoved one into Walker's hand. Tabib sidled up to join the conversation.

"I still have questions regarding your part in everything that has happened, but it appears that the Vadi Kabile owe you a debt," Osmanek admitted.

"We're happy to help," replied Walker. Leaving out that they had been forced to help at the point of a spear.

Taichi joined Osmanek and took Walker by the arm.

"I owe you a debt for your returning Aygul," said Taichi bowing. "However, my daughter has been dishonored. At the time she was a prisoner in the troll's camp. She has been tarnished, as has our family honor."

239

Walker spotted Cengiz across the room. Their eyes met and Cengiz looked away. He didn't see any sign of Aygul.

"What are you saying?" asked Walker. "Aygul was a prisoner. She was brave and helped us warn your village about the trolls."

"Taichi is correct," added Tabib. "Aygul has been sullied. She is unclean."

"Unclean?" sputtered Walker. "You can't be serious? What kind of people are you?"

"This is not your tribe," hissed Tabib. "You know nothing of us. You have no right to sit in judgement of our ways."

"No? "You said that you owe me a debt," he reminded them both. "Then repay me by forgetting about this. Aygul should be praised for her bravery and resolve, not condemned by your fanaticism."

"This is my family's honor; it has nothing to do with you." added Taichi.

"Tabib is right," added Osmanek. "This is not your business."

"So, what happens now?"

Osmanek took Walker by the elbow and led him away from the others.

"That depends on you."

"Just what does that mean?"

"Taichi feels he has lost face. Tabib agrees."

"And?"

"And there is no place for Aygul here anymore."

"Really? A daughter of your tribe?"

"Take heed, Walker. I am a man of my word." Osmanek lowered his voice. "But our traditions run deep among my people. It appears you hold Taichi's daughter in higher regard than he does. But you should not have brought Aygul back to this village."

"So, what then? I should just take her and go?"

"No, that would only make things worse," whispered Osmanek. "My people are intolerant to affronts to their honor. Trying to steal Taichi's daughter would only make things worse. No, if you have any regard for Aygul's safety, there is only one way to salvage her family's honor."

"And that would be?"

"Ask Taichi for his daughter's hand." answered Osmanek. "He owes you a debt, so he will gladly acquiesce. You will be saving his family honor, and maybe Aygul's life."

Walker suspected this was Osmanek's plan all along. Save face and avoid further questions regarding his leadership. But it was true, Walker couldn't leave Aygul with these barbarians.

Walker nodded and turned to the group.

"Taichi," Walker called out, making sure he got everyone's attention. "For saving your daughter from the ogres, I ask you, her father, for her hand."

Hairy's jaw dropped.

But if Taichi was surprised by the request, he didn't show it.

"I am honored oh great warrior," replied Taichi. "I give you, my blessing."

"Then it is settled," replied Walker. "Have her brought to me immediately; I am leaving as soon as the moon has risen."

Osmanek made a show of clapping Walker on the back. He turned to join his tribe as they began to sing some atonal tribal song. With everyone else's attention thus diverted, Walker turned to Hairy, and he shrugged. Signing that he would explain later.

At moonrise, Osmanek, Tabib, Volkan and Cengiz met Hairy and Walker at the longhouse.

Taichi appeared, leading a woman who looked like an older, harried version of Aygul. The woman was struggling under the weight of a heavy bundle. Walker recognized traces of purple on her face, recent as well as old bruises.

Aygul followed in their wake.

"I have instructed Aygul to be a dutiful wife and to obey you without question," stated Taichi. "And my wife carries my daughter's dowry."

Cengiz looked abashed and stood, avoiding eye contact with Walker.

Walker looked at Osmanek. It occurred to him that rather than feeling gratitude, the tribal chieftain resented Walker. Whatever aide Walker had provided was an embarrassment for the village chieftain. Was this real compassion for Aygul, or subtle revenge for whatever slight Osmanek was feeling toward Walker?

Walker nodded a mute reply to Taichi and Osmanek and turned to the girl.

"Aygul," said Walker. "If you would like to say goodbye to your mother, I'll be waiting outside."

Walker nodded to Hairy. He would stay behind to keep an eye on Aygul just in case.

Shouldering his pack, Walker stepped around the longhouse and walked to the edge of the village.

Stopping to wait, Walker heard a rustling from the brush and spun about, spear at the ready.

A dark gray mountain separated itself from the forest.

A bull auroch.

The beast stopped, framed in the moonlight on the center of the path, tendrils of vapor trailing from its nostrils. The auroch appeared to appraise Walker, weighing the danger he represented.

Walker looked the bull in the eye. Ignoring the Auroch's massive horns, he slowly set his spear on the ground. Then Walker spread his arms, palms up, in a gesture of submission. He wasn't a threat.

Then, in his most soothing voice.

"Don't bother that big, beautiful head about me," said Walker. "I'm just a fellow traveler taking the night air."

The auroch twitched an ear. And after a few moments, the giant turned its head and ambled off into the forest.

Walker eased himself down onto his hands and knees and smiled in relief.

"Walker?" asked Aygul, stepping out of the darkness with Hairy "Are you alight?"

"Sure," he said, smiling in return. "Ready?"

In the Valley of the Auroch

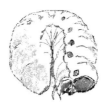

By the time they reached the top of the ridge the sun was up. The three turned for one last look at the beautiful valley Aygul had called home. To Hairy and Walker, it shone with that same emerald glow from the first time they'd seen it.

"Okay, you two," said Walker, turning his back on the valley. "How about we head back to Aurignac and start over?"

Turning to Aygul Walker added.

"I hope you like fish."

And with happy nods from both Aygul and Hairy Walker turned and led them down the trail.

END.

Hairy and Walker

In the Valley of the Auroch

HISTORY, IN PERSPECTIVE

This historically-based novel is set in southern Europe, approximately 100,000 to 250,000 years ago (paleontologists aren't in agreement on just when homo-sapiens first appeared).

This was a time of real monsters—lions twice the size of African lions, saber-toothed tigers, 12-foot cave bears, baboons the size of gorillas, giant Haast eagles and 8-foot-tall terror birds. It was also a time of such fantastical creatures as woolly mammoths and rhinoceroses, elk with 12-foot-wide antlers, huge cattle-like aurochs, car-sized glyptodonts and ground-sloths the size of elephants.

And more than one species of people.

Today all of the humans inhabiting the world, despite our diverse appearances are Homo-sapiens. But the reality is that we Homo-sapiens, are the sole survivors. We are the last of several species that as recently as a hundred thousand years ago, included many other classifications of people. We don't know what these folks called themselves; they didn't leave written records. Instead, we've assigned them names—Homo-Erectus, Homo-Floresiensis, Denisovan, Homo Heidelbergensis, and Neanderthals.

Unfortunately for paleontologists, there are no Homo-Erectus graveyards, no Neanderthal family albums, no Denisovan newspapers or Homo-Floresiensis holiday cards. All we have are some of their bones. So, what happened to all these people? Where did they all go, and why are we, Homo-sapiens, still here?

The answers to these questions are not apparent. The fact that our past is unclear is because time wreaks havoc on the historical record. Unless very carefully preserved, paper and wood disintegrate quickly. Unless protected from scavengers, bone is eaten. Steel rusts, glass weathers into sand. Even plastic, which we worry will remain in the environment forever, ages faster than most people think.

Hence—the disintegration of the remnants of our past.

The oldest known buildings in the world—the megalithic temples in Malta, Shahr-e Sūkhté in Iran, and the Pyramid of Khafre—are less than 6000 years old. The Paestum (Temple of Hera) in Greece, at 2600 years old, is comparatively young—and the Colosseum in Rome at only 2100 years old, is younger still.

The Egyptian dynasties began around 3100 B.C., over 5000 years from their beginning to the present day.

But go back just 250,000 years--not really that long, but long enough that 50 Egyptian dynasties could have risen and fallen, back-to-back. But while there were homo sapiens that whole time, there's are no records of what they did.

What was lost? What stories did we will never know?

With modern technology, scientists are beginning to piece together our long-lost past.

In 2018, researchers discovered more than 60,000 previously unknown, 600-year-old Mayan ruins in Guatemala.

LIDAR laser technology allowed researchers to look beneath the forest canopy, revealing buried homes and palaces covering an area twice the size of medieval England, which would have had an estimated population of around five million people.

Goes to show that we don't know what we don't know.

Just think about that, the Mayan empire—a culture that collapsed around the time that the Notre Dame de Paris was being completed and yet a major part of their history had been hidden until now.

Paleontologists believe that Homo-erectus, Homo-Denisovan and Homo Heidelbergensis probably died out before Homo-sapiens arrived on the scene, but what if they didn't? The fossil record is admittedly spotty and researchers make new discoveries all of the time. Who knows what's hidden, beneath modern Persia and Europe?

Now, a word about our ancestors; It's often assumed that primitive people were superstitious and religious, but that generalization isn't entirely accurate.

While the term "atheist" is relatively new, the concept is quite old. The word atheism first emerged in the 16th century; however, the root of the word dates back to the 5th or 6th century BC. For the ancient Greeks it is defined as "without gods".

Also, regarding the way my characters talk. I've written this story to reflect a contemporary idiom for the characters. To the people I've depicted, their manner of speaking would have seemed entirely normal—to them; they would not hear their accents or dialects any more than we hear ours.

It is my intention for my characters' speech to sound like that of contemporary people. When watching a movie, it bothers me when actors— "speaking" their language but in English—have accents. In film, it's probably unavoidable, but something easy to avoid in books.

The question of whether or not Neanderthals, Homo-erectus could speak at all is one I find frustrating. Gorillas and chimpanzees can learn sign language and parrots, like Alex—Irene Pepperberg's famous African Grey—could speak English and even understood math.

These creatures manage to this with brains smaller than those of our ancient ancestors' or in the case of Alex, smaller than an almond. I have no trouble believing Neanderthals and even Homo-erectus would have had language too.

Finally, I've set this story in France, in the Gorges de l'Ardèche. This is an area occupied by hominids (of one kind or another) for maybe 300,000 years. The valley is spectacular, with natural formations that have changed little over that time.

Over 2,000 caves are located in the gorge, some adorned with elaborate wall paintings, preserved from the elements. These paintings hint histories and stories lost in time.

Our ancestors probably had countless adventures in the Gorges that we know nothing about. This could be one of those the stories.

Enjoy!

References

From Wikipedia;

The Gorges de l'Ardèche is made up of a series of gorges in the river and locally known as the "European Grand Canyon", Located in the Ardèche, in the French department Ardèche, forming a thirty-kilometer-long canyon running from Vallon-Pont-d'Arc to Saint-Martin-d'Ardèche. The lower part of the gorge forms the boundary between the Ardèche department and the Gard department. The canyon is a tourist attraction, drawing over a million visitors per year, in addition to a rich historical and archeological site.

Most of the canyon is protected; it is governed by the Réserve Naturelle Gorges de l'Ardèche. Notable sights along the canyon include the Pont d'Arc at the beginning of the canyon, a natural arch 60 m wide and 54 m high. Much of the canyon is inaccessible except by water, and canoeing and kayaking are popular sports on the river. Overnight camping is not allowed, except for at two bivouac shelters.

The cliffs offer habitat to rare birds such as the Bonelli's eagle. (As of 2013 there were only two pairs in the Ardèche, and no more than thirty in all of France.)

Humans have lived in caves in the area for over 300,000 years. Over 2,000 caves are found in the gorge, some of them painted; the best-known painted cave in the gorge is the Chauvet Cave.

The Ardèche (Occitan: Ardecha) is a 125-kilometre (78 mi) long river in south-central France, a right-bank tributary of the River Rhône. Its source is in the Massif Central, near the village of Astet. It flows into the Rhône near Pont-Saint-Esprit, north-west of Orange. The river gives its name to the French department of Ardèche.

The Valley of the Ardèche is very scenic, in particular a 30-kilometre (19 mi) section known as the Ardèche Gorges. The walls of the river here are limestone cliffs up to 300 meters (980 ft.) high. A kayak and camping trip down the gorge is not technically difficult and is very popular in the summer. The most famous feature is a natural 60-metre (200 ft.) stone arch spanning the river known as the Pont d'Arc (arch bridge).

The Ardèche Gorge, the largest natural canyon in Europe, angles through southern France, northwest of Avignon. Its craggy limestone cliffs rise as high as 1,000 feet. The Ardèche River begins in the massif central, cuts through the gorge and crosses the plateau to flow into the Rhone.

https://europeupclose.com/article/the-caves-of-frances-ardeche-gorge/

The best-known landmark of the gorge is Vallon Pont d'Arc, a huge natural bridge arching far above the river. A pleasant way to spend part of a day is to rent kayaks and paddle along the river to the awe-inspiring bridge, perhaps stopping at a beach along the way for a picnic. Shortly after passing under the bridge you can come ashore, where the kayak rental company will meet you with transportation back to your car. Being on the water allows for an intimacy with the place that tourists who only watch from high on the cliff never experience.

Millennia ago, prehistoric people may have floated the river too, in hand-carved boats. You can see remnants of their lives on the plateau above the river, where standing stones remain, the dolmens and menhirs that had deep meaning in ancient times. In caves dotting the cliffs, arrowheads and knives are often found and, in some, paintings from Paleolithic times.

Chauvet Pont d'Arc Cave, along the cliff road are signs to the grottes (caves) or avens (deep holes). The most famous by far is Grotte

Chauvet, near the Pont d'Arc. Discovered in 1994, its walls have more than 300 designs painted and engraved some 30,000 years ago. There are rhinoceroses, lions, bears, owls, mammoths and more, all beautifully rendered and in amazing perspective. The Chauvet works are the oldest found in the world so far.

The cave is closed to the public, but there's an excellent exhibit in the nearby village of Vallon Pont d'Arc, open from mid-March to mid-November. It shows cave painting replicas and much more. There are artifacts from archeological finds, a reconstruction of a prehistoric dwelling, and full-size animal reproductions. At the end, there's a movie that shows more about Chauvet Cave.

Quite different is Grottes de St-Marcel d'Ardèche, which is open to visitors. Walking down the long main passageway, you come to an array of beautiful rimstone pools, perhaps a hundred of them. Continuing through this enchanting place, you arrive at the last chamber, full of stalactites, stalagmites and other mineral formations. Classical music and lighting add to the effect.

L'Aven Grotte de la Forestiére, discovered in 1966, is open April to September. The cave has several levels, formed at different time periods. Near the surface are roots from trees that grew into the cave for its water. On a lower level, hundreds of animal bones were found, some from animals now extinct. In one Grotte de la Madeleinechamber, the animals and fish that once lived here adapted to the dark environment and were eyeless and colorless.

The Grotte de la Madeleine contains beautiful and irregular formations set off by special lighting. This cave, set into the side of the cliff, can be reached from the river or from the plateau above. There's a gift shop, snack shop, and a viewpoint overlooking the gorge.

Aven-marzal Aven de Marzal was investigated in 1892 but left and forgotten until 1949, and now is open for guided tours daily between

April and October. It has numerous stalactites, stalagmites, cauldrons and multi-colored crystals. A museum shows the equipment used for early explorations. There's also a "zoo" with life-sized models of prehistoric animals.

Finally, there is the splendid Aven d'Orgnac, an enormous cavern filled with strange and eerie shapes, all carved by nature over eons. A staircase and pathway descend into the cavern, where lights show off the formations (you return to the top by elevator). It is open year-round.

Written by Marilyn McFarlane for EuropeUpClose.com

Filed Under: France, Western Europe Tagged With: Provence & Cote d Azur, ardeche, caves

https://en.wikipedia.org/wiki/Gorges_de_l%27Ard%C3% A8che

Gorges de l'Ardèche. From Wikipedia, the free encyclopedia

https://en.wikipedia.org/wiki/Vallon-Pont-d%27Arc

Vallon-Pont-d'Arc. From Wikipedia, the free encyclopedia

https://en.wikipedia.org/wiki/Elf

Ängsälvor (Swedish "Meadow Elves") by Nils Blommér (1850)

An **elf** (plural: elves) is a type of human-shaped supernatural being in Germanic mythology and folklore. In medieval Germanic-speaking cultures, elves seem generally to have been thought of as beings with magical powers and supernatural beauty, ambivalent towards everyday people and capable of either helping or hindering them. However, the details of these beliefs have varied considerably over time and space, and have flourished in both pre-Christian and Christian cultures.

The word elf is found throughout the Germanic languages and seems originally to have meant 'white being'. Reconstructing the early concept of an elf depends largely on texts, written by Christians, in Old and Middle English, medieval German, and Old Norse. These associate elves variously with the gods of Norse mythology, with causing illness, with magic, and with beauty and seduction.

After the medieval period, the word elf tended to become less common throughout the Germanic languages, losing out to alternative native terms like zwerc ("dwarf") in German and huldra ("hidden being") in Scandinavian languages, and to loan-words like fairy (borrowed from French into most of the Germanic languages). Still, beliefs in elves persisted in the early modern period, particularly in Scotland and Scandinavia, where elves were thought of as magically powerful people living, usually invisibly, alongside everyday human communities. They continued to be associated with causing illness and with sexual threats. For example, a number of early modern ballads in the British Isles and Scandinavia, originating in the medieval period, describe elves attempting to seduce or abduct human characters.

With urbanization and industrialization in the nineteenth and twentieth centuries, beliefs in elves declined rapidly (though Iceland has some claim to continued popular belief in elves). However, from the early modern period onwards, elves started to be prominent in the literature and art of educated elites. These literary elves were imagined as small, impish beings, with William Shakespeare's A Midsummer Night's Dream being a key development of this idea. In the eighteenth century, German Romanticist writers were influenced by this notion of the elf, and reimported the English word elf into the German language.

From this Romanticist elite culture came the elves of popular culture that emerged in the nineteenth and twentieth centuries. The "Christmas elves" of contemporary popular culture are a relatively recent tradition, popularized during the late nineteenth-century in the United States. Elves entered the twentieth-century high fantasy genre in the wake of works published by authors such as J. R. R. Tolkien; these re-popularized the idea of elves as human-sized and human-like beings. Elves remain a prominent feature of fantasy books and games nowadays.

Not objectively real

From a scientific viewpoint, elves are not considered objectively real.

However, elves have in many times and places been believed to be real beings. Where enough people have believed in the reality of elves that those beliefs then had real effects in the world, they can be understood as part of people's world view, and as a social reality: a thing which, like the exchange-value of a dollar bill or the sense of pride stirred up by a national flag, is real because of people's beliefs rather than as an objective reality. Accordingly, beliefs about elves and their social functions have varied over time and space.

Even in the twenty-first century, fantasy stories about elves have been argued both to reflect and shape their audiences' understanding of the real world, and traditions about Santa Claus and his elves relate to Christmas.

Over time, people have attempted to demythologize or rationalize beliefs in elves in various ways.

Demythologizing elves as indigenous peoples

Some nineteenth- and twentieth-century scholars attempted to rationalize beliefs in elves as folk-memories of lost indigenous peoples. Since belief in supernatural beings is so ubiquitous in human cultures, however, scholars no longer believe that such explanations are valid. Research has shown, however, that stories about elves have often been used as a way for people to think metaphorically about real-life ethnic others.

Etymology

A chart showing how the sounds of the word elf have changed in the history of English.

The English word elf is from the Old English word most often attested as ælf (whose plural would have been *ælfe). Although this word took a variety of forms in different Old English dialects, these converged on the form elf during the Middle English period. During the Old English period, separate forms were used for female elves (such as ælfen, putatively from common Germanic *alβ(i)innjō), but during the Middle English period the word elf came routinely to include female beings.

The main medieval Germanic cognates are Old Norse alfr, plural alfar, and Old High German alp, plural alpî, elpî (alongside the feminine elbe). These words must come from Common Germanic, the ancestor-language of English, German, and the Scandinavian languages: The Common Germanic forms must have been *alβi-z and alβa-z.

Germanic *alβi-z~*alβa-z is generally agreed to be cognate with the Latin albus ('(matt) white'), Old Irish ailbhín ('flock'); Albanian elb ('barley'); and Germanic words for 'swan' such as Modern Icelandic álpt. These all come from an Indo-European base *albh-, and seem to be connected by the idea of whiteness. The Germanic word presumably originally meant "white person", perhaps as a euphemism. Jakob Grimm thought that whiteness implied positive moral connotations, and, noting Snorri Sturluson's ljósálfar, suggested that elves were divinities of light. This is not necessarily the case, however. For example, because the cognates suggest matt white rather than shining white, and because in medieval Scandinavian texts whiteness is associated with beauty, Alaric Hall has suggested that elves may have been called "the white people" because whiteness was associated with (specifically feminine) beauty.

A completely different etymology, making elf cognate with the Rbhus, semi-divine craftsmen in Indian mythology, was also suggested by Kuhn, in 1855. In this case, *alβi-z connotes the meaning, "skillful, inventive, clever", and is cognate with Latin labor, in the sense of "creative work". While often mentioned, this etymology is not widely accepted

https://en.wikipedia.org/wiki/Kobold

The **kobold** (occasionally cobold) is a sprite stemming from Germanic mythology and surviving into modern times in German folklore.

Although usually invisible, a kobold can materialize in the form of an animal, dolls, fire, a human being, and a candle. The most common depictions of kobolds show them as humanlike figures the size of small children. Kobolds who live in human homes wear the clothing of peasants and often inhabit dolls; those who live in mines are hunched and ugly; and kobolds who live on ships smoke pipes and wear sailor clothing.

Legends tell of three major types of kobolds. Most commonly, the creatures are house spirits of evil nature; while they sometimes perform domestic chores, they play malicious tricks if insulted or neglected. These Kobolds usually show up to a residence to haunt its inhabitant. They are widely believed to have been created by ancient German satanic cults to kill entire lines of their enemies. They enjoy making animals sick and feeding off of their misery. Hundreds of people report descriptions of these creatures in their homes, however, due to the nature of the description most are not taken seriously. Kobolds are often not discovered, however if they are, they can lie dormant while following their cursed prey for years. Famous kobolds of this type include King Goldemar, Heinzelmann, and Hödekin. In some regions, kobolds are known by local names, such as the Galgenmännlein of southern Germany and the Heinzelmännchen of Cologne. Another type of kobold haunts underground places, such as mines. A third kind of kobold, the Klabautermann, lives aboard ships and helps sailors.

Kobold beliefs are evidence of the survival of pagan customs after the

Christianization of Germany. Belief in kobolds dates to at least the 13th century, when German peasants carved kobold effigies for their homes. Such pagan practices may have derived from beliefs in the mischievous kobalos of ancient Greece, the household lares and penates of ancient Rome, or native German beliefs in a similar room spirit called kofewalt (whose name is a possible root word of the modern kobold or a German dialectal variant). Kobold beliefs mirror legends of similar creatures in other regions of Europe, and scholars have argued that the names of creatures such as goblins and kabouters derive from the same roots as kobold. This may indicate a common origin for these creatures, or it may represent cultural borrowings and influences of European peoples upon one another. Similarly, subterranean kobolds may share their origins with creatures such as gnomes and dwarves and the aquatic Klabautermann with similar water spirits.

The name of the element cobalt comes from the creature's name, because medieval miners blamed the sprite for the poisonous and troublesome nature of the typical arsenical ores of this metal (cobaltite and smaltite) which polluted other mined elements.

Origins and etymology

The kobold's origins are obscure. Sources equate the domestic kobold with creatures such as the English boggart, hobgoblin and pixy, the Scottish brownie, and the Scandinavian nisse or tomte; while they align the subterranean variety with the Norse dwarf and the Cornish knocker. Irish historian Thomas Keightley argued that the German kobold and the Scandinavian is predate the Irish fairy and the Scottish brownie and influenced the beliefs in those entities, but American folklorist Richard Mercer Dorson has discounted this argument as reflecting Keightley's bias toward Gotho-Germanic ideas over Celtic ones.

Kobold beliefs represent the survival of pagan customs into the

Christian and modern eras and offer hints of how pagan Europeans worshipped in the privacy of their homes. Religion historian Otto Schrader has suggested that kobold beliefs derive from the pagan tradition of worshipping household deities thought to reside in the hearth fire. Alternatively, Nancy Arrowsmith and George Moorse have said that the earliest kobolds were thought to be tree spirits. According to 13th-century German poet Conrad of Würzburg, medieval Germans carved kobolds from boxwood and wax and put them "up in the room for fun". Mandrake root was another material used. People believed that the wild kobold remained in the material used to carve the figure. These kobold effigies were 30 to 60 cm (one to two feet) high and had colorful clothing and large mouths. One example, known as the monoloke, was made from white wax and wore a blue shirt and black velvet vest. The 17th century expression to laugh like a kobold may refer to these dolls with their mouths wide open, and it may mean "to laugh loud and heartily". These kobold effigies were stored in glass and wooden containers. German mythologist Jacob Grimm has traced the custom to Roman times and has argued that religious authorities tolerated it even after the Germans had been Christianized.

Several competing etymologies for kobold have been suggested. In 1908, Otto Schrader traced the word to kuba-walda, meaning "the one who rules the house". According to this theory, the root of the word is chubisi, the Old High German word for house, building, or hut, and the word akin to the root of the English 'cove'. The suffix -old means "to rule". Classicist Ken Dowden has identified the kofewalt, a spirit with powers over a single room, as the antecedent to the term kobold and to the creature itself. He has drawn parallels between the kobold and the Roman lares and penates and the Anglo-Saxon cofgodas, "room-gods". Linguist Paul Wexler has proposed yet another etymology, tracing kobold to the roots koben ("pigsty") and hold ("stall spirit").

Grimm has provided one of the earlier and more commonly accepted etymologies for kobold, tracing the word's origin through the Latin cobalus to the Greek koba'los, meaning "rogue". The change to the word-final -olt is a feature of the German language used for monsters and supernatural beings. Variants of kobold appear as early as the 13th century. The words goblin and gobelin, rendered in Medieval Latin as gobelinus, may in fact derive from the word kobold or from kofewalt. Related terms occur in Dutch, such as kabout, kabot, and kaboutermanneken. Citing this evidence, British antiquarian Charles Hardwick has argued that the house kobold and similar creatures, such as the Scottish bogie, French goblin, and English Puck, all descend from the Greek kobaloi, creatures "whose sole delite consists in perplexing the human race, and evoking those harmless terrors that constantly hover round the minds of the timid." In keeping with Grimm's definition, the kobaloi were spirits invoked by rogues. Similarly, British writer Archibald Maclaren has suggested that kobold beliefs descend from the ancient Roman custom of worshipping lares, household gods, and penates, gods of the house and its supplies.

Another class of kobold lives in underground places. Folklorists have proposed that the mine kobold derives from the beliefs of the ancient Germanic people. Scottish historical novelist Walter Scott has suggested that the Proto-Norse based the kobolds on the short-statured Finns, Lapps, and Latvians who fled their invasions and sought shelter in northern European caves and mountains. There they put their skills at smithing to work and, in the beliefs of the proto-Norse, came to be seen as supernatural beings. These beliefs spread, becoming the kobold, the Germanic gnome, the French goblin and the Scottish bogle. In contrast, Humorists William Edmonstoune Aytoun and Theodore Martin (writing as "Bon Gaultier") have proposed that the Norse themselves were the models for the mine kobold and similar creatures, such as dwarfs, goblins, and trolls; Norse miners and smiths "were small in their physical proportions, and usually had their stithies near the mouths of the mines among the hills." This gave rise to myths about small, subterranean creatures, and the stories spread across Europe "as extensively as the military migrations from the same places did".

German writer Heinrich Smidt believed that the sea kobolds, or Klabautermann, entered German folklore via German sailors who had learned about them in England. However, historians David Kirby and Merja-Liisa Hinkkanen dispute this, claiming no evidence of such a belief in Britain. An alternate view connects the Klabautermann myths with the story of Saint Phocas of Sinope. As that story spread from the Black Sea to the Baltic Sea. Scholar Reinhard Buss instead sees the Klabautermann as an amalgamation of early and pre-Christian beliefs mixed with new creatures.

Characteristics

Kobolds are spirits and, as such, part of a spiritual realm. However, as with other European spirits, they often dwell among the living. Although kobold is the general term, tales often give names to individuals and classes of kobolds. The name Chim is particularly common, and other names found in stories include Chimmeken, King Goldemar, Heinzchen, Heinze, Himschen, Heinzelmann, Hödekin, Kurd Chimgen, Walther, and Wolterken. Local names for kobolds include Allerünken, Alraune, Galgenmännlein (in southern Germany), Glucksmännchen, Heinzelmännchen (in Cologne), Hütchen, and Oaraunle.The Heinzelmännchen are a class of kobolds from Cologne, and the Klabautermann is a kobold from the beliefs of fishermen and sailors of the Baltic Sea. Many of these names are modifications of common German given names, such as Heinrich (abbreviated to Heinze), Joachim, and Walther.

Kobolds may manifest as animals, fire, human beings, and objects. Fiery kobolds are also called drakes, draches, or puks. A tale from the Altmark, recorded by Anglo-Saxon scholar Benjamin Thorpe in 1852, describes the kobold as "a fiery stripe with a broad head, which he usually shakes from one side to the other..." A legend from the same period taken from Pechüle, near Luckenwald, says that the kobold flies through the air as a blue stripe and carries grain. "If a knife or a fire-steel be cast at him, he will burst, and must let fall what which he is carrying." Some legends say the fiery kobold enters and exits a house through the chimney. Legends dating to 1852 from western Uckermark ascribe both human and fiery features to the kobold; he wears a red jacket and cap and moves about the air as a fiery stripe. Such fire associations, along with the name drake, may point to a connection between kobold and dragon myths.

Kobolds who live in human homes are generally depicted as humanlike, dressed as peasants, and standing about as tall as a four-year-old child. A legend recorded by folklorist Joseph Snowe from a place called Alte Burg in 1839 tells of a creature "in the shape of a short, thick-set being, neither boy nor man, but akin to the condition of both, garbed in a partly-colored loose surcoat, and wearing a high-crowned hat with a broad brim on his diminutive head." The kobold Hödekin (also known as Hüdekin and Hütchen) of Hildesheim wore a little hat down over his face (Hödekin means "little hat"). Another type of kobold known as the Hütchen is said to be 0.3–1 m (0.98–3.28 ft) tall, with red hair and beard, and clad in red or green clothing and a red hat and may even be blind. Yet other tales describe kobolds appearing as herdsmen looking for work and little, wrinkled old men in pointed hoods. Some kobolds resemble small children. According to dramatist and novelist X. B. Saintine, kobolds are the spirits of dead children and often appear with a knife that represents the means by which they were put to death. Heinzelmann, a kobold from the folklore of Hudermühlen Castle in the region of Lüneburg, appeared as a beautiful boy with blond, curly hair to his shoulders and dressed in a red silk coat. His voice was "soft and tender like that of a boy or maiden."

https://en.wikipedia.org/wiki/Troll

Troll

A troll is a class of being in Norse mythology and Scandinavian folklore. In Old Norse sources, beings described as trolls' dwell in isolated rocks, mountains, or caves, live together in small family units, and are rarely helpful to human beings.

Later, in Scandinavian folklore, trolls became beings in their own right, where they live far from human habitation, are not Christianized, and are considered dangerous to human beings. Depending on the source, their appearance varies greatly; trolls may be ugly and slow-witted, or look and behave exactly like human beings, with no particularly grotesque characteristic about them.

Etymology

The Old Norse nouns troll and tröll (variously meaning "fiend, demon, werewolf, jötunn") and Middle High German troll, trolle "fiend" (according to philologist Vladimir Orel likely borrowed from Old Norse) developed from Proto-Germanic neuter noun *trullan. The origin of the Proto-Germanic word is unknown. Additionally, the Old Norse verb trylla 'to enchant, to turn into a troll' and the Middle High German verb trüllen "to flutter" both developed from the Proto-Germanic verb *trulljanan, a derivative of *trullan.

Smaller trolls are attested as living in burial mounds and in mountains in Scandinavian folk tradition. In Denmark, these creatures are recorded as troldfolk ("troll-folk"), bjergtrolde ("mountain-trolls"), or bjergfolk ("mountain-folk") and in Norway also as troldfolk ("troll-folk") and tusser. Trolls may be described as small, human-like beings or as tall as men depending on the region of origin of the story.

https://en.wikipedia.org/wiki/Ogre

Ogre

An ogre (feminine ogress) is a term used in myth and folk tales for a variety of abominable and brutish hominid monsters, informally large, unpleasant, grotesque, predatory, and typically cannibalistic towards normal human beings, infants, and children. Ogres and similar creatures feature in mythology, folklore, and fiction around the world, appearing in many classic works of literature and fairy tales.

Ogres vary in size depending on the depiction, ranging from moderately large and heavyset by human standards to inhuman and disproportionate giants. Common features include disproportionately large heads, abundant hair, unusually colored skin, strong body, a voracious appetite, and a generally hideous appearance, odor, and manner. Ogres overlap heavily with giants in mythology and may be considered a subtype thereof; they also overlap with human cannibals in fiction.

Etymology

The word ogre is of French origin, originally derived from the Etruscan god Orcus, who fed on human flesh. Its earliest attestation is in Chrétien de Troyes' late 12th-century verse romance Perceval, li contes del graal.

https://en.wikipedia.org/wiki/Heraclitus

Heraclitus was famous for his insistence on ever-present change as being the fundamental essence of the universe, as stated in the famous saying, "No man ever steps in the same river twice" Ancient atheist

https://en.wikipedia.org/wiki/**History_of_atheism**

Atheism (derived from the Ancient Greek ἄθεος atheos meaning "without gods; godless; secular; denying or disdaining the gods, especially officially sanctioned gods") is the absence or rejection of the belief that deities exist. The English term was used at least as early as the sixteenth century and atheistic ideas and their influence have a longer history. Over the centuries, atheists have supported their lack of belief in gods through a variety of avenues, including scientific, philosophical, and ideological notions.

Philosophical atheist thought began to appear in Europe and Asia in the sixth or fifth century BCE. Will Durant, in his The Story of Civilization, explained that certain pygmy tribes found in Africa were observed to have no identifiable cults or rites. There were no totems, no deities, and no spirits. Their dead were buried without special ceremonies or accompanying items and received no further attention. They even appeared to lack simple superstitions, according to travelers' reports. The Vedas of Ceylon admitted only the possibility that deities might exist but went no further. Neither prayers nor sacrifices were suggested in any way by the tribes

https://www.ancient.eu/Neolithic/

Violatti, C. (2014, August 05). Neolithic. Ancient History Encyclopedia. Retrieved from https://www.ancient.eu/Neolithic/

Violatti, Cristian. "Neolithic." Ancient History Encyclopedia. Last modified August 05, 2014. https://www.ancient.eu/Neolithic/.

Violatti, Cristian. "Neolithic." Ancient History Encyclopedia. Ancient History Encyclopedia, 05 Aug 2014. Web. 13 Mar 2018.

https://www.goknapping.com/stone_knives.html

How to Make and Use Primitive Stone Bladed Knives

How to Flintknap

https://www.wikihow.com/**Flintknap**

https://cognitivearchaeologyblog.files.wordpress.com/2017/04/wynn-t-1998-did-homo-erectus-speak-cambridge-archaeological-journal-8-78-81.pdf

Did Homo Erectus Speak? Thomas Wynn Department of Anthropology, University of Colorado

The Origin of Language - Could Homo erectus and other hominids speak?

https://www.nature.com/scitable/knowledge/library/homo-erectus-a-bigger-smarter-97879043

Homo erectus - A Bigger, Smarter, Faster Hominin Lineage By: Adam P. Van Arsdale (Department of Anthropology, Wellesley College) © 2013 Nature Education

Citation: Van Arsdale, A. P. (2013) Homo erectus - **A Bigger, Smarter, Faster Hominin Lineage**. Nature Education Knowledge 4(1):2

Ötzi. From Wikipedia, the free encyclopedia

https://www.washingtonpost.com/news/worldviews/wp/2018/02/07/**meet-cheddar-man-first-modern-britons-had-dark-skin-and-blue-eyes**/?utm_term=.37d0725ef9a7

Meet Cheddar Man: First modern Britons had dark skin and blue eyes, By Jennifer Hassan

https://science.howstuffworks.com/science-vs-myth/what-if/what-if-neanderthals-were-still-alive.htm

What if Neanderthals were still alive? by Laurie L. Dove

https://www.seeker.com/**could-a-human-not-in-our-species-still-exist-**1770629076.html

Could a Human Not in Our Species Still Exist? New fossil discoveries continue to push the known boundaries of human evolution. By Jen Viegas

https://www.nbcnews.com/science/science-news/neolithic-europe-hunter-gatherers-farmers-coexisted-no-sex-f8C11373348

Neolithic Europe hunter-gatherers, farmers coexisted – but no sex, by Tia Ghose

http://www.bbc.com/earth/story/20150929-why-are-we-the-only-human-species-still-alive

Why are we the only Human species still alive? By Melissa Hogenboom

https://www.livescience.com/28954-ancient-europeans-mysteriously-vanished.html

Ancient Europeans Mysteriously Vanished 4,500 Years Ago, By Tia Ghose, Senior Writer

https://galleryofskulls.cool/blogs/blog/**what-neanderthals-really-looked-like-or-hey-good-looking**

What Neanderthals Really Looked Like or "Hey Good Looking". By Robert Schott

https://www.nature.com/scitable/knowledge/library/neanderthal-behavior-59267999

Neanderthal Behavior. By: Gilliane Monnier (Department of

Anthropology, University of Minnesota)

https://www.newhistorian.com/neanderthals-extinction-may-rest-not-coat/7008/

Neanderthals' Extinction May Rest on Not Having a Coat. Posted By: Ginger Perales

http://www.daynes.com/en/hominids-reconstructions/homo-erectus-sangiran-17-14.html

https://www.nature.com/scitable/knowledge/library/homo-erectus-a-bigger-smarter-97879043

Homo erectus - A Bigger, Smarter, Faster Hominin Lineage. By: Adam P. Van Arsdale (Department of Anthropology, Wellesley College)

https://en.wikipedia.org/wiki/Homo_sapiens

Homo sapiens. From Wikipedia, the free encyclopedia

https://en.wikipedia.org/wiki/Australopithecus

Australopithecus. From Wikipedia, the free encyclopedia

https://en.wikipedia.org/wiki/Homo_habilis

Homo habilis. From Wikipedia, the free encyclopedia

https://www.britannica.com/science/human-evolution

Human evolution. by Russell Howard Tuttle

https://en.wikipedia.org/wiki/Human_evolution

http://www.pnas.org/content/pnas/113/25/6886.full.pdf

Early farmers from across Europe directly descended from Neolithic Aegean's Edited by Eske Willerslev, University of Copenhagen, Copenhagen, Denmark

http://www.archaeologyonline.org/Documents/FoodDrink.pdf

FOOD AND DRINK IN EUROPEAN PREHISTORY

https://en.wikipedia.org/wiki/History_of_the_forest_in_Central_Europe

History of the forest in Central Europe. From Wikipedia, the free encyclopedia

https://www.first-nature.com/trees/index.php

Native and naturalized trees of Britain and Ireland

https://draxe.com/mullein/

Dr. Axe.; Mullein: **The Medicinal Herb that Fights Infections & Inflammation**

https://www.motherearthliving.com/Plant-Profile/herb-to-know-mullein-verbascum-thapsus

Herb to Know: Mullein (Verbascum thapsus)

https://en.wikipedia.org/wiki/Neolithic_long_house

https://www.theguardian.com/culture/2014/jun/02/neolithic-houses-recreated-at-stonehenge

Neolithic houses built at Stonehenge - but not without modern tools. Maev Kennedy

http://www.ancientcraft.co.uk/Archaeology/stone-age/stoneage_living.html

https://www.nature.com/news/**neolithic-chefs-spiced-their-food-**1.13585

Neolithic chefs spiced their food. Mineral grains from garlic-mustard seeds found in 6,000-year-old cooking pots. by Mark Peplow

http://www.survivopedia.com/survival-uses-of-moss/

by Theresa Crouse for Survivopedia.

https://blog.survivalfrog.com/moss/

You Really Shouldn't Underestimate Moss's Survival Uses. By Donald Willey

https://en.wikipedia.org/wiki/**Sphagnum**

https://www.primalsurvivor.net/**making-rope-from-plants**/

The Survivalist's Secret to Making Rope from Plants. By Jacob Hunter

https://www.signingsavvy.com/sign/WE/471/1

https://www.handspeak.com/word/

American Sign Language Dictionary

http://www.stjo.org/site/News2?page=NewsArticle&id=5673

Lakota (Sioux) Culture - Four Directions. St. Joseph's Indian School.

http://indians.org/welker/greeting.htm

The Indigenous Peoples' Literature pages were researched and organized by Glenn Welker.

https://www.britannica.com/event/Neolithic-Period

Neolithic Period, anthropology. Written By: The Editors of

Encyclopaedia Britannica

https://en.wikipedia.org/wiki/Prehistoric_Europe

Prehistoric Europe. From Wikipedia, the free encyclopedia

https://en.wikipedia.org/wiki/Neolithic_Europe

Neolithic Europe. From Wikipedia, the free encyclopedia

https://en.wikipedia.org/wiki/List_of_extinct_animals_of_Europe

List of extinct animals of Europe. From Wikipedia, the free encyclopedia

https://en.wikipedia.org/wiki/Fauna_of_Europe

Fauna of Europe. From Wikipedia, the free encyclopedia

https://en.wikipedia.org/wiki/Elasmotherium

Elasmotherium. From Wikipedia, the free encyclopedia

http://www.bbc.com/earth/story/20150518-the-epic-history-of-rhinos

The story of rhinos and how they conquered the world. By Chris Baraniuk

https://en.wikipedia.org/wiki/Cave_bear

Cave bear. From Wikipedia, the free encyclopedia

https://en.wikipedia.org/wiki/Panthera_leo_spelaea

Panthera leo spelaea. From Wikipedia, the free encyclopedia

https://en.wikipedia.org/wiki/Woolly_mammoth

Woolly mammoth. From Wikipedia, the free encyclopedia

https://en.wikipedia.org/wiki/Woolly_rhinoceros

Woolly rhinoceros. From Wikipedia, the free encyclopedia

https://en.wikipedia.org/wiki/History_of_lions_in_Europe

History of lions in Europe. From Wikipedia, the free encyclopedia

https://depositsmag.com/2016/07/12/the-saber-toothed-cat-of-the-north-sea/

Dick Mol (Netherlands)and Wilrie van Logchem (Netherlands)

https://en.wikipedia.org/wiki/Aurochs

Aurochs. From Wikipedia, the free encyclopedia

https://en.wikipedia.org/wiki/Astacus_astacus

Astacus, the European crayfish. From Wikipedia, the free encyclopedia

https://en.wikipedia.org/wiki/Tsavo_Man-Eaters

Tsavo Man-Eaters, From Wikipedia, the free encyclopedia

https://www.livescience.com/58735-man-eating-lions-analyzed.html

What Drove Tsavo Lions to Eat People? Century-Old Mystery Solved

https://en.wikipedia.org/wiki/Man-eater

Man-eater. From Wikipedia, the free encyclopedia

The Hamlyn Guide to Edible and Medicinal Plants of Britain and Northern Europe by Edmund Launert

https://wagwalking.com/horse/condition/crown-vetch-poisoning

Wildwood Wisdom by Ellsworth Jaeger

Bushcraft 101 by Dave Canterbury

Extreme Food by Bear Grylls

Survive by Les Stroud

Wilderness Survival Guide by Creek Stewart

Native Harvests by Barrie Kavasch

The Curious Cookbook by Peter Ross

The Penguin Atlas of Ancient History by Colin McEvedy

https://forest.ambient-mixer.com/middle-europian-forest

https://en.wikipedia.org/wiki/Hurrian_language

https://www.dailymail.co.uk/news/article-2729455/**Why-bitter-berries-summer-s-sweetest-fruit-Mixed-bag-weather-results-early-burst-sloe**.html

And importantly;

The War against the Rull by A. E. Van Vogt

But most importantly;

Jim Gaffigan on Camping

https://www.youtube.com/watch?v=sZg4Df_6gEA&t=29s

ABOUT THE AUTHOR

Peter Alan Thelin lives with his wife Sue in Point Richmond California. A precision optician by trade, Peter has worked for Lawrence Livermore National Laboratory since 1988.

Peter's hobbies include working on interesting old cars, older sailboats, recumbent trikes, hovercraft, parrots, science fiction, local politics and living on the water (a floating home).

Peter is also a contributor (self-appointed know-it-all) to Quora.com, the online Q&A website with over 4 million views.

Made in the USA
Middletown, DE
23 October 2023

41216855R00168